Jackie Kabler is an award-winning crime writer, whose psychological thrillers have been Amazon Number One hits in the UK and Canada and made the *USA Today* bestseller list. Her novels have been translated into eight languages.

Before becoming a writer Jackie spent twenty years as a news reporter for GMTV, BBC and ITV news, covering major stories around the world including the Kosovo crisis, the Asian tsunami, famine in Ethiopia, the Soham murders and the disappearance of Madeleine McCann. She now combines writing with her job as a presenter on TV shopping channel QVC; she is also an ultramarathon runner and keen gardener.

Born in Coventry but spending much of her childhood in Ireland, Jackie lives in Gloucestershire with her husband.

www.jackiekabler.com

X x.com/jackiekabler
instagram.com/officialjackiekabler

CW01499920

Also by Jackie Kabler

Am I Guilty?

The Perfect Couple

The Happy Family

The Murder List

The Vanishing of Class 3B

The Life Sentence

THE REVENGE PLOT

JACKIE KABLER

One More Chapter
a division of HarperCollins*Publishers*
1 London Bridge Street
London SE1 9GF
www.harpercollins.co.uk
HarperCollins*Publishers*
Macken House, 39/40 Mayor Street Upper,
Dublin 1, D01 C9W8, Ireland

This paperback edition 2025
1
First published in Great Britain by
HarperCollins*Publishers* 2025
Copyright © Jackie Kabler 2025
Jackie Kabler asserts the moral right to
be identified as the author of this work
A catalogue record of this book is available from the British Library

ISBN: 978-0-00-854459-1

Printed and bound in the UK using 100% Renewable Electricity
by CPI Group (UK) Ltd

Part I

ELLA

Chapter One

I don't notice at first. I'm running late. It's already 6:50am, twenty minutes after my usual arrival time at work, and there's a delivery due at seven. I'm feeling flustered and muttering to myself as I drive too fast down the cul-de-sac, swerve onto the forecourt and slam the brakes on.

'Lights, coffee machines, water the plants … errrm … *what*?'

I turn the engine off and stare at the building in front of me. Have I driven down the wrong street? No, of course I haven't. There's Clancy's Car Repair on my left, no sign of life this morning, the chipped green paint around the upstairs windows a sickly orange under the glow of the sodium streetlight. It'll be closed all week, I remember; Eric and his wife have gone skiing in Austria. But if I'm not in the wrong street – *how*? What's happened to the café? I rub my eyes, as if that will make the slightest difference, and stare for a few moments longer, then clamber out of the car and take a few hesitant steps towards the door.

'Seriously – *what*?' I say out loud, then shiver and wrap my long black coat across my chest as a gust of chill February wind lifts my hair from my shoulders. My heart rate is speeding up now, my gaze whipping from left to right as I try to process what I'm seeing. It's ... gone. Not the building, obviously. That's still there, the creamy brown brick, the white door, the small window next to it, the grey roller shutters. They're closed now, of course, but it's always one of my favourite moments of the day, pressing the button to open them, watching them glide upwards to reveal another, much larger window, flooding the small space behind it with light. But – where's everything else? Where's the sign, the café name sign, that should be screwed into the wall? Where's the heavy A-board, the one I write the day's specials on, the one that's normally chained to an iron loop next to the door, so I don't have to lug it outside every morning and bring it back in every evening? Where's the *bin*, for pity's sake? The bin that usually sits on the little forecourt, receptacle for sandwich wrappings and coffee lids, for those who like to start eating their lunch as they walk back to their own units on this small trading estate. Gone.

It's all ... *gone*.

It's Monday morning. Did someone come here last night, or over the weekend, when much of the estate is deserted, and steal it all? But why? What use would those things be to anyone else?

'You *bastards*!'

Suddenly, I'm furious, heat rushing through my body despite the near-freezing temperature. I march to the door, reach into my coat pocket and pull out my phone, my hand shaking a little as I search for the torch app and switch it on. I angle the beam through one of the glass panes and gasp.

No. Please, no.

Frantically, I move to the small side window to get a better view, hoping desperately that I'm not really seeing what I think I'm seeing. I am, though. It's … empty. The tables and chairs, the high stools along the counter, the coffee machines, the mugs and cutlery, the dozens and dozens of plants … gone. Vanished.

This can't be happening. How? *How?*

I stand back again, eyes sweeping across the front of the building. There's no sign of a break-in, no broken glass, the door and shutters looking just as they always do, no visible damage. This doesn't make *sense*. I fumble in my pocket again, find my keyring, and with fingers slippery with sweat now push the café key into the door lock, wriggling it desperately as it jams.

Shit. Shit. *OK, calm down, Ella. Take your time*, I think.

I take a breath, then pull the key out and insert it again, forcing myself to turn it slowly. Nothing. What's wrong with it? I pull it out and bend down, peering at the lock, and then at the key in my hand. The key is brass; the lock is stainless steel. Shiny, new-looking.

Somebody's changed the lock. Somebody's taken *everything* and changed the bloody lock.

What the hell do I do now?

Chapter Two

W hat I actually do is stumble back to my car on trembling legs, then collapse into the driver's seat, close the door and cry. I just can't get my head around this. Did whoever took everything just break the lock to access the place, and that's why there's no other damage? But what sort of burglar goes to the trouble of bringing a brand-new lock with them, and replacing the old one before they run off with the stolen goods? And why didn't the alarm go off? I set it as usual when I left on Friday, I *know* I did. But if it had gone off, security would have called me…

Think, Ella. *Think.*

I wipe my tears away with the backs of my hands and look at the clock on my dashboard. *Dammit.* The delivery truck will be here any second. OK, well, that's my first job then, I'm going to have to call them and cancel it. Maybe, if I explain what's happened, they won't charge me for all the wasted food?

I scroll through my phone, looking for the number, half expecting to see the van's headlights appearing in my rear-view mirror even as I dial, but the street remains dark and quiet. As the call connects, I inhale and exhale slowly, trying to steady myself.

'Hello? Is that Shawna? Shawna, it's Ella Leonard from Mug & Meadow. I'm *so* sorry to do this with so little notice but I'm going to have to cancel today's order. Something bizarre has happened...'

I launch into the story of the past few minutes, but I've only got to the bit about the missing café name sign when Shawna interrupts me.

'But ... Ella, I'm a bit confused!' she says. 'You cancelled today's order last Wednesday, don't you remember? You cancelled *all* future orders. You said the place was closing down. I don't understand...'

'What? I said ... *what*? But ... I didn't even speak to you on Wednesday. Are you getting me mixed up with someone else?'

'No, of course not. It was definitely you. Mug & Meadow, Redthorpe Park Trading Estate, Gloucester. We even talked about all your lovely plants, and what you were going to do with them. I was really sorry to hear you were leaving so soon, even though I always knew it was just a pop-up. Ella, are you telling me that *wasn't* you? It sounded just like you, I didn't even question it ... I don't get it...'

Shawna's voice tails off.

'I ... I don't get it either.'

I can feel a bead of sweat running down my forehead. I open my mouth to say something else, then close it again. I have no idea *what* to say. Somebody – somebody who was definitely *not* me – called the supplier last Wednesday to tell

8

them the café was *closing down*? Does that mean this wasn't a break-in, after all? But Lena wouldn't do that to me, would she? Of course she wouldn't, there's absolutely no way. There must be some other explanation. There *must* be.

I clear my throat.

'Shawna, I'm so sorry about this. Something really weird is going on here, and I need to get to the bottom of it. Let me just make a few calls and I'll get back to you, OK?'

'Erm ... sure. OK. Bye, Ella.'

I end the call and sit, rigid, staring at the phone in my hand. Is this some sort of elaborate prank, maybe? Because it can't be a normal burglary, not now. No thief would be considerate enough to not only change the locks but also cancel deliveries for their victim's business in advance. That would be ridiculous. But, equally, who would play a prank like this? Do something so extreme, for fun? It doesn't add up.

I stare bleakly at the now strangely bare-looking façade of the building in front of me. I'd been so hopeful, so *happy*, when I arrived here six weeks ago, just before Christmas. It was to be a fresh start, an exciting new chapter in my life. It's just a pop-up for now, yes, but it could be the start of something *big*. A chain of speciality 'coffee slash plant' shops, all over the country. When my boss, Lena, had first approached me with the proposal, I'd loved the idea immediately.

'I want to put them in unexpected places,' she'd said, her eyes sparkling. 'In amongst high-rise flats. On industrial estates. You know, places where you might normally just find food trucks or coffee vans or grubby little takeaways? They'll be little oases in concrete jungles. Small coffee shops that serve really good food and drinks, but also sell plants. Exotic plants, *beautiful* plants. People can come and sit and take a break surrounded by greenery and foliage and then buy a plant to take home. Recreate the experience in their own kitchen. It's going to be great, Ella. We'll start with a little pop-up, just for a few months, as a trial run. But it's going to work, I know it is. And you're the *perfect* person to kick it off.'

She was right – it *was* a good fit. I love coffee, and I adore plants. I've never been lucky enough to have my own garden, not as an adult. But everywhere I've lived, even in the grottiest bedsits and house shares, I've always found room for a few cacti, an aspidistra, an aloe vera. Something to take care of, a living organism that makes few demands and yet responds so gratifyingly to a little love and attention. OK, so running a coffee shop was never exactly in my life plan, but then whose life ever goes exactly to plan? I spent too long with my head in the clouds, dreaming of a life of riches and glamour. I even lived it for a while. But nothing lasts for ever; I needed to get real. And this was a chance to be in at the beginning. Who knew where it could lead?

'If it takes off, I'll make you regional manager first, and then … well, the sky's the limit, Ella,' Lena had told me, squeezing my hand. 'I've got so many other things going on I'll need a right-hand woman to oversee things. This could be amazing for you. I'm calling it Mug & Meadow. What do you think?'

'I think I'm in,' I told her, and we'd both squealed with excitement. I quit my job and gave notice on my London rental that very afternoon. A few weeks later, I packed my bags and drove my clapped-out old Fiat up the M40 to Gloucester, and moved into the sweet little one-bed apartment Lena had sorted for me as part of the deal. She popped up briefly twice to give me the keys to the café, and to check I was OK with all the equipment, and then ... well, then I was on my own, and I *loved* it. I spent Christmas sorting the place out, sending Lena regular updates and pictures, revelling in her ecstatic replies.

'*It looks amazing! We're going to smash this!*' she said, the night before opening day. I was slightly disappointed that she'd had to fly to New York on a business trip on the first of January and so couldn't be there to see the place open its doors on the second. Then, I was slightly relieved she *wasn't* there, because for the first few days I only had a trickle of curious customers venturing in. I'd done *some* local advertising ahead of time, but had I done enough? Had I messed up before I'd even had a chance to get going? I'd worked as a barista and assistant manager in a number of places previously, but I'd never been in charge before, and I was suddenly terrified that I'd taken on too much, that I was out of my depth. But then, in week two, Mug & Meadow suddenly took off. I never doubted the quality of what I was serving: hand-roasted coffee, home-made speciality syrups, delicious fresh cakes and sandwiches bought in from local farm shops and suppliers, everything organic, every dietary need catered for. And the plants of course, each one carefully selected by me, filling the window and every spare surface. Outside, the January skies may have been grey, rain hammering on the corrugated iron roof, but inside was my own five-hundred-square-foot tropical paradise. I was astounded though at how quickly news of our arrival spread after that first week. First, dozens of people working on the industrial estate became daily visitors; then, they were rapidly joined by passing trade and residents of nearby housing developments. By week three, I was run off my feet all day, every day – there was no budget for me to take on any additional help, for now at least – and it was *wonderful*.

'We've done it!' I messaged Lena when I totted up that week's takings.

'I knew we would. Knew YOU would! We'll have a second one open in no time!' she replied, and promised me a slap-up celebratory meal just as soon as she could get away from London for a few days.

Except now … I groan and sink my face into my hands. Maybe this is down to a competitor, someone who's doing something similar, who's trying to sabotage us. But how would they know who our suppliers are? Have they been spying on us, somehow, maybe? I don't know that much about Lena's other enterprises – I haven't even known her that long. We met when she became a regular customer at my previous coffee shop, but we became close very quickly and I do know she has a finger in lots of pies, always travelling, always flying off to meet investors and potential business partners. And yet, she saw something in me, trusted me. How can I tell her about this? How can I tell her everything was fine on Friday, and now today this entire new business has just … *disappeared*?

I can't, not yet. I *can't*. I need more information, need to try to work out what's happened here. I'll leave it, just for a few hours. I tear my eyes away from the building in front of me and twist in my seat, looking down the road behind me. The first faint streaks of dawn are now visible in the sky, and soon customers are going to start arriving, expecting my usual 7:30 opening time, demanding their favourite vanilla lattes and coffee smoothies to kick off the day. That was my creation, the breakfast-in-a-cup smoothie: coffee, rolled oats, banana and a hint of cocoa. We sell dozens every morning. What are they going to think, all these people, when they turn up and see – nothing?

I can't worry about that now. Action, that's what's needed, I think.

First stop, the estate security office. And then, I'm calling the police. I have no idea what's going on here, but I'm damn well going to find out.

Chapter Three

The security office is staffed twenty-four hours a day, and it's just around the corner, so I lock the car and walk. On the outskirts of Gloucester city centre, Redthorpe Park is a small trading estate with around twenty-five units; four cul-de-sacs branch off Main Street, which is used as a cut-through between two busy A roads. The traffic is already building, commuters and commercial vehicles whizzing past me. As I walk, shivering again now and wishing I'd brought my gloves, I curse the fact we didn't bother installing CCTV cameras at the café. There's no central system here; each business is expected to fit its own cameras according to its needs, and because we were a pop-up, planning to stay for just a few months, Lena had decided it probably wasn't worth the expense.

'The place has an alarm, all the buildings do,' she told me. 'And they're all linked up to the security office, and there's someone there round the clock, so they'd be alerted if anyone tried to break in. And all the equipment's insured, so I think we'll be fine, don't worry.'

But now we're *not* fine, are we? I march briskly down the street, eyeing the cameras on the other properties. I desperately need to find out *who* cleared out our place. Maybe one of these cameras picked up some unusual behaviour over the weekend? Then I sigh. There's an endless stream of cars, vans and lorries driving up and down Main Street every day and night; even if one of the security cameras captured footage of a van turning into our road, that would prove nothing. It could just be someone heading for the handy little parking area next to Mug & Meadow, used by both mine and Eric's customers and often random others too, a convenient place to stop and eat a sandwich or make a phone call. I need footage from our actual street: from Eric's camera next door, possibly? There are just three buildings in our little cul-de-sac – Eric's garage on the left, Mug & Meadow at the end, and a large, currently vacant unit on the right – so Eric's is really my only hope. Except I can't ask him for help, not today; he shut up shop on Friday for his holiday and won't be back until this coming Sunday.

Typical of my luck. Just typical, I think, then abruptly stop walking, realising I've reached the security office. I push the door open and am instantly enveloped in welcome, if rather muggy, warmth. Henry, one of several security guards who work shifts to provide the twenty-four-hour service, is sitting behind his battered wooden desk, a large mug of steaming coffee, an open packet of chocolate digestives and a newspaper laid out in front of him. He looks up and grins. He has one front tooth missing, and that combined with his shiny bald head always makes me smile; he looks like an overgrown, happy baby.

'Mornin', Ella,' he says, with a fine spray of biscuit crumbs. He frowns and wipes his mouth with the back of a meaty hand. 'Sorry. What can I do for you this fine Monday? Actually, it's feckin' miserable out there, ain't it?'

'It's not great,' I say. 'And honestly, Henry, I've had better starts to a week.'

'Aww, mate. What's up? Sit down and tell me all about it,' Henry says, and points to the only other piece of furniture in the small, overheated room: an ancient-looking swivel chair, its black plastic upholstery ripped in several places. I give it a quick, surreptitious once-over, but it looks clean enough, so I lower myself onto it and sigh.

'Something *awful* has happened,' I say.

When I've finished explaining – I leave out the bit about the orders being cancelled, because that just feels like an added complication he's unlikely to be able to help with – Henry frowns and taps the keyboard on his desk, squinting at his computer screen.

'I'm just finishin' my shift now,' he mutters, 'and there was definitely nothing untoward 'appenin' overnight. Quiet as the grave. And I'm just checkin' back over the weekend...'

He pauses, leaning forward in his chair, which creaks ominously.

'Nope. That's right back to Friday lunchtime now, and not a single report of an alarm goin' off anywhere on the estate. So, I hate to say this, mate, but if someone entered your property without triggering the alarm, they must 'ave 'ad a key. *And* the alarm code.'

I stare at him.

'But nobody has a key except me and my boss,' I say. 'And, I guess, whoever she rented the place from. But I've got *my* key, and Lena hasn't been down here for weeks, and I hardly think the landlord's going to come and steal all our stuff. Could someone have disabled our alarm, somehow, and then just broken in?'

Henry shakes his head.

'Absolutely not,' he says vehemently. 'If any of the alarms are disabled, as opposed to just turned on or off with the code, that flags up on our system. We'd know. If there's no other damage, it seems to me that someone used a key, switched off the alarm, emptied the place and then changed your lock for some reason. Have you *asked* your boss?'

It's my turn to shake my head.

'No … not yet. I wanted to … well, to try and get some more information about what's happened before I call her. I feel so … *responsible*. I *know* I locked up properly, and I *know* I put the alarm on, but I still feel like it's my fault, you know? I just don't understand … but, OK. Thanks, Henry. I'll call Lena in a bit, but I know what she'll say – she'll ask me if I've reported it to the police. I'll do that first.'

Henry looks doubtful.

'I mean – sure. I suppose if all your stuff's been removed … but if there's no sign of a break-in, and no damage, and the alarm didn't go off…'

He shrugs.

'I know,' I say. 'I know.'

I can feel panic rising, a hard knot in my stomach. I stand up slowly, say goodbye to Henry, and walk out of the office into the cold morning air. Then I pull my phone out of my pocket and dial 101.

Chapter Four

'I reckon that camera's just pointed down at his own forecourt. That won't capture anything of the parking area, or your property. I mean, I could be wrong, but...'

The police officer turns back to look at me, and shrugs. *She's probably right*, I think, with a sinking feeling. We've just checked the position of the security camera on the wall above the closed shutters of Clancy's, and it does indeed seem that it's angled downwards, which is logical, after all. Eric's going to want to see what's happening right outside his garage, not what's going on elsewhere in the street. Even so, the disappointment is crushing.

'Ask him if you can have a look anyway, when he gets back,' the officer is saying. 'But I'd be surprised if you got anything of any use. And honestly, I think you really need to get hold of whoever runs your place as soon as you can. There's probably a simple explanation. It doesn't really feel like a crime's been committed here, you know? More like bad communication within the company, I'd say. I mean, if someone cancelled all your food orders in advance, and told your supplier the café's closing down, and there's been no damage, no alarm going off, a brand-new lock…'

She holds her hands out in a 'what-can-I-say' sort of gesture, and she and her male colleague, who's been listening to our conversation with a bemused expression, exchange glances.

'Agreed,' he says. 'I'd make some phone calls, and then if there really is reason to suspect all your stuff's *actually* been stolen, then get back to us, OK?'

He smiles, and it's a nice smile, on an attractive face with green eyes and a light smattering of stubble. He was definitely checking me out earlier – they always think they're being subtle, don't they, but I saw the way he was eyeing me – and on any other day I might flirt a little, but today is not that day.

'But … that call to my supplier,' I say. 'She said the caller claimed to be *me*. That's … impersonation or something, isn't it? Isn't that illegal?'

I'm clutching at straws now, but I'm starting to feel desperate.

The male officer shakes his head.

'Not by itself. Not unless you're a police officer or a solicitor,' he says. 'If the impersonation carries on, and whoever's doing it uses your identity to commit fraud or something, that's a different matter. But right now, it doesn't sound like much harm's been done. Your orders have been cancelled, but you can just reinstate them, can't you? If the place *isn't* actually closing down, I mean. It's annoying for you, but it's not a crime, unless it keeps happening, when you might be able to claim harassment, possibly. But right now…'

It's his turn to shrug.

'Did you sign a contract, when you took the job?' he continues. 'You said it was a pop-up, so maybe it just…well, popped *down* again? Popped *off*. And they forgot to tell you.'

He grins, and his colleague smiles too. I swallow, the knot in my stomach now seemingly having moved to my throat.

'No … well, it's on its way,' I say. 'My contract, I mean. I was paid cash up front for the set-up time and first month because Lena – my boss – wanted to get the ball rolling and get the café open straight after Christmas. It all happened so quickly she didn't have time to get the contract drawn up before I left for Gloucester so she just said she'd give me a lump sum to keep me going and she'd sort all the paperwork as soon as she could in the New Year. I was expecting it to come through any day now…'

My voice tails off, as I notice the deeply sceptical, raised eyebrow looks on the faces of the two officers.

'Riiigghhtt…' the woman says, slowly. 'Well, our advice, Miss Leonard, would be to speak to your boss. I'm sure she'll be able to clear this up, and if not, well, as Gary here said, give us a call. But I'm not sure there's anything else we can help you with right now.'

They leave, and as I watch their car move slowly down the street, tears spring to my eyes again. I get it, I do … the more I explain to people what's happened here, the sillier and more gullible it makes me sound. But I *know* Lena. I know how excited she is about Mug & Meadow, the high hopes she has for the future, how thrilled she's been about the success of the past few weeks. We last spoke on Friday afternoon, and she was buzzing, telling me how brilliantly I was doing and to make sure I had a restful weekend because I deserved it.

'You're killing it there, seriously, Ella,' she said, adding that she already had her eye on at least two more potential sites, one in Bristol and another in Birmingham. The idea that she just changed her mind overnight and closed the place down without even bothering to inform me is ludicrous. And anyway, Shawna said the orders had been cancelled last *Wednesday*. So Lena just 'forgot' to tell me about that on Friday? No. Something else is going on here, and I *will* get to the bottom of it, but there's no getting away from it now: I'm going to have to call her, and confess that somehow, I've managed to lose *everything* over the weekend, and I am *not* looking forward to that conversation. I sniff loudly, then get back into my car (still parked on the café forecourt, to my relief; I'd been half expecting *that* to have vanished too, when I arrived back from my visit to Henry) and root around in my bag for my notebook and pen. I rip out a page, write 'CLOSED UNTIL FURTHER NOTICE HUGE APOLOGIES FOR ANY INCONVENIENCE' in large capital letters, then open the glove compartment, where I know there's a roll of heavy-duty sticky tape, last used to rather unsuccessfully repair an annoying tear in the driver's side floor mat. I keep catching my heel in it, and new car mats have been on my shopping list for a while. I'd been hoping this new job would finally give me some financial security – maybe, I'd thought, I could even buy a new *car*, not just new accessories for this old banger – but now…

'Don't think about it,' I hiss under my breath. 'Just crack on. Do what needs doing, one thing at a time…'

I find the tape and get out of the car to stick the notice onto the café door. While I was talking to the police, at least half a dozen customers wandered down the street, gaped at the building with confused expressions. then came over to ask me what was going on, and I had to tell them I wasn't really sure, to astonished reactions. I can't bear to face any more of them so, after gazing through the window at the sad, empty interior for a further few seconds, I give myself a mental shake and head for home. As I drive, I call Shawna back, thankful to find the line is busy and I'm diverted to voicemail. I really can't handle speaking to her again right now, and so I leave a message, confirming that I do, after all, want to confirm that all further deliveries should remain cancelled for now. My voice sounds shaky even to my own ears.

I'm desperate to get the place up and running again, and I know Lena said all the equipment is insured, but even so, it's going to take time to source and order replacements, and then there's the insurance claim, all the paperwork ... My stomach is churning as I pull into my allocated parking space outside my apartment building and switch off the Fiat's engine. I'd dismissed the thought earlier when I was talking to Henry, but *could* it be the property's landlord who's done this, some sort of misunderstanding about the length of the lease? Could *they* have come and taken the stuff and put it into storage maybe, because they need the building for a new tenant? We didn't change the alarm code when we moved in, so that wouldn't have posed a problem. But why change the lock? And, that call to Shawna. That's the bit that's bugging me, the bit that doesn't fit. The possibility still needs to be investigated, though, I think, as I climb the stairs and let myself in to number 9, slip my coat off and hang it on the peg inside the door, then head for the kitchen. I'm starting to feel nauseous, and I suddenly realise it's after ten and I haven't had so much as a sip of coffee this morning yet: I normally eat breakfast at work, while I prepare the café for opening time.

I flick the kettle on and push a slice of bread into the toaster, pondering on the landlord thing. The problem is, I still need to speak to Lena first, because I don't even know who our landlord *is*. She organised all that: finding the premises, hiring the equipment and arranging the short-term lease. I had enough to do with dealing with food suppliers, planning menus, sourcing the plants, writing copy for local advertising, and all the squillions of other little jobs that had to be done to get the place up and running. It's not as if the entire trading estate is owned by one company, either – that would be far too straightforward. I don't know who owns our building, but I do know that some of the units are owned by the businesses they house – Eric owns his garage, for example – but others are owned by property firms who lease them. Why didn't I *ask*? I really am stupid, aren't I? This is information I should have, information that might help me to sort this mess out without having to bother Lena. But I'm new to this, and I just didn't *think*.

Bugger. Bugger, bugger, BUGGER.

I force myself to eat, nibbling at my toast with little appetite and slowly sipping an instant coffee. I may sell an extensive selection of superb speciality coffees at work, but all I have at home right now is a screw-top jar from the supermarket. A proper coffee machine is right at the top of my shopping list, once I have some spare cash.

I drain the last, slightly bitter, drops from my mug and brace myself. I can't put it off any longer. I hesitate for a few seconds, then pick up my phone and dial Lena's number.

Darn it. Voicemail.

It's not really a surprise: Lena spends half her life in meetings, and it's rare she answers the phone straightaway.

But this news isn't something I want to share in a voice message, so I keep it short.

'Lena, hi, it's me,' I say, trying to sound upbeat and confident. 'Something rather – erm – unexpected has happened at Mug & Meadow this morning. I really need to speak to you, urgently. Can you call me back as soon as you get this? Thanks.'

I put the phone down on the table and look around. My kitchen is tiny, but cheerful; white walls and units, a sunshine yellow blind, and of course my little collection of plants on top of the fridge – a peace lily, a feathery, delicate lace fern, and my favourite, the rather retro – it was hugely popular in the 70s, but not so much nowadays – burgundy rubber plant, its glossy leaves standing proudly on sturdy stems. Off the kitchen there's a small, cosy living room, and then a windowless bathroom and one bedroom. It's not much, but it's all mine and, even better, there's no rent to pay. I'd been delighted when Lena threw accommodation in as part of my package, but it suddenly dawns on me now that if the café really is closed for good, then I'll have to move out of here too. It makes me even more certain that Lena isn't behind this. There's no way she'd kick me out of my home with no notice, and everything seems fine here anyway, thank goodness. So – the landlord? Or ... I consider again the possibility that the café thing is some sort of massive prank. *Who*, though? Who would do something like this? OK, I definitely pissed off a few people back in the day, there's no doubt about that. I'm the first to admit I wasn't always the easiest person to be around when I was younger, but that's all very much in the past now. I've grown up. I've changed, hugely. I look back now and feel mortified by how I behaved sometimes, how entitled and bratty I was. But didn't we all have our moments, in our teens and twenties? And that was all such a long time ago. Surely it can't have anything to do with any of this? It's not like it's even my business. It's much more likely this is someone with a grudge against *Lena*, if it *is* a prank. But again – a prankster could break the lock, but how would they be able to switch off the alarm, or know which supplier to call to cancel our orders? Did they come into the café for a sneaky look around, maybe? Did they spot some packaging or boxes with Shawna's company name on them? I don't know, I just don't *know*.

My head is beginning to throb. This is hopeless: I could go over and over it all day and drive myself mad, but there's no point in speculating, is there? Not until I can speak to Lena. Practical action, that's what's needed. So, what next?

I pick up my phone again and open my banking app. How's the cash situation? The lump sum I was paid before Christmas is almost gone. Lena had said she'd start paying me monthly from February, with payday on the fifteenth of every month. It's the third today, so twelve days to go, and I have … I tap on my current account and check the balance. Two hundred and twenty-two pounds left. Plus twenty or thirty quid in my purse. OK, I can manage with that. I topped up my mobile at the weekend, so that should last me for a while, and I don't need anything else urgently, other than food. I don't have a credit card; I never have had. It's one of the things that was drummed into me in my childhood – 'live within your means' – and somehow stayed with me. I *never* use credit, but I've always coped so far. I can again. Will I still be paid, though, if the café has to remain closed for a while? I'm sure I will. Even though I do feel responsible for all this in some strange way, none of it is *really* my fault, is it? Lena will understand that. And this is all I have now. It *has* to work. I can't go back to London; there's nothing for me there any more. And I certainly can't go home. I burned *that* bridge a long time ago. No. This is just a blip, something we'll laugh about in years to come when Mug & Meadow is a UK-wide success story. Hey, maybe even a *global* success story. Every new business has teething problems. It's going to be fine.

I look at my phone again, willing there to be a message, one I didn't hear coming in, but the screen remains dark. No messages. Call me back, Lena. *Please*. Quickly.

Chapter Five

L ast night wasn't fun. I tried to get hold of Lena multiple times before finally going to bed, but a second (and then third) voicemail, two texts, a WhatsApp message and an email all remained unanswered. After eventually drifting off just after two, I then began waking what felt like every half an hour and checking my phone, finally giving up on sleep at 6 am and, still in my pyjamas, relocating to the kitchen. I'm still here now, nearly four hours later, and I've lost count of how many bad coffees I've drunk.

Where *is* she? All my messages have stressed how urgent it is that I speak to her, and it's just not like her not to respond, so I'm really worried now. What if it's not just Mug & Meadow that's been a target? What if something's happened to Lena too?

I just don't know what else to do. She doesn't have an office as such; she works from home or from wherever she happens to be each day, and if there's a PA or other support staff, then I've never had any dealings with them. I've always just spoken to Lena directly. I don't have details of any of her family or friends either, no one else I can contact to find out if she's OK. I *think* she's single; if she's been dating recently, she certainly hasn't mentioned it to me. But I don't even know where she's originally from, just that she lives somewhere in the Notting Hill area of London. And her surname, Fox: it's not exactly common, but it's not that unusual either. Just to pass the time, I did a Google search earlier: more than 64,000 people with the name Fox in the UK. I can't exactly start trying to contact them randomly and ask them if they happen to have a daughter or sibling called Lena. And I can't call the police either, can I? Not yet, anyway. Not just because I've been waiting twenty-four hours for replies to a few messages. They'd laugh at me, *again*.

Something really doesn't feel right here though. The disappearance of everything at the café was one thing, but this silence from Lena … there's something very wrong, I know it. My scalp is prickling, my muscles tense, and every time a news alert or an email pops up on my phone, I nearly jump off my chair, adrenaline surging through my body so quickly it makes me feel light-headed. I've made a few more phone calls in the past hour, suddenly realising I'm due a plant delivery from the nursery tomorrow and a fresh batch from the coffee roastery on Thursday. Those orders *hadn't* been cancelled in advance, and so I just told my surprised-sounding suppliers that the place has had to close temporarily due to a water leak, and that I'll be back in touch as soon as it's fixed.

Will it be, though? *Will* this be fixed? *When*? As the hours tick by, my fear and confusion grow. I make myself get dressed, drag a comb through my hair, eat an apple, but I'm finding it hard to sit still, wandering restlessly from room to room, my stomach rolling.

Come on, Lena. Just call me back. Tell me this is all just some crazy misunderstanding, please, I think.

By two o'clock, I can't stand being cooped up in the flat for a moment longer, and so even though the sky is leaden, the clouds a murky, threatening grey, I pull on my coat, stuff my phone in the pocket and go out. There's a park about ten minutes away, so I walk there, head down against the buffeting wind, my pale denim jeans darkening as the rain begins, a spattering at first, then a relentless downpour. I trek on, past the empty play area and basketball court, the bandstand and aviary, not caring that my coat isn't actually waterproof or that my body is starting to ache with cold. I just need to keep moving, to keep *thinking*. I did, briefly, when Lena first offered me this job, wonder if it was all a bit too good to be true, but my doubts had been quickly swept away by her enthusiasm, her passion for her new project contagious. The lump sum she was offering to start me off with had been hard to resist too. I was pretty broke back then, living hand to mouth; my job as barista and deputy manager in a chic Kensington coffee shop paid better than similar roles in the chain cafés, but when you take the cost of living in London into account, well … even though I'd just been renting a single room in a grimy, rundown shared house for most of the previous year, barely socialising or buying new clothes, I'd still been struggling to muddle through to the end of each month. The house came with parking, and so I'd managed to keep hold of my car, reluctant to part with it and always keeping it sparkly clean and ready to go although I rarely drove it – I couldn't afford the fuel, or the London Congestion Charge. But that was about my only luxury, so Lena's offer, when it came, seemed like something I'd have been insane not to grab with both hands, a life raft in an increasingly stormy, hostile sea.

It hasn't always been like this though. I'm thirty-two now, but back in my twenties I had a few golden years. I was a model and, for a while, a successful one. I'm not classically beautiful, or particularly tall or slender, the attributes models used to be expected to have, like those glossy glamazons of the 80s and 90s, the Naomi Campbells and Cindy Crawfords. I was one of the new breed of models, the quirky, the pierced, the tattooed: a full sleeve in my case, my right arm the canvas for an intricate, monochrome masterpiece, a black rose bush cascading from my shoulder to my wrist. Suddenly, people like me were on the front of magazines and strutting down catwalks, the fashion industry's beauty standards becoming more diverse, more inclusive.

I'm not – well, *plain* – I'm not saying that. People have always told me I'm attractive; my hair is thick and naturally blonde, and my eyes are green and rather cat-like in shape, often commented on. But my nose, although straight, is probably a little too long, and I've always been conscious of my ears; they're a bit pointy at the top, like what's-his-name from *Star Trek*. I'm pretty flat-chested too; 'bijou boobs', as Matt, one of my exes, used to joke. Despite my self-perceived flaws, though, I somehow found the confidence at twenty to give it a go: to walk into a model agency I knew represented those who were a little different – the plus-sized, the disabled, the more mature – and just *try*. And, they *loved* me. They signed me on the spot. I hadn't been in a great place at the time. I'm not stupid; I left school with three A-levels, but my home life wasn't ideal back then and I'd lacked direction, not wanting to go to university, persuading the owner of a local fashion boutique to take me on as a sales assistant instead. It had been the first in a string of casual, short-lived jobs, used to fund a party-girl lifestyle, and after a year of me paying no rent and basically using our home as somewhere to sleep and do my laundry, my mother had enough and threw me out.

Well, there was a bit more to it than that, if I'm honest. The final straw was ... something a little more serious. I don't blame her for wanting me gone, put it that way. Anyway, by the time I got my modelling deal a year or so later, I *still* hadn't managed to get my shit together and was officially homeless: still working in crappy jobs and, although not quite on the streets, sofa-surfing and terrified that the tolerance of the few friends I had was about to run out, especially as most of them were struggling too, living in tiny studio flats with barely enough room for their own belongings, never mind an extra fully-grown adult.

The modelling contract changed everything. Almost overnight, the money began to flow in, and for the next five years or so I lived the good life. London Fashion Week, even Paris and Milan a couple of times; a few big campaigns, including several for Topshop; regular magazine fashion spreads. Enough money to rent my own smart little apartment, to holiday in Ibiza and on Greek islands. I didn't save of course; I was young, and living the high life, and I thought it would last for ever, so it was spend, spend, spend. And then, it all started to go wrong again. Gradually, the work began to dry up, and that was, I can admit now, not really because I no longer looked as good, or because I was getting older, or because tattoos were no longer cool. It was because of *me*, because of the person I was back then. It was because of how I *behaved*. It wasn't just my mother I managed to piss off;

somehow, I was *always* falling out with people – photographers, bookers, other models. Some liked me, or liked how I looked, anyway. Straight men, gay women: people who wanted to sleep with me, basically. It sounds arrogant now, but it was just a fact. But those who weren't trying to get me into bed … not so much. I appreciate the friendship of other women so much more these days, but back then … well, I wasn't always a girl's girl, I guess. I never had a tight circle of female friends like others seem to have. I got on fine with some of my non-model housemates, but at work I just kept on messing up. Maybe it was my own insecurities, the highly competitive nature of the business, a reaction to the constant judging and criticism that came along with auditions and castings, but I was definitely a bit of a diva at times, and modelling is a tight industry; word gets around.

At that point in my life though, when the bookings began to slow down, I'd at least learned a bit more about how to look after myself. I was more savvy, more financially aware, and although the modelling didn't grind to a *complete* halt, I knew I needed a back-up, something to keep me going during the lean months. I thought hard about what that should be, and then it came to me – coffee. My favourite drink. Models *live* on coffee. And when does a good coffee shop ever struggle for business, especially in London? So, I decided to do it properly. At twenty-six, I let my fancy apartment go and moved into a house share again to save money, found a café that agreed to take me on and trained partly on the job, partly at college, investing some of my remaining modelling money in a number of courses. Twelve months later I emerged with a food and beverage service diploma, a barista skills award and a food hygiene qualification. I landed a better job in a more upmarket coffee shop and squeezed in the modelling jobs that still occasionally came my way. Life was OK for a while, nice even. Gradually though, over the next few years, the intervals between calls from my agency grew longer and longer. It's a fickle business; there are always new trends, new faces knocking at the door. And when you still, despite huge efforts to shake it off, have a lingering reputation for being 'difficult', you're rarely at the top of anyone's list, and eventually, you slide off the bottom, into that inelegant heap labelled 'former models'.

By the time Lena appeared on the scene, my life had almost turned full circle. I'd lost motivation, lost confidence. I felt stuck in a rut; my job in Kensington was fine, but even though I had the qualifications for a much better role in the catering industry, I was no longer sure if it was right for me, and I kept putting off the chore of looking for a new place to work. And without the modelling side hustle, I was back to just about getting by, spending the last few days of every month surviving on the slightly stale pastries and filled baguettes the café let us take home if they were still sitting unsold in the chiller cabinet as they reached their sell-by date.

Lena changed everything. This new opportunity changed everything. A new, grown-up life, being close friends with my boss, getting on with people, being popular with my customers and the other business owners on the trading estate. I've been happy, really happy, finally. And now it's all gone, and Lena seems to have vanished too.

'Fuck! Fuck, fuck, FUCK!'

I stop walking, suddenly overcome with frustration and rage, and spit the words into the damp air. I'm right next to the duck pond in the middle of the park, and a mallard, pecking in the dirt and clearly startled by my sudden outburst, flaps its wings and lands in the water with a splash, quacking indignantly, its iridescent green head bobbing as it swims rapidly away.

I take a deep breath, then another, fighting back tears, trying to calm myself. Then I pull out my phone.

Nothing. No messages. Right, I've had enough of this. I stab at the screen, feeling furious.

Lena! I'm sorry but this is getting ridiculous. I NEED to speak to you! CALL ME! TODAY!

I hear the familiar *whoosh* as the email vanishes, and I stand stock still for a few seconds, the rain plastering my hair to my face. What now? Go home? Sit there for another long night, just waiting?

Ping.

I jump as an email arrives in my inbox, and instantly I feel my heart rate quicken.

Lena? I tap on the message, but … it's *not* Lena.

It's the email I've just sent her, bouncing back to me, two stark lines of text added at the top.

Delivery to this recipient failed permanently.
Reason: user unknown.

Chapter Six

I stare at my phone, my throat tight, my breathing rapid.

User unknown?

What? Has Lena closed down her email account? Has somebody *else* closed it? My hands are shaking as I dial her number, hoping desperately to hear her cheery voice saying hello, apologising for being so slow in getting back to me, but expecting to hear, yet again, her voicemail, the words so familiar now I can recite them along with her.

'Hi, this is Lena Fox. I'm busy right now but please leave a message and I'll call you back as soon as I possibly can. Thanks!'

Instead, there's no sound at all on the line for a couple of seconds, and then I hear an automated voice, saying words that make my mouth drop open.

'The number you have dialled has not been recognised.'

No. Come on. *Please.*

I cut the call and dial again. I'm trembling so much now I almost drop the phone as I raise it to my ear, but nothing's changed. The same message, the same sick, sinking feeling deep in my guts.

No email address, and now no phone number. I need to think, need to focus, but it's as if my brain and entire body have gone into slow motion as I walk home. I feel as if I'm dragging myself along the pavement, the rain coming down unabated, soaking through my clothes, stinging my face, half blinding me. One minute my mind is racing, searching desperately for answers; the next, it seems frozen, and twice I stop dead at junctions, unsure if I should be turning left or right, confused even about how to get back to the apartment. By the time I finally do, I'm feeling frantic and panicky; I struggle out of my sodden coat and abandon it on the hall floor and then, shivering violently, I grab my laptop and sit down at the kitchen table, panting.

OK, calm down. Calm. Down. It's OK. She'll be here somewhere. You can find her, I think.

I grip the edge of the table, trying to steady myself. I know that, like me these days, Lena doesn't use social media, so there's no point in looking there – she always says she appreciates the power of Instagram and TikTok as business tools, and that we'd set up accounts for Mug & Meadow once it was off the ground, but that she really can't be bothered for herself.

'It's just a timewaster,' she told me once. 'I know what I'm like; I could waste hours scrolling through cat videos and things like that. I'm too busy for it.'

I got it. I used to be all over socials when I was modelling; I can't be bothered these days. But where else can I look? There must be a contact form on her website, right? I've only visited it once or twice, back when she first offered me the job, and I haven't saved it in my bookmarks, so I type the name of her company – Foxy Eats Ltd – into Google. Nothing. Nothing comes up.

What?

I try again, leaving off the 'Ltd', just in case, but there's still nothing: no website, no details whatsoever of any company owned by Lena Fox and encompassing numerous food-related businesses. I stare at my laptop screen, my stomach contracting, my damp clothes clinging uncomfortably to my cold skin. Where is her website? Seriously, where is it? Has that been taken down too? But *why*? Her entire *company* can't have vanished.

'This is *impossible!*' I shout and thump the table so hard my laptop jumps an inch into the air, then lands again with a clatter. I push my hair back off my forehead, my whole body trembling. I've never felt so bewildered in my life. It was *there*, just a few weeks ago. A company website, a glamorous photo of Lena on the home page, all the details in the 'About Us' section of how she'd begun her little empire. How she started offering catering services to fellow students for birthdays and other celebrations while studying business at university, and how now, just fifteen years or so later, her portfolio includes everything from cookery classes to a string of seaside ice-cream trucks to an organic baby food range. I'd been so impressed, so excited when the first Mug & Meadow had been added to the list, so hopeful that one day my picture might be added too, as Lena's business partner. And now … it's gone. No website, no trace of there ever having been one.

I sink my head into my hands and claw at my scalp. Then, a

vague memory pops into my head, and I sit up straight again and gulp in some air. Hang on. Lena did tell me she was in the process of having the website redesigned, didn't she? I remember now…

'The company's getting so big, and so diverse,' she said. We were at Mug & Meadow on that first day in December, when she drove from London to hand over the keys and check the equipment, and she'd been chatting away while I wandered around the café only half listening to her, my mind full of the possibilities offered by this fresh, white space that was to be all mine to shape and grow.

'It's so exciting! I'm planning a bit of an online relaunch in the new year,' she went on. 'I just need to find time to sit down with a web designer. It's a bit basic right now, the website, isn't it? No proper links to the various arms of the business or anything. It's not really my area, the tech stuff. We can do some photos of this place for it, though, can't we, when it's ready?'

'Sure, whatever you need,' I'd replied. 'Ooh…!'

I'd been distracted by pulling the shiny new coffee grinder from its cardboard box, and she'd laughed and changed the subject. I'd forgotten all about the darn website, but now I wonder if that's all it is – has the website been taken down because Lena's finally got round to redesigning it? It's just that the timing's so suspicious, with everything else that's going on…

OK, so think. How else can I get hold of her? God, I'm so cold though…

I push the laptop away and stand up. I need to get warm and dry first; I can't concentrate properly feeling like this. I go and get changed, throwing my wet clothes into the laundry basket in the bathroom and pulling on a thick sweatshirt and leggings, then blasting my hair with my hairdryer. Back in the kitchen, I make some coffee and put a couple of chocolate biscuits on a plate, and then, feeling a little better, sit down at the table again.

Right. Let's do this. Be methodical, I think.

I start with Google, but although the name 'Lena Fox' brings up numerous results, none of them is the right Lena. I spend several minutes scrolling through images, but her face doesn't appear, and the same thing happens when I search LinkedIn. My heart's starting to thump again, niggly little doubts beginning to creep into my head. Even if her own website is down, someone with as many businesses as she has should have some sort of online presence. There should be mentions of her all over the place. Why can't I find her? And why didn't I do this before, when she first offered me the chance to work with her? She sent me the link to her website, and I looked at that, but I didn't do anything else, did I? No proper research. I just didn't feel the need; she seemed so genuine. And it's all been fine up until now. *Better* than fine. It's been fantastic. But ... what do I know about Lena Fox, really, in the short time we've been friends? And yet ... she paid me all that money. She set me up in this apartment. She provided everything I needed to get Mug & Meadow up and running. If it was all some sort of scam, *why*? What would she gain from it? There must be some logical explanation for all this, there *must* be.

I stand up and start pacing the kitchen, thinking about last October when Lena became a regular at the Kensington coffee shop. She started coming in every day, always around ten, when the breakfast rush was over and before the busy period we always got mid-morning, and she'd sit there tapping away on her laptop or chatting earnestly on the phone, sipping a latte and nibbling a pain au chocolat or a cinnamon and raisin Danish as she worked. She stood out, even though most of our customers were well dressed and well spoken. Her sleek blonde bob, her expensive leather handbags, her beautifully tailored coats. After a while, we got chatting, and she told me she was overseeing the catering operation at a nearby art gallery which had had to outsource for six weeks while its kitchen facilities were upgraded. As the days went on, she opened up even more, and told me so many interesting stories about her other business interests that her arrival each morning became the highlight of my day.

'Wow,' I remember saying. 'You're not much older than me, are you? And look how much you've achieved! It's amazing.'

She shrugged modestly, but I could tell she was pleased by the compliment. After that, she seemed to take an even keener interest in me, even inviting me to join her at her favourite window table every now and again when I was due a break and she didn't have any urgent phone calls to make. Even though, as I've said before, I've sometimes found female friendships tricky, that hangover from my modelling days, now and again someone comes along whom I really click with, and that's what happened with Lena. I told her all about my former career, and about how becoming a barista and moving into café management had been my back-up plan. I told her about the courses I'd done and the qualifications I'd earned, and about my anxiety about the future. I guess all of that got her thinking, but it was the plants that really did it in the end.

There'd been a few in the place when I joined, dotted around on the tables and the counter, but I felt it needed more; I wanted that feeling of stepping into a leafy hideaway, that sense of nature surrounding me in busy west London, and so I persuaded the manager to let me do a little green makeover. The customers loved it, and when Lena realised it had been my idea she clapped her hands with glee. That was when she offered me the Mug & Meadow job.

'Honestly, if you move out of London, you'll get so much more for your money too,' she said, when she first mooted the idea. 'Property, cost of living … you won't know yourself. I know it would be a big change, and that's scary, but from what you've told me, you're ready for this, Ella, I know you are.'

And the rest, of course, is history.

But now, as I sit at my kitchen table, I have a growing sense of dread. What if I'm evicted from this apartment too, now that everything else seems to be disappearing? What do I do when my money runs out? I don't even have Lena's bank details, do I? Maybe I could have traced her through them, but she paid me in cash, which I put straight into my own bank account.

Bank account. Wait a minute…

I may not have Lena's bank details, but there's a business account for Mug & Meadow, the one I used to pay the café takings into. Is there any way I can trace her through that? Maybe if I call the bank and tell them it's an emergency?

My hand shaking slightly, I make the call, but twenty minutes later, after first being held in a queue and then finally having a very brief conversation with a business adviser, I put my phone down again feeling close to tears.

Closed. The business account for Mug & Meadow was closed yesterday. They couldn't tell me anything else, but the fact that it's no longer open doesn't even come as a surprise now. It's just gone, like everything else.

'BULLSHIT!'

I scream into the quiet room, my hands balling into fists. Why didn't I insist on a proper contract from the off? Why did I just take her word for everything? That's me all over though; did I even *read* my first modelling contract, when the agency gave it to me to sign? Of course I didn't. I just scrawled my name, whooped and went off to the pub to celebrate. Have I ever properly read any employment contract since? Nope. Always too grateful to be offered a job, too eager to accept, whatever the terms and conditions might be. It was no different this time. I took a job that seduced me with a wad of cash and a nice apartment and the promise of a bright future, and signed absolutely nothing.

Idiot. Absolute fuckwit.

I stare at my screen for a few seconds, blinking away angry tears. Then another thought strikes me. *Companies House.*

A memory has flashed into my head of a lecture at college about the steps we'd need to take if we ever wanted to set up our own business. Companies House registers company information; as far as I can remember, you don't have to register if you're a sole trader, but a limited company must. And Lena's company is called Foxy Eats *Ltd.* Companies House makes information available to the public; might there be a way of tracking her down there? I bring up the website and, my stomach clenching, click on 'get information about a company', then type the name into the search bar.

And … surprise, surprise, nothing. It's just not there. Lots of similar names, but not the right one. No Foxy Eats Ltd. I scroll up and down the page, eyes scanning every line, desperate to find it.

Come on. Come *on*. Where are you?

A little sob escapes me. What's the point? It's not here, is it?

It's not here, and if it was a proper limited company it would *have* to be here. So what does that mean?

Slowly, I push the laptop away from me. I know exactly what it means.

It means Lena's company doesn't exist.

Chapter Seven

Wednesday morning, and I feel wobbly and nauseous after another horrible night of little sleep and raging anxiety. At 3am, I found myself sitting up in bed manically dialling Lena's number over and over again, as if it might have magically reconnected itself in the early hours. It hadn't, of course, but that didn't stop me then emailing her repeatedly instead, only to see the bounce-back message over and over again.

I've given up now. What's the point? My head is throbbing. I'm not usually a headachy sort of person, but this seems to be literally hurting my brain. I simply don't understand any of it, and until I can find someone who does, there's no benefit in sitting here with everything going round and round in dizzying circles in my head. I'm going to drive myself insane. At nine, not knowing what else to do, I swallow down a couple of paracetamol and a piece of toast then drive back to the industrial estate. I pull up onto the café forecourt and as I cut the engine I frown, immediately spotting something.

The notice I stuck on the door. Where is it? And what's that, in its place?

I get out of the car and walk quickly towards the building, then gape at the small, square red and white sign that, somehow, has appeared *inside* the central glass panel of the door.

Available for rent, it says, followed by an agent's name, address and number.

'It's flipping *not* available for rent,' I mutter out loud. 'It's *already* rented.'

Then, I realise what this sign means. This is a *good* thing. Finally! Finally someone I can talk to. Someone who might be able to shed a bit of light on this holy mess.

I pull out my phone and take a picture of the sign, then get back into my car and dial the number.

A man answers.

'Burton and Grant Commercial, good morning. How can I help?'

'Erm … hi, my name's Ella Leonard, and I've been running Mug & Meadow, the new café on the Redthorpe Park Trading Estate? This is going to sound a bit strange, but when I arrived for work on Monday the place had been … well, cleared out and locked up. I've had trouble getting hold of my boss and I didn't actually know how to contact the landlord or anything until just now when I saw your sign in the window. Can you tell me what's going on? I mean, someone's changed the lock and taken all the equipment and cancelled the suppliers and everything…'

'Just hold the line, please. I'm putting you through to Adrian Grant.'

There's about thirty seconds of silence, and I've just started jiggling my knees up and down impatiently, nerves swirling in my stomach, when another male voice says:

'Adrian here. Miss ... Leonard? Peter tells me you apparently weren't aware of the short-term nature of the let at the Redthorpe Estate? I'm very sorry you weren't kept in the loop, but I can assure you everything's above board. The rental was for a month initially, with the agreement it would be renewed on a weekly basis thereafter. We were given notice ... let me check ... yes, on Friday the twenty-fourth of January. We agreed that last Friday, the thirty-first, would be the café's last day of trading and that the premises would be cleared over the weekend. That happened as planned on Sunday morning. Unfortunately, the door lock was accidentally broken during the process but the team who did the removals very efficiently fitted a new one the same day and handed us the new keys. I'm not sure what else I can tell you.'

'But ... but...' I stutter.

How can this be right? We were supposed to be there for several months, not just a matter of weeks. Again, none of this is ringing true. If someone – Lena, presumably, because who else? – gave notice over a week ago, why wouldn't she have told me?

I make a mental note of 'Sunday morning', but I need more information.

'Adrian, can you tell me who gave notice on the premises?' I ask. 'And who came to clear the place? Do you have those details?'

'Erm...'

Adrian Grant pauses.

'Well, obviously I can't give out any confidential information. But ... well, I do have the email here in front of me. It's from Lena Fox? Your boss, I presume? I think you really need to speak to her…'

Blood roars in my ears, and for a few seconds I can't speak. Then I gulp in some air.

'Yes, yes, I will,' I manage to say, but in my head I'm thinking:

What now? What else do I need from this man? Because an email from Lena's now defunct address is no help to me at all…

'Do you … do you know who came and took all the contents away? It's just that … well, I left a couple of personal items in the café, and I don't know who to contact to get them back.'

It's a lie, but it just might work, and I grip the phone tightly, my whole body tensing as I wait for Adrian to reply. He's muttering under his breath now, and I can hear papers rustling on the other end of the line.

'Hmmm,' he says. 'I was here when they popped in with the keys, but I don't think…'

Another pause.

'I'm really sorry, Ms Fox seems to be the only contact I have. I do remember she was with two men though, when we did the handover…'

'Lena? Lena came herself? Are you sure? What did she look like?'

My throat is tightening, my chest constricting, the panic rising again.

'Well … I don't like to comment too much on a woman's appearance, everything gets misinterpreted these days,' says Adrian, with a little laugh. 'But … well, she was very attractive. Blonde hair. Smartly dressed.'

I swallow hard.

'And – the two men? Do you remember anything about them?'

'Not really. One came in with her, but I didn't pay him much attention. Thirties, dark hair, wearing overalls I think? They were in and out, just handed over the keys and signed a document for me. It only took a minute or so. The other guy was waiting outside in the van... My desk is right by the window, so I watched them drive off, but I'm afraid I couldn't see him clearly at all.'

Shit. Shit.

'And the van? Did it have a company name or anything on it?' I ask, and even I can hear the desperation in my voice.

'I don't think so,' he replies slowly. 'Just a rental, I think. I don't remember the company though. Sorry, but I don't really think I can be of much more help. If you need your things back, I suggest you go through Ms Fox. I'm sure she'll be able to assist.'

'But ... I can't...'

Tears have unexpectedly sprung to my eyes, and I stop talking for a few moments, trying to gather myself.

'Look ... this is really, really important,' I say. 'Do you have any CCTV maybe, of the people, or the van outside? I'm really struggling to get hold of Lena, and I need...'

'Gosh no, I'm afraid not,' Adrian says. 'We're a small office, and we don't keep any valuables or cash on site, so we simply don't need security cameras. Contact Ms Fox, that's my best advice. And I'm afraid I have another call coming in, so I'm going to have to go now. I'm sure you'll get everything sorted. Good luck, Miss Leonard. Bye now.'

Chapter Eight

I feel numb as I drive back to the apartment.

Lena. This *was* Lena.

Or at least, it now *appears* it was she who terminated the rental agreement; she too who came, along with whoever those men were, to close the place down. So – nothing's happened to her, has it? She's fine. It's me that's in the shit. But why? *Why?* I give up. It's unfathomable, and I still can't quite believe it, but what can I do? Maybe this is how she does business. Maybe she's a completely different person to the one I thought I knew, and all the 'nicey-nicey' was just an act. I was just a naive idiot. Even though she seemed thrilled with how well the café was doing, she just changed her mind about keeping it going.

And didn't bother to tell me? Who does that? Who the fuck *does business like that?* I think.

Well, that's clearly what's happened. The more the realisation sinks in, the more I feel sick, actually physically sick. I'm trying to stay angry, but I know what I really am now is scared, more scared than I think I've ever been in my life. I know I just have to accept this, and move on. But to where? Where do I go now? What do I do?

I drive on autopilot, and when I reach my building I sit in the car park for a solid ten minutes, unable to summon up the energy to even get out of my car. When I do, finally, slowly climb the stairs to the second floor, I stop abruptly on the landing, and stare at what's piled outside my door.

What ... what are all those? Have I come to the wrong landing?

My gaze moves to the door, to the dull brass number 9 nailed to it. It *is* my apartment. My chest tightens, and I look back at the floor, at the little stack of cardboard boxes. Boxes that are full, I know immediately, even without opening them, of my belongings.

And there we have it. The obvious next step. I've been evicted, haven't I?

I feel strangely calm, my hand surprisingly steady as, just in case, I pull out my door key and try it in the lock. It won't budge. I'm locked out. Of course I am. *Fuck.* I've only been gone an hour, an hour and a quarter at most. Were they outside, Lena and her cronies, watching? Waiting for me to leave the building so they could run in and do this? Pack up my pathetic little life and leave it for me to collect? Good at changing *stinking* locks quickly, aren't they?

'AAAAGH!'

The fury is building again, and suddenly it's white-hot, crashing over me like a wave. I kick viciously at the nearest box, immediately wishing I hadn't, as pain shoots up my big toe, and then up, up, into my stomach, my chest, my throat. I groan, and sink to the floor, my legs crumpling under me. This isn't really physical pain, though, this sensation that's sweeping over me. It's the pain of betrayal. The pain of suddenly knowing, without any doubt whatsoever now, that, for reasons I still can't comprehend, this *has* been done to me deliberately. Lena Fox gave me everything, then ripped it away again, leaving me with nothing. *Nothing.* No job, no home, and soon, I realise with a shiver of fear, no money either. This isn't just bad business practice, this is personal, I'm sure of it now. All orchestrated by a woman who, as far I'm aware, I'd never even met until a few months ago. Who is she, really? *Do* I know her, from my dim and distant past, maybe, and just didn't recognise her? Or did someone put her up to this? But why?

'WHY?'

I howl the word. It bounces off the magnolia-painted walls of the landing, echoing back at me, and I drop my head onto my knees and sob. I'm not sure how long I've been sitting here, my shoulders heaving, my cheeks wet, but suddenly I feel a gentle tap on my shoulder and I jump violently.

'Sorry … gosh, I'm so sorry, I didn't mean to frighten you? It's just, I heard … Are you OK? What's happened?'

It's a woman I vaguely recognise, older, in her sixties maybe, with short, greying dark hair and an anxious expression on her lined, kind-looking face. She lives downstairs, I recall now, as I rub my hands across my face and stand up.

'I'm OK. Well, sort of,' I say, and she frowns, gesturing at the sad pile of cardboard boxes.

'I heard you shouting. Have you … have you been kicked out or something?' she asks.

'Looks like it,' I reply. 'I don't suppose you saw who did

this? I only popped out for an hour or so. Looks like they've changed the lock and everything.'

'Well, yes, I did see some people earlier actually. A blonde woman and a man coming in the main entrance. The man had a toolbox. I just assumed they were doing some repairs or something. I didn't pay them much attention really; I was just nipping out to the bins. Is it some sort of mistake? Can you call the landlord and sort it out?'

No, I can't. Because Lena arranged this place for me, and I have no idea who the landlord is, I think. *Because I'm a dimwit, who never asked. But you can guarantee that even if I did find them, it would be the same story as the café. A short-term let, which has now been terminated…*

'Yeah, I'm sure I can,' I say casually. 'Erm … do you think there'd be any CCTV footage of them? The two people? I've never really noticed if there are security cameras around. You know, just in case it *was* a mistake, and the landlord needs to know who they were?'

She shakes her head, looking confused.

'They didn't break in though, did they? Is some of your stuff missing? There aren't any cameras outside or inside in the public areas, I'm afraid. All the apartments are privately owned; I was one of the first to move in and we all decided we'd just deal with our own security, to keep the building service charge down. I have a camera outside my front door, a few of us do. But if they used the stairs from the lobby and came straight up here they wouldn't be seen on that. If your apartment or number 8 have cameras they'd be on those though…'

She looks up at the wall above number 9, and then turns to look at the door of the adjacent apartment, the only other door on this floor apart from the one that opens onto the stairwell.

'Oh,' she says. 'Neither of you have one. So – no, then. I doubt there'd be any footage.'

'OK ... never mind. It's fine,' I reply, but I feel like screaming.

How do I find out who they are, then? It's almost certainly Lena, or the woman I know as Lena, this blonde woman. But what about these men who are helping her? Do I know *them*? Give me a frigging break, universe, please...

'Look ... I need to go now, I'm expecting my daughter any minute,' the woman is saying. 'As long as you're OK? I hope you get it all sorted.'

She smiles, and pats me on the arm, and I smile back and thank her, fighting an irrational urge to cling to her like a frightened child and beg her not to leave me, to ask her if I can stay with *her* tonight, even though I don't even know her name. As she disappears through the door to the stairs, I turn slowly back to the boxes, trying not to burst into tears again. They're not sealed, and I open a few, to check. There's no food or drink, not that I had much in the fridge anyway, but everything else looks OK. My clothes, my toiletries, even my plants; it all seems to be here, nothing obviously damaged or missing. I travelled light when I left London. I didn't have much anyway, having always lived in furnished rentals, but I wanted a fresh start, so I sold the few bits I did have – a few vases, an antique chair, a bedside table – and moved to Gloucester with just the essentials. I'd started acquiring a few extra bits in the past few weeks though, and now I'm deeply regretting it. Will I even fit all this in my little car? And where am I going to sleep tonight? A hotel, until I can make some sort of plan and find a new job? The little money I have left won't last long if I have to pay for hotels…

I realise I'm biting my lower lip so hard it hurts.

OK, stop overthinking. One step at a time. Load up the car first.

It takes me six trips, up and down, up and down, cursing the fact the building doesn't have a lift. Finally though, everything is crammed into my Fiat, the boot, back seat and passenger footwell full of all my worldly goods. Then I realise I need to take some of them out again for tonight, so I spend another ten minutes rooting through the boxes, pulling out cosmetics and clothes and cramming them into a holdall. By the time my overnight bag is ready, the anger is back, and I've made a decision. I'm going to go to the police, again, because what was it that officer said to me on Monday?

'…it's not a crime, unless it keeps happening, when you might be able to claim harassment…'

I mean, what is this, if it's not harassment? I've done absolutely nothing wrong, and yet suddenly I've lost my job *and* my home, with no warning whatsoever. This can't be legal, can it?

I may be still completely in the dark about who's really behind this, and why. But if they think I'm just going to meekly accept it, they're very, *very* wrong. I pull my seat belt on, ease the car out of its parking space and head towards Gloucester police station.

Chapter Nine

I perch on the end of the narrow single bed and take a sip of tea from a thick white ceramic mug, trying to remember what day it is. Thursday. Day four of this horrible new chapter of my ludicrous life.

Outside, the city is just waking up, the traffic beginning to build, streaks of silver piercing the graphite grey sky. I spent the night in a city centre B & B, after a fruitless, frustrating chat with a police officer who, although sympathetic, told me she really couldn't offer me any help whatsoever.

I'd asked to speak to one of the officers I met on Monday, but they weren't available, which meant I had to wait first for someone else to become free, and then for her to track down the details of my case. When I finally got to sit down with her in a small, windowless interview room, she listened patiently, then shook her head slowly.

'Look, I do understand this isn't very nice, and that it's put you in an unfortunate position,' she said. 'But … like my colleagues earlier in the week, I can't really see that any crime's been committed here. I mean, none of your belongings have been *stolen*, have they?'

'No,' I said. 'But...'

'And if the apartment came with the job, and the job is finished, and you didn't have any sort of contract...' she continued. 'Well ... my advice is to make sure you have a contract in future, and check the small print. I'd say your boss has certainly acted a bit ... well, *unethically*. But this isn't a criminal case. You could try getting some legal advice, see if there's any sort of civil court claim you can make, but I'm not sure you'd even have a leg to stand on there. It sounds to me that you were paid a nice sum of money to run a pop-up food place for a short time, with accommodation thrown in, and that short time is now over. I'm sorry. There's really nothing we can do.'

I sat in my car and cried for a bit after that. It's becoming a habit. Then I pulled myself together and logged on to my banking app to remind myself of the sorry state my finances were in. I still had £30 and a few coins in my purse, plus precisely £180 left in my account. I'd filled the car with petrol on my way to the police station, realising I was almost on empty, and I cursed myself for wasting the forty or so quid it cost me. But then I thought:

No, I need to keep the car on the road. If I have to find another job, and somewhere else to live, it's probably going to be cheaper to drive around than to keep forking out for public transport. And I can live on this for a while, can't I, if I'm careful?

I don't want to go down the claiming benefits route, not unless things get really desperate. It's something I've never done, *ever*, and I know that's what the system is there for, but as far as I know a new claim takes weeks to process and while there's probably some sort of emergency payment I might qualify for, given my circumstances, that's for people in real need, not people like me. I can sort this out myself, I *can*. I'll be back on my feet soon. I just need to live on a very tight budget for a bit.

And so I went online and scoured local accommodation websites until I found a cheap guesthouse with decent reviews, costing just £35 a night, with parking for an additional £8. I could have added breakfast for another tenner, but when I checked in – it was dated and shabby, but at least it was clean – I found tea and coffee plus a kettle and tiny fridge in the room, so I nipped out to the little grocery on the corner of the road and bought a couple of prepacked sandwiches, an apple, a banana and a bag of cheese and onion crisps. Dinner and breakfast covered for a few quid.

Now, I wipe a breadcrumb from my top lip and stare out of the window at the street below, watching as two men in luminous yellow jackets haul barrels of beer from the back of a lorry and roll them into the pub opposite. I made myself eat, but now my stomach is cramping, and I'm feeling shaky with worry. My phone credit situation is OK for now, but with the money I have left, even if I spend as little as possible on food, I can still only really stay here for three nights, max. I've completely ruled out returning to London, which means I need to find another job, here, *today*. Ideally, one that will pay me weekly, although even surviving a week is going to be a massive struggle at this rate. And I'm so, so tired. Did I sleep at all, last night? I'm not sure I did, my mind in turmoil, my heart rate as high as if I'd just run a marathon.

I'm still racking my brain, trying to work all this out. Last night, I plucked up the courage to call Karen, my old manager in Kensington, to ask her if she'd seen Lena recently. I didn't hold out much hope – she'd only become a café regular because of her art gallery contract, which ended ages ago – but Karen is brilliant at remembering customers' faces, even if they only pop in once a week.

If Lena, or whoever she really is, is *still using the place, maybe I will go back to London for a few days and try and find her there,* I reasoned.

Unfortunately and, in retrospect, completely unsurprisingly, Karen did *not* sound delighted to hear from me and was clearly not in the mood to be helpful.

'Seriously, Ella? You quit with a few weeks' notice, when you know I'm already short-staffed, and swan off to your fancy new job without a backward glance? And now it's all gone tits up you expect me to track down your runaway new boss for you?' she said, coldly. 'Well, I haven't seen her since you left, I'm afraid. And if you don't mind, I'm going to go now because I just got in from work and there's a hot bath waiting for me. My bloody feet are killing me.'

I couldn't blame her. Me, very briefly slipping back into behaving like stupid old model me again. Too over-excited about my new job, my sunny new future. Why was I so inconsiderate? Karen was a good boss, and I *didn't* give her a proper notice period; I *did* walk out without looking back, even though I knew she'd probably struggle for cover. I should be ashamed of myself; I *am* ashamed, both of treating her so carelessly and of being such a trusting fool. Another life lesson learned, and if I get out of this mess, I'll never make either of those mistakes again. And I *will* get out of it. I'm a shambles right now, but I still have a bit of fighting spirit left in me. Lena might have royally screwed me over, but she can't stop me starting again. I still have my car, and my skills. She can't take those from me.

And so I go out – stopping in the hallway to say good morning to my host and booking in for another two nights – and, on foot for now so as not to waste my precious petrol, I start pounding the streets, pausing at every café, coffee shop and restaurant to look for 'staff wanted' notices in the windows. As almost always in this industry, I find several, and two hours later, almost to my own astonishment (because how appalling has *my* luck been recently?), I have a job.

Well, not a proper job, exactly, but a trial shift for tomorrow in Cloisters, a decent-looking traditional style tearoom on a cobbled side street not far from Gloucester cathedral. It's not exactly a step up for me – they need someone who can both work behind the counter and help clean the place – but I can't afford to be fussy, and the frazzled-looking manager, Donna, doesn't ask me too many awkward questions about my previous job, for which I'm deeply grateful. She simply nods approvingly when I quickly run her through my experience and qualifications, then gives me a temporary employee form to complete and asks if I can do a paid trial day starting at seven in the morning, adding that she can probably offer me four or five shifts a week if things work out. I hesitate before filling in the requested home address on the form; a guest house, I know, is unlikely to be acceptable, and so I write down the address of the apartment I've just been kicked out of. She's not likely to check, after all, and I can always say I've moved, if this turns into anything more permanent.

As I plod back to the B & B, though, my brief feeling of elation is slowly nudged out by worry curling its way back into my thoughts. Donna does pay weekly, I checked, but even if tomorrow goes well, which I'm determined it will, it could be the middle to end of next week before I get any money, and how much will depend on how many shifts I actually end up being given. I can't afford to stay anywhere after tomorrow night, which means that on Saturday morning I'll be homeless. If I was a normal person, a person who actually had a supportive family or a solid group of friends, I could phone someone and borrow some money now, just until I get myself sorted. Maybe even go and stay with someone for a few days. But I'm not a normal person, am I? I'm Ella Leonard, professional plonker. I try hard, and I'm so much better at it all these days, but right now I'm on my own again. So I'll just have to manage, somehow.

I pause at the door of the guesthouse, and look at my car, parked in the small walled yard to the side.

I can sleep in that, I think. *Just for a few nights. It'll be fine. I'll do some research this evening, find somewhere safe to park up. Somewhere I can go to get showered and changed. A local swimming pool, possibly? Something like that. They don't cost too much to get into, do they?*

Yes, that's what I'll do. It'll be OK. And I can get a second job too, maybe. Find some even cheaper accommodation for the next few weeks. Try to save enough money for a deposit on a room in a shared house again, just for now. Just until I get myself back on my feet again.

I push open the front door and head for the stairs up to my room with a new feeling of determination, combined with a ripple of fresh anger.

I can and I will get myself out of this hole. And once I have, I'm coming after you, Lena Fox, or whoever you are. I assure you, you are not going to get away with it.

Chapter Ten

I bring the car to a stop and cut the engine, then look around warily. I'm home, if you can call a layby on the A38 just outside Gloucester 'home'. It's going to have to do for a few nights though, if I want to eat for the next week. After some extensive research, I decided this would be my best bet: a spacious layby separated from the busy dual carriageway by a grass reservation, with hedges and fields on the other side, and just a fifteen-minute drive from my new workplace. Having never done this before, I wasn't very clear on whether it's even *legal* to sleep in your car, but apparently it's fine, as long as you obey the parking rules of the area you've stopped in and don't cause an obstruction. And as long as you're not over the alcohol limit for driving, which could lead to you being charged with being drunk in charge of a motor vehicle. Not that *that's* going to be an issue; I'd kill for a nice big gin and tonic or a glass of red wine, but I absolutely can't afford to buy booze at the moment.

It was *where* to park that was tricky. I ruled out proper car parks because they all charge money, of course, and some – even at motorway service stations – have maximum stay limits, often just four hours. I didn't want to risk a residential area either, fearing too much curiosity from locals, and when I started looking at laybys I had to rule out several of those too, after a Google search brought up a few websites recommending them for hook-ups and dogging. Those sorts of encounters I can *definitely* do without. But this one seems OK. Other than my little car, there's just one lorry parked in it right now; I've tucked in behind it, its bulk giving me a sense of protection. It's already dark, but up on the left I can see a couple of rubbish bins, which is handy; there are no toilets, but I made sure I went before I left the café and if I do need a wee in the night, I'll just have to go in the bushes. Needs must.

I make sure the doors are locked, then slip off my seat belt.

It's fine. It's going to be fine, I tell myself.

My trial shift at Cloisters went well yesterday; I could tell Donna was impressed with my barista skills, and when I didn't grumble when she asked me to pop in and give the toilets a quick once-over after what she said was a particularly busy lunchtime, she took me aside and told me she'd already made up her mind, and was happy to keep me on, albeit on a zero-hours contract.

'I have two regulars who are higher up the pecking order, I'm afraid, love,' she said. 'But Kev is off sick this week and Anita often has short-notice childcare issues, so, you know … I'll give you as much work as I can, OK?'

I accepted gratefully. Deep down, I know I'm worth more than this; I know I could get a much better job, if I wasn't so desperate, so short of cash. But right now, with so much going on in my head, this is about all I can manage, and as it turns out Donna asked me to come in again today and has already told me she'll need me on Monday and Tuesday too, which is great. She's closed tomorrow, Sunday; being so close to Gloucester cathedral she opens seven days, she told me, from Easter, when tourists begin to flock to the mediaeval building and work up an appetite for tea, coffee and cake. But now, in quiet, dreary February, she makes the most of having Sundays to herself. I'm not sure what *I'm* going to do tomorrow; maybe I won't think about that just yet. There's tonight to get through first.

There's a little yard behind Cloisters where staff can park for free during the day, and before I left this evening I spent some time assembling everything I'd need overnight and stacking it on the passenger seat. All my belongings on the back seat are covered with a blanket, just in case; I don't really have much worth stealing, but I'm worried that one of the other staff will ask why my car is bulging with so much *stuff*. They haven't yet, thankfully; Donna walks to and from work, and maybe those who do use the yard simply haven't noticed; maybe they have and have just decided it's none of their business. If they did peer in, they might wonder about the plants though; they're crammed into the passenger footwell, a mini, knee-high jungle, and I've been switching their positions every day, trying to make sure they all get their share of daylight. I dearly wish I could just stay *there* overnight, in that private little back yard, safe and relatively quiet, but I can't, of course, because I lied to Donna about where I live, and I can't risk her returning to the tearoom unexpectedly and finding me dossing in my car.

And, other than shower and toilet facilities, I have enough to get by, don't I? I think, trying to remain optimistic, as I pull a fleece blanket from the pile next to me and wrap it over my knees. The apartment Lena organised for me was fully furnished, right down to pillows and duvets, but I had a couple of cushions and throws of my own, and they'll do for my makeshift bed this evening. I'm a little anxious about how cold it's going to be; I've checked the weather forecast, and it's likely to drop to around minus three tonight. But I plan to sleep in my clothes; I have thick socks and several jumpers if I need them, and I can always switch the engine on and turn the heating up full blast for a few minutes if it's really freezing. I don't want to do that too often, conscious of wasting fuel, but it's an option. Hygiene-wise, I have antibacterial wipes, cleanser, cotton wool and several bottles of water, and I'll just have to get out of the car and spit in the bushes when I clean my teeth. I have a couple of magazines someone left on a table in the café earlier to keep me entertained, and I made sure I fully charged my phone before I left work, so I can use the torch on that for extra light if I need it. I even managed to come away with a free dinner; Donna handed me a leftover sausage roll and an iced vanilla cupcake at the end of my shift. It's not the healthiest meal, but it will keep me going until morning.

There's a leisure centre a couple of miles away, and that's where I'm planning to shower and change. It opens at six in the morning on weekdays, eight at weekends; you have to book a session in the pool to get access to the changing rooms, but I've already done that for tomorrow, Monday and Tuesday, at a cost of £5 a day. My bank balance is dwindling frighteningly fast – I'm surviving on the cheapest, sell-by-date-about-to-expire supermarket sandwiches, and I now have about forty quid left – but if I keep my spending on food to a minimum, and hopefully get my hands on some more café leftovers, I'll just about make it to Wednesday, when Donna said she'll pay me. And there'll be tips too, hopefully.

'So here we go,' I say aloud to my rubber plant, and reach out a finger to stroke one of its smooth leaves. 'Night number one. Let's do this.'

Three hours later, I'm bored. I've read the magazines, eaten my dinner and drunk a bottle of water, sharing it with my plants, and the traffic thundering past – so heavy at times that my little car shook – has started to diminish, rush hour over. The few vehicles that pull into the layby behind me from time to time don't stay long, and now it's after nine and there's just me and the HGV still parked in front of me. I haven't seen the driver, so I assume he or she is sleeping. I only got out of the car once, my hood up against the light drizzle, a plastic bag and a roll of toilet paper clutched in my hands. I squeezed through a gap in the hedge to squat uncomfortably and pee, then put the used tissue into the bag and deposited it in the layby bin.

How on earth has my life come to this? I mused, as I got back into the car, but I immediately pushed the thought away. It's happened, and for now all I can focus on is getting through each day, until I have money again and can sort myself out.

Now, I pull on a second pair of socks and lower my seat back as far as it will go, which isn't very far, thanks to the mound of my possessions on the rear seat. It's far from comfortable – my legs aren't that long, but this car is tiny, and I can't stretch out fully – but I have my two plump cushions for my head and neck and my two blankets to snuggle under, and suddenly I feel bone-tired and mentally exhausted. I'll sleep, I'm sure I will.

And I do. I drift off quickly, but I wake again around

midnight, stiff and shivering. It's *freezing*. I rub my numb fingers and feet, trying to warm them up, but I'm so cold my teeth are chattering, so I give in and switch the engine on for fifteen minutes or so, along with the radio for a bit of company. There's little traffic passing now, and I feel small and alone and vulnerable, even though I keep telling myself I'm in a locked car, where nothing bad can really happen to me. I can just drive away, can't I, if I feel threatened? When I've thawed out I reluctantly turn the engine and the late-night music show off again. I've got my warmest coat over me now too, but I can see my breath in the air, each exhale forming a ghostly little cloud above my head. I must have fallen asleep again though, because it feels like hours later when something makes me open my eyes suddenly. I didn't hear anything, no noise at all. But … I can *feel* something. A presence. Is somebody out there?

My head whips to the right. It's still dark outside, and it takes me a couple of seconds to process what I think I see. Am I imagining it? And then I blink, and realise I'm not. There's a pair of eyes, a face. Somebody is standing inches from my car window, looking right at me.

Chapter Eleven

Their eyes are narrowed, squinting, as if they can't quite see me properly but are trying very hard to focus. I say *they*, because this face is wearing a beanie hat pulled down over the eyebrows, and a scarf wrapped around them right over the nose, meaning all I can see are those eyes, dark and piercing. Suddenly I'm shaking uncontrollably, and not just from the cold, and then I hear a scream, and then another, and realise they're coming from me, that I'm screaming so loudly my throat hurts. I back away from the window, my back arching over the mound of belongings on my passenger seat, and the eyes outside widen. Then the person they belong to turns tail and runs. I drag myself back into a sitting position, my breathing ragged and my heart pounding, and see them leap into a car that's now parked alongside mine. Seconds later, they're driving off at speed. I press my face against my window, but all I see is a flash of headlights and then a set of rapidly disappearing red taillights; what type of car it is or even the colour, I have no idea. I spend the rest of the night bolt upright in my seat, sleep impossible, turning the engine on for a few minutes once an hour to stop myself freezing to death.

That was Saturday night. I've had better. Now, it's seven forty-five on Monday morning, and I've just pulled up outside Clancy's Car Clinic, next door to what used to be Mug & Meadow.

I'm safe, I'm OK, I keep telling myself, but I know that deep down, I'm not OK at all, images of the face at the window on constant replay in my head. A random, curious motorist, or someone connected to everything that's happened to me recently? It was still dark, of course, and my panicked brain was in too much turmoil to notice anything useful at all, but my feeling now is that it was a man; something about the eyes, the lashes. They didn't look female to me. So, a late-night driver who'd stopped in the layby to stretch his legs and spotted a sleeping woman in the car in front of his? It's human nature, isn't it, to look at people, to be a bit nosy? Or could it have been one of the men who's been helping Lena over the past week? Are they watching me, following me? But *why*?

Once daylight arrived yesterday, I drove to the leisure centre and had a long hot shower, followed by a mug of tea and a bacon sandwich in the on-site cafeteria. I knew I shouldn't be spending the money, but I needed to feel human again, to feel *normal*. It helped, but now as I sit in my car, waiting for Eric – hopefully back safe and sound from his skiing trip – to arrive to open up at eight, and looking at my little café building, closed and shuttered, the letting agent's sign still in the window, I can't believe it's only a week since I arrived here for work and found what I found. One week.

Seven days. How can my life have changed so much in such a short time?

I slept in the yard behind Cloisters last night. There was no way, absolutely no way I could stay in the layby, so I took a chance, knowing the tearoom is closed on Sundays and setting the alarm on my phone for six so I could leave again well before Donna arrived for work this morning, which is usually around seven. There don't seem to be any security cameras – I had a good look around when I arrived yesterday afternoon, while it was still bright – and even if the worst comes to the worst and she does find out I've parked there overnight, well – it's not as if I'm doing any harm, is it? I can say I locked myself out of my apartment or something. It'll be OK, and the overnight thing is just for two more nights, for now anyway. Come Wednesday, payday, I can stay in a B & B again. One day, one night, at a time.

There aren't any toilets in the yard, but there's a twenty-four-hour supermarket a five-minute walk away and it has a customer loo. Not ideal in the middle of the night, but I have a strong bladder and I rarely need to get up to go anyway, so I knew I could manage. I parked up mid-morning yesterday and spent the rest of the day wandering around Gloucester, first going in and out of clothes shops and even trying the odd thing on, just for something to do. When I got bored of that, I visited the Cathedral, feeling guilty as I walked past the voluntary donation box at the entrance.

Suggested donation, £5 per adult

I couldn't afford to pay, and thankfully nobody seemed to notice. I can see now why the place is so popular with tourists though. I spent ten full minutes gawping at the Great East Window alone. It's the size of a tennis court, the detail in the mediaeval stained glass extraordinary.

After that, I went on the hunt for some reduced-price dinner, returning to my car with a slightly stale bread roll, a single bruised peach and a tub of cream cheese, my fingers trembling as I paid for them and realised how very little cash remained in my purse. Then I had another realisation – the fact that I don't have a knife – so I broke the bread roll and smeared the cheese onto it with my fingers, cleaning up afterwards with wet wipes. I went for another walk around the city, gazing longingly through the windows of cosy-looking bars and restaurants. And then I returned to my car, for another uncomfortable night, waking with cramped limbs and an aching neck, but thankful for no early-hours prowlers this time. A quick shower at the leisure centre followed by just a mug of hot tea and now I'm here, waiting for Eric. I know it's probably a waste of time, but for my own peace of mind I want to see if there's anything of interest on his CCTV footage from last weekend, before I head to work for 9:30.

I can eat there, I hope. Sneak a piece of toast when no one's looking, I think, my stomach growling. *Come on, Eric*.

I look in my rear-view mirror, hoping to see his red truck turning into the cul-de-sac, and frown. There's a car, a blue Audi, sitting just at the entrance to the street, and it looks familiar. When I drove out of the leisure centre car park this morning, I'm sure that car was right behind me. I noticed it because I used to have a blue Audi myself, a little TT, back in my modelling days, and although this car is an A3, I think, it's the same shade of blue. I squint at it, trying to see who's inside. There's a figure in the driver's seat, but I'm too far away to see it clearly, and suddenly, on impulse, I reach for my door handle and jump from my car. I'm bloody well going to go and *see* who it is, and if they *are* following me…

Dammit.

As I start to march down the street, the blue car begins to move, rapidly performing a three-point turn at the end of the cul-de-sac. Seconds later, it's turning left and disappearing down the main road. I sprint to the junction, but it's too late. There's no sign of it, and I didn't even manage to note the registration, not that it would have been of much use to me. It's not as if I have access to police databases and can go and look it up, and I'm pretty sure the police aren't going to do that for me on such flimsy grounds.

Am I just being paranoid, though? Was it simply a motorist parking up for a minute to make a phone call or drink a coffee? Was it even the same car I saw earlier this morning?

The questions nag at me as I traipse back to my Fiat, but I can come up with no answers. And then I hear the sound of a throaty engine approaching, and turn to see a vehicle I definitely do recognise, a red Mitsubishi pick-up, Eric beaming at me through the windscreen. I raise a hand and he waves back, but as he pulls up onto his forecourt his smile is replaced by a confused expression.

'What's happened here?' he says, as he gets out of the truck, and gestures at the café building to the right.

'Oh Eric. Did you have a good holiday? It's a long story,' I say. I fill him in with the basic details, omitting the stuff about being evicted from my apartment and the now apparent non-existence of Lena and her company and simply telling him I've as yet been unable to contact her to get to the bottom of all this, and his mouth drops open.

'Shit,' he says. 'That sounds friggin' shady if you ask me. Can't the cops do anything?'

'They just say that because it was a pop-up, and I didn't actually sign a contract – I know, I know – there isn't really much they can do. But I just thought if I could have a look at your CCTV footage from last weekend, maybe there's something there that might help? It was Sunday morning, from what I've been able to gather. I mean, it does look as if your cameras are just pointing down here'—I gesture at the forecourt we're standing on—'but you never know. Can I have a look?'

'Course you can, love. Come on in. I'll make you a cuppa.'

Eric rests a chunky hand on my forearm and gives me a sympathetic smile. He's a nice man; a bit older than me, probably early forties, with a shaven head and a soft belly hanging over the edge of his tightly belted jeans, and he likes me, I think. And not in a creepy way either. I got so used to all the male attention in my modelling days – attention that was really only focused on one thing – that I still find it strangely touching when a man just likes me for *me*. When I first arrived on the trading estate and was getting everything set up he'd often pop in to see if I needed a hand with any heavy lifting or little DIY jobs, but it all seemed so genuine. I do still get it now and then, men watching me with that look, a combination of awe and lust. I don't even mind it, sometimes, if I'm in the right mood. But with Eric, I've always felt … *safe*, I suppose. Now, he opens up the garage and I follow him as he lumbers into the little kitchenette behind his main workshop. He makes me a coffee and offers a shortcake biscuit, which I happily accept, then leads me into his office off to the right, a cramped space just big enough for two ancient-looking wooden chairs and a desk, piled high with oil-stained invoices and receipts but upon which sit two surprisingly up-to-date looking computer monitors.

Eric lowers himself into the chair behind the desk and taps a few keys, then angles one of the monitors in my direction.

'Last weekend. Here we go. Do you know what time Sunday? Shall I start at what – 5am, to be safe?'

I nod and lean forward eagerly, but as the footage starts playing, my heart sinks, and I know instantly that this is going to be yet another waste of time. The camera outside the garage is, as I suspected, only capturing footage of the forecourt directly outside. You can't see the road, or even the pavement; no images of vehicles or people passing by at all.

Shit. I knew this was likely, but it's still *so* frustrating.

I let Eric fast-forward for a minute or so, but this is clearly getting me nowhere, so I tell him not to worry after all, and thank him for everything, then say I'll keep in touch and let him know if Mug & Meadow is reopening. I even give him a hug as I leave, and he stands there and waves, a sad smile on his face, as I drive away, feeling unexpectedly bereft. I strongly suspect I'm never going to see Eric again, and I'm going to miss him.

It's another busy shift at Cloisters, and by the time five o'clock comes I'm feeling too shattered to go through my planned charade of saying goodbye, leaving in my car and driving around until Donna locks up and leaves and the coast is clear for me to return for the night. Instead, I offer to help with the pre-closing clean-up, even though it's not on my list of duties today, telling my boss I'm meeting a friend in a bar down the street at six so I might as well hang around for a bit, and she gratefully accepts my assistance, and tells me to help myself from the counter, not just from the 'almost past its best' pile, before I leave.

'If you're going boozing, you might as well have an easy dinner when you get home,' she says with a grin, watching me select a cheese and onion pasty, a small tub of fruit salad and a chocolate brownie, and I nod and agree, my heart twisting with sadness as I think about my dinky little apartment kitchen. How I yearn to sit *there* for dinner tonight, instead of in the cramped, cold front seat of my car.

We say goodbye as Donna locks the tearoom door, and I walk swiftly away, then stop a hundred metres or so down the road to check she's disappeared in the other direction. She has, so I head back and around to the rear of the building, down the short alley that leads from the street to the yard. When I reach it, I fumble in my handbag for my car key, then look up and gasp.

What…? Oh no, please, no. Not this…

My car is still there, parked in the far corner of the small, paved courtyard. But where the passenger window was there's now an empty space surrounded by jagged shards of glass, and on the ground there's a clump of brown soil and a plant pot I recognise, terracotta with white stripes, broken into three pieces. It's the pot from my lace fern.

No, no, no…

I rush to the car, almost tripping over a loose paving stone in my haste, and hit the remote to open the central locking. My car's been broken into, that much is obvious. But why didn't the alarm go off? This is right outside the back of the tearoom, surely we'd have heard it, or someone would have alerted us to it? And – more to the point – what's been stolen? Everything I own is in this car, and I'm whimpering as I scan the interior, bending to peer into the back seat. Some of my bags are still here, but they've clearly all been rummaged through, and there are gaps: one of my blankets is gone, two of my three beloved plants, a bag of shoes. Random bits and pieces, things that surely can't be of much value or use to anyone else, but to me....

Suddenly, it's all too much, and I slide down the side of the car and land in a heap on the cold flagstones.

'Why? Why me? *WHY*?'

My wail echoes around the yard, but there's nobody here to answer me, and I cover my face with my hands and sob. I like to think I'm tough – I *am* tough – but right now I've never felt so disorientated, so frightened. And so utterly alone.

Chapter Twelve

Wednesday. It's finally payday, thank *goodness*, because I am now almost totally broke. I just about managed another trip to the leisure centre this morning for a shower, thinking as I washed my hair about how grateful I am that my period isn't due for another couple of weeks; having to buy tampons would pretty much clear me out. Now, as I reverse into my parking spot in the yard, making sure to get the passenger side as close to the wall as possible, my stomach aches with hunger.

Broke and *ravenous*.

I cut the engine and lean across to check that my broken window, now covered with cardboard, plastic and sticky tape, is still as secure as it can be after the drive, then get out of the car, lock it and head into the tearoom. I haven't told anyone about Monday's break-in. Yes, I know I should have gone to the police, but I just *couldn't*. For a start, there's the small issue of my car insurance being up for renewal two days ago, and me not being able to afford to pay for it. They can check things like that on the spot, can't they? That could mean a fine, penalty points, possibly even being disqualified from driving. And if they seize my car, well … what do I do then? Although there aren't any security cameras in the yard itself, I'm sure the thief will have been captured on cameras out in the main streets when he left the alleyway with the loot, aka my precious belongings. The plants alone would have been enough to make him pretty easy to spot. But, much as I want the scumbag to be caught, I'm just going to have to let it go, because pursuing it will get me in even more trouble than I'm already in. Aside from the insurance thing, I'm quite sure the police would also tell me my car's not safe to drive like this – I found some cardboard and a couple of plastic bags in a bin and used them for my makeshift repair – but without insurance I'd have to pay to get it fixed myself and again, I can't afford to do that. If I get stopped by police on the road, I'll just have to say I'm on my way to a garage, and that the broken window was an accident. A kid with a ball, something like that. *Can* you break a car window with a football? Maybe not. I'll come up with something though.

I'll say the same to Donna and my other Cloisters colleagues too, if they ask. Again, I haven't told them because I just don't want the hassle of the explanation it would require, or the questions about what's been stolen. With my car parked tightly against the far wall of the yard, the smashed glass isn't really noticeable, and so far I've got away with it. I still don't understand why the alarm didn't go off, though. I've tested it since, and it's working fine. Was it a temporary malfunction of some sort? I have no idea, but I no longer have the space in my head to think it through; I don't even care any more if this was just an opportunist thief, who wandered into the yard and saw a car full of things that might be valuable, or someone connected to all the rest of this ongoing weirdness. I've been too busy just trying to survive to dwell on it.

It's been *so* cold. Nights in the car in this February weather were bad enough when all my windows were intact; now, it's like sleeping in a freezer, and although I say 'sleeping', I'm barely getting any rest at all, terrified that if I allow myself to drift off for too long, I'll end up with hypothermia. My body actually aches from shivering so violently for so many consecutive hours, and if it wasn't for those gloriously hot leisure centre showers to thaw out in I think I'd be in real trouble by now. I know I can't go on living like this, that I need to make some sort of proper plan, but for the past few days it's almost as if a fog has descended on my brain, a sluggishness which means that although I can function hour to hour, do my job, do what I need to do to get through each day, anything else just feels completely beyond me. This morning though, with the prospect of having some cash again in just a few hours' time, I feel a little brighter, a little less afraid.

When I get paid, and into a B & B for a couple of nights, I'll feel better, I tell myself now as I say good morning to Donna, and head into the staff room to hang up my coat. This Wednesday shift was a last-minute request last night, and I'm grateful for it; Donna has already said she won't need me again now until Saturday. I've worked out that I'll take home just under four hundred pounds for the five days I've worked so far, and I've found a guesthouse even cheaper than my first one, a little further out from the city centre. It's just £29 a night, parking included, and although it looks very basic in the online photos, the reviews are OK, and anything's better than another night in my car. I'm getting good at eating and living cheaply, and although I need to visit a launderette this week – I'm rapidly running out of clean clothes – I think I can make this money last until next week's payday, even save a few pounds. I won't be able to sort out the car insurance, not yet, so I'll just have to drive really carefully and hope I don't get into any accidents. But I'm hoping I won't have to *sleep* in my car again, and maybe I can find that second job now too, and juggle both. Start getting myself together again, back up where I should be. Free up some head space too, and carry on trying to find Lena, or whatever her real name is.

Yes, today is a good day, I think, and I find myself grinning as I tie my apron and head out into the tearoom.

'Right, who's next?' I say cheerfully, as I slip behind the counter.

The morning whizzes by, the place busy as always, and at lunchtime Donna asks me to do a quick check on the loos. I nod and grab the wire basket of cleaning products and rubber gloves from the cupboard under the counter, then head into the small restroom area. There are just two non-gender-specific cubicles and a communal hand-washing area, and everything looks pretty tidy, so I give the basin a wipe, squirt some bleach around the toilet bowls and leave again.

'All good,' I say, as I return the basket to its shelf.

'Fab,' says Donna. 'And that's the rush over for now, by the look of it. Fancy a cake and a latte?'

'Absolutely!' I say, and she smiles and turns to the coffee machine, while I slip back out into the dining area and clear a couple of recently vacated tables. I've just put my loaded tray down next to the dishwasher when there's a shout from behind me. I spin around to see a young man, who I remember serving with a pot of tea and an egg and cress ciabatta twenty minutes or so ago, stumbling through the door from the restroom, red in the face and coughing violently.

'HEY!' he shouts, his voice raspy, and he coughs and splutters again, clutching at his throat. 'What the hell's going on in your toilets? There's some sort of chemical thing...'

He bends double, wheezing, and Donna and I exchange shocked glances.

'Ella, what's he talking about? Didn't you just check the loos?' she says sharply.

'Yes! They were fine when I...'

But I can smell it too now, a sharp, acrid odour, getting stronger by the moment. I walk quickly towards the toilets, sidestepping the man who's still hawking and gasping, and as I push the door open I recoil.

What the...?

It smells like bleach, like the bleach I used in here just a few minutes ago, but a hundred times stronger, pungent and toxic, stinging my eyes, burning my throat. Instantly, I know what this is, and I slam the door shut.

'I think we need to evacuate,' I say. 'Donna, everyone needs to go, *now*.'

Her eyes widen, but she nods her understanding then turns to the dozen or so customers dotted around the tearoom.

'Guys, I'm so sorry, we need to close urgently. Bit of a ... a plumbing emergency. Look, if you can come back tomorrow, lunch is on me, OK?'

There are a few startled exclamations, but within seconds everyone's on their feet, picking up coats and grabbing bags, and a minute later, the place is empty. The coughing man is the last to leave, glaring at me as he stumbles through the door to the street, Donna still apologising. She closes and locks the door then turns to me.

'Well? What on earth is it?'

'I'm pretty sure it's chloramine,' I say. 'When I was doing my diploma, we had a module on general restaurant hygiene and they did this bit where they warned us about the consequences of mixing certain types of cleaning products. So, bleach and vinegar can give off chlorine gas, or if you use hydrogen peroxide and mix it with vinegar, you get some sort of acid, I can't remember the name, but it's quite corrosive, you know, to your skin and eyes and so on. But the smell in the loos now…'

I sniff, and I can still smell it, even though the restroom door is closed.

'That's chloramine. I remember it distinctly. It's caused by mixing ammonia with bleach, and it can be really dangerous if you inhale too much of it. But I don't understand what's happened, Donna, because I was the last one to clean in there, and everything was fine. I threw some bleach in the loos, but I didn't mix it with anything else…'

The expression on Donna's face has grown increasingly horrified as I've been speaking, and now she frowns and scurries around the counter to the cleaning products cupboard, pulling out the basket and picking up each bottle in turn, squinting as she reads the labels.

'It'll be OK, though,' I say quickly. 'We just need to air the place out, it'll all be fine in an hour or so…'

My voice tails off as Donna lifts a bright yellow bottle of drain cleaner and waves it at me.

'Ammonia,' she says, and there's anger in her voice now. 'There's ammonia in *this*. Why would you do that, Ella? With your experience how could you make such an *idiotic* mistake? Now we've probably lost the rest of today, and I'll be out of pocket tomorrow too if that lot come back for their freebies, to say nothing of the damage to our reputation if they tell their friends...'

'But I *didn't*!' I say. 'I told you! I didn't *touch* the drain cleaner. I wiped the handbasin down with that'—I point to the blue bottle of all-surface cleaner—'and then I just put some bleach round the toilet bowls. I promise you. This wasn't me, I wouldn't be so stupid...'

But Donna's shaking her head.

'I'm sorry, Ella, but you're the only one who's been in there with the cleaning basket in the past couple of hours. If it wasn't you, then it's a bit of a coincidence that this ... this chloramine or whatever you call it suddenly starts floating around in there minutes after you emerge. It was *obviously* you, unless you're suggesting one of our customers decided to do a bit of housework while they were in there spending a penny?'

'No, of course not, but...'

Donna sighs heavily.

'I had high hopes for you, you know. But if you're capable of making a cock-up like this, I can't risk keeping you on. I'm sorry, Ella. I'll pay you in full for the week you've worked, but I won't be using you again. Go and get your things, and I'll sort your wages. I'll pay you in cash, make it easier for you.'

'Donna, please! Honestly, it wasn't me!'

I can feel tears filling my eyes, and I blink them away. Suddenly my legs feel weak, and I grab onto the back of the nearest chair for support.

How can this have happened? I can't lose this job, I can't ... I think.

'Please, Donna. Please don't let me go, I really need…'

'Ella, I've made up my mind. Please go and collect your things.'

She's not even looking at me any more, busying herself at the till, stuffing notes into a brown envelope. As I stand there, staring at her, unable to take this in, she turns and slaps it on the counter.

'Your money,' she says coldly. 'Now go.'

Chapter Thirteen

I sit in my car, staring blankly out at the tearoom yard, waves of despair washing over me. I need to go and book myself in to that new guesthouse. I need to somehow find another job now too. There are so many things I need to be doing, *have* to do, and yet I can't seem to move. There's just one thought crashing around my head.

How did that *happen*? Because it *wasn't* me who mixed those chemicals, I know it wasn't. But Donna was correct when she said nobody else went in to clean the toilets. Other than the two of us, there was just Anita on duty today, and she was in the kitchen all morning, churning out finger sandwiches, scones and teacakes. The chloramine gas *did* appear not long after I carried out my lunchtime check. So *how*…?

And then it hits me. What did Donna say, albeit sarcastically, about who else could have caused this?

'…unless you're suggesting one of our customers decided to do a bit of housework while they were in there spending a penny…'

That man, the one who alerted us. The man who emerged

from the loo not long after I'd been in there, and made a big scene, coughing and spluttering. He was wearing a backpack. A black canvas backpack, plenty big enough to hold a couple of bottles of cleaning products...

My breath catches in my throat, and I squeeze my eyes shut, trying to picture his face. I didn't recognise him, I know that. Although, to be fair, I barely looked at him, too concerned about what was making him cough like that, and the suffocating smell emanating from the toilets. But I know he was ... ordinary. Dark jacket, dark hair. Probably nobody I'd remember, even if I had met him before. Could he have been one of the men who helped Lena clear out the café, and my apartment? Didn't the guy at the letting agents say the man who came in to drop off the café keys with the woman I assume was Lena had dark hair? But ... millions of men have dark hair. And maybe when I cleaned the restrooms at the end of my shift yesterday, I accidentally used the drain stuff instead of toilet cleaner, and then the bleach I used today interacted with it. Maybe it *was* my fault. And yet ... the end of yesterday's shift was about twenty hours ago. I flushed the loos after cleaning them – I always do – and they'd have been flushed goodness knows how many times this morning. Customers are in and out all the time. How can there have been enough chemical left in those toilet bowls to react so strongly with the bleach I added an hour ago? There can't have been.

I think about the dark-haired man again, the unpleasant look he threw my way as he left the tearoom, and I shiver. I look around my car, at the broken, poorly patched-up window, at the depleted pile in the back seat, and at my handbag, the brown envelope of cash protruding from its opening. And, in a flash, I make a decision. I'm *not* going to go and check in to that B & B. I'm *not* going to try and get another job in Gloucester. I can't do this any more. I need help, and at a low point last night, when I was lying awake in the dark, trembling with cold, I suddenly realised there *is* one person I might possibly be able to turn to. One person who might not turn me away, in what's now become a true emergency.

Not my mother, or any other relative, not that we have many. Not anyone from my modelling days, or from my old job in Kensington either.

But – *Harriet*.

Harriet might help me. We had a special bond once, me and Harriet. She was one of the few women I knew when I was younger that I really did feel very close to. And OK, we haven't seen each other for a while, for *years*, but even so. She's a good person, and the more I think about her, the more I think she might be there for me, just for a little while. Just until I get myself together again.

I swallow hard, and check my face in my rear-view mirror, wiping away a smear of black mascara from under my right eye. I looked last night, and I still have her number in my phone, and even if she's changed it, well, she should be pretty easy to track down. She's a doctor, a consultant paediatrician, at a London hospital, and they're all listed on the hospital websites, aren't they? It's just … how do I tell her what's been going on, and why I need her help so badly, after so long? It's so hard to explain, when *I* don't even understand what's happened. And it's *embarrassing*. I'm supposed to be a strong, capable, independent woman, and to have ended up in a state like this … it's *humiliating*. And yet … it's Harriet. Kind, compassionate. The more I think about her, the more I think it won't even matter that we haven't seen each other in years. She'll get it. She'll help me, I really think she will.

I start the car engine, and drive slowly out of the yard. If I'm going to drive back to London, I'll need to go and fill up with petrol, so I'll do that first, and then I'll call her. Ask her if I can come and stay for a few days. We lived together for a bit back in the day. It'll be like old times. And I really have often thought about her, often intended to give her a call. It's just … time slips by, doesn't it? And she was always so busy, with her job, as was I. But now…

I should have thought of her sooner, a week ago; maybe things wouldn't have got quite so bad if I'd called her then, instead of trying to struggle through on my own. But hey – I'm doing it now, aren't I? Better late than never.

At the garage, I transfer the notes from the brown envelope into my purse and go and fill up the car. Then I move from the pump to one of the customer parking spaces at the side of the building, and pick up my phone, scrolling through my contacts until there she is. Harriet Hart. *Doctor* Harriet Hart. My hand shaking slightly, I take a deep breath and dial her number.

Part II

ELLA AND HARRIET

Chapter Fourteen

HARRIET

'She's five minutes away. She just called. I told her where to park,' I say, and George nods, then plucks at the towel that's wrapped round his waist.

'I'd better get dressed,' he says. 'Best not be half naked when I meet her. And then shall I stick the kettle on or open a bottle of wine?'

I hesitate.

'Wine, I think. It's been a long time, but I'd bet my life she still drinks. White will be fine.'

He gives me a thumbs-up sign and heads for the bedroom, while I lick my lips nervously and run my hands over my hair. I was surprised, to say the very least, to get the call from Ella. I was still at the hospital when she phoned, trying to reassure the distraught mother of a three-month-old baby with a severe chest infection, and I'd had to ask her to call me back in half an hour. *Exactly* thirty minutes later – I have a habit of noting the times of phone calls – she did. And, long story short, she'll be arriving on our doorstep any moment now, to stay for a few days, something my husband is still trying to get his head round.

'But – you *never* have friends to stay,' he said, gaping at me, when he arrived home to find me plumping the duvet in one of our spare bedrooms. He looked exhausted, dark circles under his eyes and his dark brown hair, badly in need of a cut, flopping onto his forehead. He pushed it back with an irritated 'tsk!' and slumped into the black velvet armchair in the corner of the room, watching me as I began rearranging the scatter cushions at the head of the bed.

'And who is she again? *Ella*, did you say?'

'Ella Leonard,' I said. 'We shared a house for a while, before you and I met. We didn't really keep in touch after she moved out, but she's got herself in some sort of trouble and she says she hasn't got anyone else to turn to. I felt sorry for her. She sounded terrible on the phone. It's nothing *illegal*, the trouble she's in, before you ask. It sounds like she's been the victim of some sort of scam. She gave up her job and house and everything in London to take a job up in the Midlands – in Gloucester – and now it's all fallen through and left her with nothing. She's been sleeping in her car, the poor thing!'

George raised an eyebrow.

'Wow. But why call you? Has she really got no one else? A family? Or savings to fall back on? I mean, if *you* haven't seen her for years … seems a bit odd? You've never even mentioned her before.'

I shrugged.

'Haven't I? Maybe not. Housemates came and went, you know what it was like. But we were pretty close at one point, so honestly, I'm quite looking forward to seeing her. I think she's been estranged from her family for ages. I certainly never met any of them. And not everyone has savings to fall back on, George. Sounds like she's been living pay cheque to pay cheque for a bit. But she's OK, I promise. And she needs help. She wouldn't have reached out to me like this if things weren't bad. Sometimes you've just got to step up and do the right thing.'

'I suppose so,' he said dubiously. 'What does she do? What's she like?'

'Well, she *used* to be a model – she was quite successful at one point. But when *we* met, she was doing these catering qualifications at college and only modelling part time. Now she's a coffee shop manager. The job she took in Gloucester was to do with starting up a new chain or something. And she's … nice. Good fun. She was a bit … well, *model-y* at times back then. You know, young and beautiful and used to everyone telling her that. A bit of a princess sometimes. But that was years ago. Don't worry. Honestly, it'll be fine.'

He still looked doubtful, but he sighed and slowly got to his feet with a grimace, his back clearly bothering him after a long day in surgery.

'OK, well … if you're sure. Whatever.'

'I'm sure. It won't be for long,' I replied.

I understood why he was a little taken aback. I *don't* often have friends to stay, as a rule. It was one of the things I remember Ella and me having in common when we first met; like me, she didn't seem to have loads of close female friends like other women did. I'm a very private person, I suppose; I find it hard to let down my walls and get close to people, but Ella and I *were* close for a while back then. Nowadays, I have a *couple* of friends at the hospital, women in similar roles who understand the pressures, women I can offload to, share a bottle of wine with on the rare nights when we go out and let our hair down. But we're not *close* close. I don't really have *time*, with the job being so full on and trying to maintain a relationship, which is tough when you're *both* hospital consultants. I can barely fit in the odd date night with George, never mind trying to squeeze in a social life. But now … it's only five years since I last saw Ella, but it seems like a lifetime ago, back when the responsibilities were fewer and having fun was a little higher on my priority list. At the prospect of us both being back under the same roof, I feel a fizz of excitement.

BZZZZZ.

Even though I'm expecting it, I still jump at the sound of the door buzzer.

She's here.

I walk quickly to the control panel on the wall in the hall, pressing the door release to give her access, picturing her walking across the marble-floored lobby downstairs, getting into the lift and hitting the button for the penthouse. I wait, counting down.

Thirty seconds, twenty, ten…

I'm at 'five' when I hear the tap on the door.

'Ella! Woah, look at you! Come in, come in!'

I stand back, grinning, and then as she hesitates, looking uncertain, I grab her hand, the one that's not clutching a black holdall, some sort of plant sticking out of the opening. I pull her inside, closing the door behind her, and for a few moments we just stand there, looking at each other.

Older, but still stunning, is my first thought. There are fine lines around her striking green eyes, and a slight puffiness, as if she's been crying, but her long blonde hair is still thick and lustrous, tumbling down her back, and her body looks lean and strong. There's a long black coat draped around her shoulders and she's wearing jeans and a navy jumper with elbow-length sleeves, the striking tattoo covering her right arm to the wrist vivid against the paleness of her skin.

She's staring at me too, but then her gaze moves to behind and around me, and those cat-like eyes widen.

'Wow. You look amazing, Harriet – but this *place*! Holy crap!"

'Thanks,' I say. 'I'll give you a tour in a minute. But come on – give me a hug, it's been forever!'

'It has. And I'm so grateful for this, Harriet, seriously. You're a lifesaver.'

She smiles and stoops to drop her bag on the floor, lifting the plant out of it.

'Here. It's a peace lily,' she says. 'The low life who broke into my car took the rest, but you can have this one. It just needs a bright spot, and don't overwater it.'

'Aww, thanks,' I say, taking the plant in its earthenware pot from her and putting it carefully down on the sideboard. 'I've been meaning to get some plants, actually. This will be a good start. Now, come here!'

She holds out her arms. Up close, she smells stale, a musty, greasy aroma rising from the soft wool of her sweater, and I remember she's been sleeping in her car, and that she's probably desperate for a shower, so after a few seconds I pull away and say, 'Right. Want the tour?'

'Definitely!' she says. 'I mean – how did you end up here? Are doctors better paid than I thought or did you win the lottery or something?'

I laugh.

'Not quite. Just inherited a decent sum of money when

someone died a couple of years ago and decided to do the sensible thing and put it into property. Two NHS salaries would never have paid for this, trust me! And I say two because my husband's also a doctor; he's just had a shower so he's getting changed, I'll introduce you in a minute. Come on.'

She raises an eyebrow.

'Living in a spectacular penthouse *and* married. You've had a busy few years, haven't you?'

'I suppose it did all happen quite quickly, yes! Gosh, we do have a lot to catch up on, don't we? Look, grab your bag and I'll show you to your bedroom.'

I always love doing this; showing off our home to people who've never visited before. And Ella doesn't disappoint, oohing and aahing as I lead her from room to room. We live in Teddington, in a three-bed, three-bath penthouse apartment topping an ultra-modern building in a small, exclusive development. The open-plan living space, with beautiful oak floors and a top-of-the-range kitchen, leads onto a vast wrap-around terrace with spectacular views of the Thames; down below, there are landscaped gardens and twenty-four-hour security. Right next door is a private members' club, simply called 'The Club'; living here gives us unlimited access to its state-of-the-art gym, tennis courts and swimming pool. When we bought the place, just after our wedding two years ago – when I, to my astonishment, lost my friend and neighbour Farah but inherited a fortune – it cost just under two million pounds. It's probably worth several hundred thousand more now, the way London property prices are going, and I thank my lucky stars for it every single day.

When I finally show Ella her room, with its king-size bed, floor to ceiling window looking onto the river, and en suite with huge walk-in shower and freestanding clawfoot bathtub, she gasps.

'Wowzers. I might never leave!'

I smile.

'Stay as long as you like,' I say. 'Why don't you freshen up and unpack, and then come and have a drink? There's plenty of hot water if you need a quick shower. We'll be in the kitchen.'

'Thank you. Thank you *so* much. I just brought a few bits in for now. My car is still full of stuff but it'll be OK down in that underground car park overnight, won't it? It's just that I've got a broken window, so I'm a bit worried about it all being nicked, but honestly I'm so knackered right now, I can't even contemplate going down there again to lug everything up here…'

She sinks down onto the bed, suddenly looking distraught, and I remember what she's been through and nod sympathetically.

'It'll be fine, don't worry. I don't think there's *ever* been a break-in down there. We'll sort it out tomorrow morning, I'm not due at the hospital until one. Take your time. See you in a few minutes.'

When she appears in the kitchen twenty minutes later, George and I are sitting at the breakfast bar, glasses of wine in hand.

'Here she is! Ella, this is my husband, George.'

George stands up, pushing his stool back and holding out a hand, and I watch as his eyes sweep over her. I don't blame him – even with her hair still damp from the shower and her face free of even a trace of make-up, she looks incredible.

It's those eyes, that bone structure, I think, and as George greets her with a cheery 'Hi Ella. Doctor George Walker, at your service!' ... I wonder for a moment if I've done the right thing in letting her stay. But I trust George implicitly, and anyway, Ella's absolutely not his type. Too edgy, too ... *tattooed*. My darling husband is conservative with a small 'c', and he can't stand tattoos. Tattoos, body piercings, colourful hair dye ... all big no-nos for George. Ella's wearing a white tank top now, with a pair of loose black jogging bottoms, her feet bare – we have underfloor heating throughout, and we keep the place at a cosy temperature, especially on these cold nights – and her tattoo is on full show: black roses, entwined stems, perfectly depicted thorns, her entire arm covered.

He won't like that at all, I think.

'Well, hello, Dr George Walker,' Ella replies playfully, then looks at me and grins.

'Look at the two of you, all gorgeous and successful in your beautiful home,' she says. 'And look at me, a walking disaster area. It's a mad life, isn't it?'

'Ahh, shit happens to all of us,' I say. 'Come on, sit down and have a drink and tell us all about it.'

Ella grimaces and pulls out a stool, as George grabs another glass and pours her wine. She raises it to her lips and takes a mouthful, then another, and then sighs heavily.

'Jeez, I needed that,' she says. 'It's been a bugger of a week, I can't tell you.'

She does though. She'd given me an outline on the phone, but by the time she's finished the extraordinary story which began when she arrived at work up in Gloucester last Monday, George is staring at her slack-jawed. We exchange glances, then I say, 'Wow. Just wow, Ella. That is ... *insane.*'

She shrugs.

'I know. For the first couple of days I thought it was a sick joke, or a big mistake, but now…'

She takes another swig from her glass and wipes her mouth with the back of her hand.

'Now, I think it was all planned, right from the start. Someone's *done* this to me, deliberately. It was just *so* well executed, you know? Every detail, right from when this Lena woman, or whoever she really is, made friends with me in the first place. I'm almost a hundred per cent certain I never laid eyes on her in my life before she started coming into the café in Kensington, so someone else must have put her up to it, although why anyone would get involved with something like that and mess with the life of a total stranger beats me.'

She sighs and pushes a strand of hair back off her face.

'Beats me too. Beggars belief,' mutters George.

'I know,' Ella says. 'And I think I've been living in such a state of high anxiety – I mean, borderline panic half the time – since it happened, I haven't really been able to think properly. But on the drive down here, I don't know … it was like my head cleared. And now, I think I *might* know who's behind it.'

'*Who*?' I say. 'I mean, who have you pissed off enough to do all that to you? I know you can be a bit of a pain in the ass, but…'

I wink at her, and she gives me a little smile.

'Yeah, yeah. But you're right. I used to be, anyway.'

The smile fades, and she adds, 'I know I didn't always behave … very *well*, when I was younger. It was the crazy world of modelling, you know? It messes with you. I've changed, I promise you. Totally different person these days. But maybe now I'm paying the price for back then.'

She looks down at the floor, flushing a little, and George turns to me and raises an eyebrow.

'So go on,' he says, turning back to look at Ella. 'Who do you think it is? Behind all this?'

She looks up, eyes flitting from his face to mine.

'I think it's my mother,' she says.

Chapter Fifteen

HARRIET

We're sitting on the sofa, Ella and I, one at each end, feet up, wine glasses in hand. George has gone to bed; he's shattered, and has an extra-early surgical list tomorrow, covering for one of his fellow orthopaedic surgeons who has, ironically, managed to break his own arm. When Ella announced she suspected her own mother of being the villain in her story, his mouth had dropped open.

'Your … your *mother*? Good Lord. What on earth did you do to her?'

Ella had looked at me, sending me a silent message, and then she'd shrugged, looking sheepish.

'Oh … just the usual teenage stuff, but I was probably a bit worse than some teenagers. A bit wilder, you know? And honestly, I don't think she ever really wanted me around. The older I got, the worse it got. I actually think she started to get jealous. Of me, how I … how I look.'

She gestured vaguely at her own face, looking embarrassed.

'I moved out ... well, she kicked me out really ... when I was nineteen. I haven't seen her since. Haven't seen any of my family, not that there's many of us anyway. But I always wondered if one day she'd come and find me. And I could be wrong, because I'm not sure how on earth she'd have the cash or the brains to come up with something this elaborate, but she's the only person I can think of who might just be ... well, *vindictive* enough. Maybe she's married a rich man or something, and decided to spend some money punishing the wayward daughter.'

'Blimey.'

George had looked astounded, but now he's gone off to bed I want to delve a little deeper. And it's only now, of course, that we can talk freely about Ella's mum. When my husband asked me before her arrival about why she wasn't seeking refuge with her family, I'd been deliberately vague, not wanting his rather rigid moral compass to make him say that if she was capable of *that*, then he'd prefer her not to stay after all. But I know *exactly* what happened between Ella and her mother. She told me all about it, back when we were housemates.

'Thank you so much for not telling him,' she says now, rubbing at a toe before tucking her bare foot under one of the sofa cushions. 'When he asked ... I didn't know what to say. I don't really like talking about it. I was such a schmuck back then.'

'That's OK,' I say. 'Weren't we all, as teenagers?'

The night she told me about it was actually not that long after she'd moved into the spare room in my shared house. Housemates changed regularly, but it had been me and two other junior doctors – Mark and Jenny – for the previous year. Then Jen moved out to live with her boyfriend, and I'd started to get lonely. Mark was spending most of his spare time with *his* boyfriend, and as the single one I was finding myself alone in the house more and more, watching far too much trashy TV and eating way too many solitary microwave meals. When we advertised for a new housemate, Mark was happy to leave it all to me, and so I made an entirely female shortlist and spent one full evening interviewing the five women who made it. Ella was the easy winner; fun, charismatic, hard-working. I didn't want to live with yet another medic, and her lifestyle seemed so much more exciting, but I liked her too. I felt she'd fit right in, and in those first few months we quickly became firm friends, which was why her confession about why she no longer had any contact with her mother had initially come as such a shock.

It had been just her and her mum for pretty much her whole life. She'd grown up in Harrow in Greater London, an only child of parents who divorced when she was just four years old. Her dad had emigrated to Australia shortly after the split, never to be heard from again, and with no other relatives living anywhere nearby, you might expect that Ella and her mother – her name is Tina – would become a solid, unbreakable unit. What actually happened, she told me one night when we were on our third bottle of cider in front of the TV, was that her mother had at first tried to compensate for the loss of her father by completely over-indulging her only daughter ('honestly – anything I wanted, I got,' she said), and then, as Ella grew into her teens, had flipped the other way, coming down hard on her for the smallest of misdemeanours.

'I think she realised she'd kind of turned me into a spoiled brat,' Ella told me. 'But of course – you know what I'm like –

the harder she tried to stop me doing stuff, the more I wanted to do it. In the end, it was outright war.'

She showed me photos, and Tina was an attractive woman – OK, definitely not quite as beautiful as her stunning daughter, but striking – and there were, according to Ella, a steady string of 'men friends', some lasting a matter of weeks, others a little longer. It was during one of these longer flings, with a man called Eddie – 'a hot builder', Ella told me – that the mother-daughter relationship finally, and irrevocably, broke down.

'I shagged him,' Ella told me, with a shrug and a grimace. 'A few times, actually. I shagged my mother's boyfriend. So … you know … not my greatest idea. But she'd really been pissing me off around then; *endless* bloody nagging, about *everything*. And he was *fit*, even if he *was* twice my age. And we got away with it for a while, until the shit hit the fan.'

Said shit had hit said fan one afternoon when Tina had come home early from work and walked in to find her boyfriend and her teenage daughter 'hard at it', to quote Ella, in her own bed. And that was it. Ella was out, for good. No further contact.

'How long is it since you've seen her? Or even spoken to her?' I ask now, putting my wine glass down carefully on the low glass-topped table in front of the sofa.

'Same answer to both questions,' Ella says. 'About thirteen years. We never spoke again after that day she chucked me out.'

Her eyes meet mine, and she sighs.

'I want to go and confront her, but to be honest I don't even know where she lives any more. I mean, she *could* still be in that house in Harrow, I suppose? How would I find out? I've had the odd look on Facebook and so on over the years and I've never found her. I don't think social media would be her kind of thing anyway. And she worked in accounts but she changed job pretty often. I Googled her name earlier when I stopped for a coffee on the way here, but there's nothing coming up. Where else can I look?'

'Right. Let me grab my iPad,' I say, and uncurl my legs, stand up and cross the room to where my tablet's sitting on the sideboard.

'I need a job too, fast,' Ella says as I sit down again. 'I got paid today but only a few hundred quid, and when that's gone...'

She sighs again and sinks her head into her hands.

'Oh, Lord. It's all such a mess,' she mumbles.

'Come on, none of that,' I say briskly. 'If you're not too fussy, there might be something going in the hospital canteen. I saw a sign on the door this morning. They need someone urgently; I *think* it said they're interviewing on Friday. I mean, it's not like your fancy coffee shop, but...'

'Oh wow, anything ... I just need to earn some money, anything will do for now!'

Ella sits bolt upright, eyes bright.

'How would I apply? Honestly, this is amazing, I can't tell you how grateful...'

'I'll find it on the website for you and send you a link in a minute. And I'll put a word in for you too – I get on well with the canteen manager. She always puts aside a piece of lemon drizzle cake for me when they have it because she knows it's my favourite. She's nice, you'd like her. And you can stay here 'til you get yourself sorted, OK?'

As I say the words, I wonder how happy George will be

about an extended stay, then dismiss the thought. It'll be fine. As I told him earlier, a friend in need and all that. And I think he's already realised Ella's OK. As he went off to bed he kissed me on the forehead and gave my arm a little squeeze, a gesture I took to mean that everything's all right. He won't have the heart to send her away, he's too good a man.

Ella opens her mouth, probably to thank me again, but I hold up a hand.

'Shush, it's OK. Not a problem. And as for your mum … what was the address in Harrow? And her full name?'

She tells me, and I type it in. Moments later – boom.

'Yep, she's still there,' I say. 'Look.'

I turn the iPad to face her.

'Electoral register,' I say.

'You can search the electoral register? I didn't realise!'

She moves closer, peering at the screen.

'Yep. There are two versions of it – the full one and the open one,' I say. 'The full one's used for elections and stuff, and you have to be on that if you want to vote. But the open one, the one that's available to the public, you can opt out of, if you want to keep your name and address private. Not everyone seems to realise that though. Your mum obviously didn't. I have an account with this online search website because I helped a young parent track down her father a while back. A bit like you, she hadn't seen him for years but then her little boy developed an illness with a genetic component and she wanted to find her dad to see if he had it too. Anyway – there you go. Your mother is still living in your family home. Well, as of the most recent electoral register update, anyway.'

'Gosh. This is incredible, Harriet. I've had such a horrible,

horrible time and now … I feel like you're literally just solving all my problems one by one.'

She reaches for my hand and squeezes it. I smile.

'It's nothing, honestly. Look, I'll send you that job link now. If you get your application in tomorrow morning, I'll mention you to Paulette in the canteen and hopefully you'll get an interview on Friday. Take it from there, OK? And now—' I yawn '—I'm absolutely knackered. Do you mind if I turn in? Feel free to stay up if you want to. The remote's there if you want to watch telly. I'll be around for a bit in the morning before work, as I said, and I'll help you bring the rest of your stuff in and get settled, OK? But just make yourself at home.'

I stand up, and Ella does the same, then bends to pick up both of our wine glasses.

'No, I'll go too. I can't tell you how excited I am at the thought of sleeping in an actual bed tonight, and that one in your spare room looks *so* good. I'll rinse these out on the way. Thanks so much again, Harriet. Goodnight.'

She leans forwards and brushes her lips against my cheek.

'Goodnight, Ella. Sleep well,' I say softly, and as she turns and walks towards the kitchen, I watch her, her lithe body, her bare feet padding silently across the wood floor.

How strange this feels, I think, *to be together again, sleeping in the same apartment, after so many years.*

I stand there for a moment longer, then turn slowly away and head for bed.

Chapter Sixteen

ELLA

Happy Valentine's Day to me.

I have a big grin on my face as I walk out of the main entrance of MediWest Hospital and turn left, heading for the bus stop. I've got a job. It's not much – a role as staff canteen supervisor – but it's a job, and it will do, for now. Harriet did as she promised, and put in a word for me with Paulette, the manager, and I've just walked out of the interview having been given the position on the spot.

'I suspect you won't stay long, with your experience,' the very pleasant Paulette had said, giving me a wry smile. 'But we need someone immediately and if you can start on Monday, on a trial basis for the first month, we'd be delighted to have you.'

I'll be reporting to Paulette, but otherwise when I'm on shift I'll be team leader, opening and closing the canteen, supervising the kitchen and being responsible for cashing up at the end of the day. None of that sounds too onerous, which is good; it frees up my headspace for trying to get to the bottom of the events of the past couple of weeks. But tonight, I'm in the mood to celebrate, not dwell on what's happened. It may be the most romantic day of the year, and a Friday to boot, but Harriet's already told me she and George have no plans to go out tonight, and so I plan to buy a bottle of prosecco in the fancy little off-licence round the corner from the penthouse, as my contribution to a nice evening in.

'We never do Valentine's Day,' Harriet said this morning, as she stood in the doorway of my room, watching me carefully apply my make-up ahead of my interview. 'It's just a load of commercial rubbish, isn't it? We tell each other we love each other every day anyway; we don't need a special day to do it. And everywhere is packed and so expensive. We'll just stay here, get a takeaway, have a couple of bottles of fizz. And maybe we can persuade George to let us watch a romcom, eh?'

I smiled at her in the mirror.

'One of the Bridget Joneses?' I said, hopefully.

I love those films.

'Maybe,' she said with a grin.

I'm still on a high on the bus journey home, and now as I pass through the security gates, smiling at the uniformed guard who already recognises me and waves me through, the bottle of prosecco wrapped in brown paper and tucked into my handbag, I feel a little frisson of pleasure. The past couple of weeks have been horrendous, but now that I have somewhere to live, even temporarily, and I'm about to start working and earning money again too, it's like a weight's been lifted from my back, bringing a lightness to my step as I walk through the manicured gardens that surround the development's three apartment blocks, admiring the planting scheme. It's right up my street, the sort of look I call 'tropical

English': lush fan palms, fatsias and tree ferns, underplanted with cottage garden favourites. There's not much colour at this time of year, but I can see foxgloves and lupins and delphiniums, cut back now but ready to burst into life with the approach of spring.

I reach Harriet's building and look up, admiring its clean, white lines, complemented beautifully by the warm wood and green-tinted glass of its balconies and terraces. As I head across the immaculate lobby towards the lift, I try to suppress a tiny stab of envy. I'm so grateful Harriet's taken me under her wing – she really, *really* didn't have to – but … holy cow. How lucky was she to inherit enough cash to buy a place like *this*? I've dreamed of living somewhere this magnificent for years, ever since my modelling days, when now and again we'd shoot campaigns in stunning manor houses or exquisite rooftop apartments. When I asked Harriet for more details about how it came about, she told me it had been sheer chance. She'd had an elderly neighbour who was pretty much alone in the world, so she'd begun popping in regularly whenever she had any spare time, keeping the old woman company, doing her shopping, cooking a little extra food when she made dinner and dropping it round. When the woman died, to Harriet's astonishment she left everything to her. And everything, it turned out, was a lot more than just the proceeds from the sale of her Edwardian terraced house and a few quid in a savings account.

'Turned out she had several other properties too,' Harriet told me. 'I knew she'd been an interior designer, she told me that. But she was clearly a very successful one back in the day, and her solicitor told me she'd been super-savvy when it came to the property market. She bought really grotty, rundown places at knockdown prices and transformed them, long before it became trendy to do that. I sold them all and managed to buy this place. Crazy, isn't it?'

Crazy indeed. And then, to top it all, she's landed a husband like George. Harriet's really attractive, don't get me wrong. Long, sleek dark hair, a neat, straight little nose, chocolate brown eyes. Pretty in a sweet, 'girl-next-door' kind of way. But George – wowsers. He looks a bit like his namesake George Clooney; not the clean-shaven version, but the bearded one. This George's hair is floppier, more auburn than grey, but he has that crinkly-eyed smile, that easy-going charisma. And he's *nice*. Not everyone would be happy to take in a complete stranger, just because she once shared a house with his wife. She's nabbed a good one there. A surgeon too. Impressive. They are a properly gorgeous couple, and I'm delighted for her. Maybe some of her luck will rub off on me while I'm here. I don't want to outstay my welcome, but this canteen job doesn't pay a lot, and I'm not sure how quickly I'll be able to save enough money for a deposit and the first month's rent on even the smallest, shabbiest studio flat. London rental prices are off the scale, and as for buying – forget it. In other parts of the country, it might be a little more unusual for a single woman in her thirties to still be renting and house-sharing, but not here. Maybe I'll need to move away again, think about looking for another job outside London instead. *But hey*, I think, as I step out of the lift, and let myself into the penthouse, using the spare key Harriet's lent me. *One day at a time. This job will tide me over. It's a start, a gentle way to begin rebuilding my life*, again.

And tonight, a pleasant evening in store, in this beautiful place. Then, tomorrow, something less pleasant, but something very necessary. I've talked it over with Harriet, and she agrees I should do it. I'm going to Harrow, to the house I grew up in. I'm going to Harrow, because the more I think about the events of the past couple of weeks, the more I've convinced myself there can only be one person behind it all. That I'm right in thinking it's my mother, the one person who just might have held a grudge for so many years, and finally decided I needed to be punished.

And tomorrow, I'm going to find her.

Chapter Seventeen

ELLA

Harrow – or, to give it its full name, Harrow-on-the-Hill, situated as it is close to a 400-foot-high hill in northwest London – is a suburb most people would consider to be *nice*. A largely affluent population, excellent amenities, decent transport links. It has a village feel about it – a mix of whitewashed cottages and Victorian terraces – albeit a village with restaurants for every possible taste, and a world-renowned public school. As I make the ten-minute walk from the tube station to Hartley Road, the memories come flooding back. There's the pub I had my first drink in, illegally of course, when I was just fourteen but looked at least five years older. And there's the building I remember as Maxim's nightclub, now a trendy-looking tapas bar with apartments on the top two floors. But the closer I get, the more apprehension twists my guts. What if she's not in? It's Saturday morning, and my mother never was an early riser at weekends, often to be found lounging in the living room in her pyjamas well past midday. But what if she's changed? What if she, I don't know, plays golf or something on a Saturday morning these days? What if she's away on holiday?

As I turn into the street, I pause, taking in a few gulps of air, trying to calm myself. Our house – I still think of it as *ours*, even though it's been more than a decade since I was unceremoniously chucked out of it – is halfway down on the left, a three-bedroom property with a tiny front and slightly larger, long, narrow rear garden. I see it immediately, noting with mild surprise that it's still the same colour as it was when I left, a shade my mother described as 'French Grey', the paint on the façade peeling a little in places now, even though the windowsills and surrounds have clearly been touched up and are a bright, fresh white. I expected it to look very different somehow, but it's as if the years have slipped away, and I'm arriving home from school, or from my job in the boutique, bracing myself for another argument, another telling off about something I have or haven't done. My footsteps slow as I approach, and as I stand at the kerbside, looking at the wood-panelled door with its decorative glass panes, I can feel my heart thudding, and wonder if I can actually pluck up the courage to lift the heavy lion's head knocker, to send that still so clearly remembered *rat-a-tat-tat* echoing through the rooms.

Just. Do. It, I think.

I take another slow, deep breath, and push open the low iron gate. And then I jump, as the front door of the house to the right opens suddenly, and a silver-haired man appears on the step.

''Ello,' he says, with a friendly smile. 'I saw you standin' out 'ere and I weren't sure you 'ad the right 'ouse. You lookin' for Tina?'

The accent is broad Cockney and feels strangely out of

place. When I lived here, our next-door neighbour was a retired headteacher called Eileen, who spoke as if she was closely related to the King, all long vowels and no discernible regional accent whatsoever, even though she'd grown up in Devon.

'Erm … yes, yes, I am. Do you know if she's in?' I reply.

'Nah, not for a while now, luv,' he says, and shakes his head, a melancholy expression replacing the smile.

'Place 'as been empty for months, which is a right shame. I miss 'er, she was a laugh. Took her into Cotsfield … hmm, let me fink … must 'ave been around November time, I reckon. Still 'anging on though, by all accounts. Bit of a miracle. Won't be long now, though, according to Michelle down at number twenty-two. She visits, y'see. Anyway, sorry, luv, I ramble a bit. Are you a work mate or…?'

I'm staring at him, confused.

'Erm … sorry, I don't really understand. They took her into where? Did you say *Cotsfield*? What's that?'

He raises an eyebrow.

'Oh. Sorry, I assumed … it's an 'ospice. End-of-life care, you know? Cotsfield 'ospice. Just out on the edge of town.'

'A … a *hospice*? She's in a hospice? But – *why*? What's wrong with her?'

My mouth suddenly feels dry, and I lick my lips, eyes fixed on the old man as he frowns, then looks furtively over his shoulder into the hallway behind him, as if trying to see if anyone might be within earshot.

'Well, I don't know if it's my place to say, if you don't already know. But … well, it's the big C, ain't it? Cancer. She's dying of cancer, luv.'

Chapter Eighteen

ELLA

I'm standing in a corridor at Cotsfield Hospice, waiting. It smells horrible – a mix of antiseptic and coffee and *illness* – and the wave of nausea that swept over me when my mother's next-door neighbour dropped his bombshell is intensifying by the second. I look around, eyes scanning for a plant pot or something else I can discreetly throw up into if I need to, but there's nothing but two faux-leather-covered armchairs, a small table between them stacked with out-of-date magazines.

Hurry up, I think.

When I explained to the woman on reception that I was Tina Leonard's daughter, come to visit her, she'd looked at me askance.

'Oh. We haven't seen you before,' she said suspiciously. 'And you're not on her visitors' list...'

'I've been working away,' I said quickly. 'And, to be honest, we haven't been ... well, we haven't been exactly close for a while now. But – could you ask her, maybe? If she'll see me? I mean – how is she? Is she still able to ... to talk and everything?'

'Just about,' the woman replied. 'I suppose I could. Follow me.'

I did, and now she's behind the closed door of the room at the end of this corridor, and I'm out here, waiting, my stomach rolling, my palms damp. I breathe deeply, trying to quell the queasiness, and then suddenly the door opens and she's back, nodding at me.

'You can go in,' she says. 'But just five minutes, OK? She's very tired.'

'Thank you,' I whisper. And then, somehow, my legs are moving and I'm walking into the room, pushing the door shut behind me. I stand there for a few seconds, getting my bearings. It's bright in here, a bigger, sunnier, altogether *nicer* room than I've been expecting. There are floral curtains at the window, views of a neat, tree-lined garden beyond them. An L-shaped sofa and low table in the corner, a flat-screen TV, a small bookcase. And then, of course, there's the bed, hospital-style, metal-framed, crisp white bedding. And in it, propped up on pillows, is a tiny form, so pale and thin that I have to look twice, for a moment wondering if this is all a huge mistake, that this is some other Tina Leonard, and not my mother at all. And then she speaks, and instantly I know. It's her. Of course it's her.

'Took your time, didn't you?' she croaks.

'I didn't know,' I reply. '*Obviously*, I didn't know, or I would have...'

I hesitate, not quite knowing how to finish the sentence. Even if I had somehow found out my mother was ill, would I really have come to see her, if recent events had never happened? Our relationship had deteriorated so much by the time we eventually parted ways that we were barely speaking; sleeping with her boyfriend wasn't my finest hour, but by then she didn't even feel like my mother, just an irritating, endlessly nagging roommate. And I know I'd driven her mad for years with my teenage rebellion, my refusal to stick to any of her house rules, my wild partying, my total lack of any contribution to household bills. But I was the child, and she was the parent, and sometimes it felt as though there was very little parenting going on. Yes, she worked hard to support us, but she played hard too, and I spent many nights alone in that house on Hartley Road while she went drinking and clubbing with Graham or Pete or Andy or whatever the latest one was called. I must have loved her once, but it was so long ago I can barely remember how it felt. And now, as I look at her frail body, her wispy hair, the sharp jut of her cheekbones on her emaciated face, I have no idea how to feel. I'm shocked, yes. Sad that anyone's life is being cut far too short by such a cruel disease. But will I mourn my mother when she dies? I don't know. I really don't know.

'Well, what do you want?' she says. 'Why now? Because if you're after money, you've come to the wrong place.'

She gives a weak little cackle, and I take a step forward, again unsure what to say.

'I'm not here for money. I just … how long have you been here?' I ask.

'Beginning of November,' she replies, then coughs. 'Should have come in earlier, really. Couldn't work for months before that, and being on my own … the savings ran out pretty quick. You don't have to pay for hospice care, did you know that?

NHS and charity donations cover it. It's good here too. They look after you...'

Her voice tails off, and she coughs again. I wonder what sort of cancer she has, but I don't want to ask, and anyway, my mind is starting to race. I met Lena in October and moved to Gloucester in December. If my mother was already sick then, already not working, using her savings to live on ... and if, as she's just said, she's single, not married to some rich man as I speculated...

It's not her, is it? I think. *It can't be. What was done to me cost money, a lot of money ... but if not her, then who? Who?*

'Anyway, you've seen me now, so you can piss off again,' she says. 'You're no daughter of mine, not any more, not after what you did. It's too late. And whatever you say, I know you're only after the money when I pop my clogs. So I'll put you out of your misery. I've got nothing left but the house, and I've instructed my solicitor to put it on the market when I'm gone, and every penny's going to this place. Do some good with it, help other people who find themselves in my shitty boat. So go on, bugger off to wherever you've been. Leave me to die in peace.'

She closes her eyes, then very deliberately turns her head away from me. I stand there for a few moments, and to my surprise feel tears pricking my eyelids. I have a sudden urge to reach out and touch her bony hand, to drop a kiss onto the papery skin of her forehead, to tell her I'm sorry, so very sorry, for all of it. To tell her I forgive her for everything she did or didn't do too, to beg her to allow me to visit her again, so we can maybe salvage something, anything, in the little time she clearly has left. I almost do it, and then ... I change my mind. What's the point? She wants nothing to do with me, does she?

She very obviously cut me out of her life a long time ago. She doesn't even care about me sufficiently to seek any sort of revenge, other than leaving me nothing in her will. Somebody else is behind what's happened, and I may never know who now. But it's not my mother, and it's time to go.

I look at her one more time, her eyes still closed, the blue-veined lids fluttering faintly. Then I turn and take the few steps towards the door.

'Goodbye, Mum,' I whisper.

I wait a few seconds, but there's no reply. I leave the room, and walk quickly down the corridor, heading for the exit.

Chapter Nineteen

HARRIET

'This has been so nice. Just what I needed. Thank you, Harriet.'

'No problem,' I say.

Ella and I are strolling along the path by the river, heading back home after a slap-up Sunday roast at The Boat Inn, about twenty minutes' walk from the apartment. Chicken for me, beef for her, plus all the trimmings, washed down by a shared bottle of rather excellent merlot. It's a chilly afternoon, the sun already low in the sky, rain threatening, but Ella seemed so low this morning I thought going out and treating her to some lunch might be the right thing to do, and it seems I was correct. George is on call at the hospital until late tonight, so it's just the two of us, and she's definitely perked up in the past hour or so, some of her fighting spirit seemingly returning.

She was *very* down last night when she got back from her planned showdown with her mum, and when she explained what she'd discovered, I leapt up from my chair and pulled her into a hug.

'Ella! That's … that's awful. I'm so, so sorry,' I said, and she let out a little sob, clinging to me briefly before pulling away, looking embarrassed.

'It's horrible,' she agreed, rubbing a hand across her eyes. 'But you know what? She hasn't wanted me in her life for years, and clearly has no interest in me being in it now, for whatever time she has left. She was delighted to tell me she's leaving me nothing too. So, what can I do? And to be honest, my biggest concern now isn't losing her, because I feel like I already did that when I was a teenager. My biggest concern is that if *she's* had nothing to do with all the mad stuff that's happened to me recently, then who the heck has? I was *so* sure…'

I shrugged helplessly, and she sighed and told me she was going to have a long bath and an early night, disappearing into her room and not emerging until nearly 11 this morning. Now though, as we stride along, walking with more purpose as dark clouds begin to gather overhead, she gives me a sidelong glance.

'I'm looking forward to starting at the hospital tomorrow. I appreciate you getting lunch, but I feel bad. They're paying me weekly, so with what I still have left from my wages from Gloucester, I'll be able to pay you some rent or whatever on Friday, OK? And contribute to the supermarket shop. I'll pay my way until I can afford my own flat.'

'Honestly, it's fine,' I say, feeling a drop of rain hit my forehead and pulling up the hood of my parka. 'Don't worry about it. I'm sure it won't be for long, and you'll be able to save more towards your deposit if you're *not* paying rent, so forget it. Just buy a bottle of wine or something now and again. And

George is on board too, with you staying, I mean. So it's all good.'

'Are you sure? That's so kind of both of you. Thank you,' she says.

I'm not being entirely honest here; George *is* on board, just about, but I had to do a little gentle persuasion to get him to agree to our temporary house guest becoming more of a long-term lodger.

'Frigging hell. For how long?' he'd groaned on Friday evening when I'd told him that Ella had landed the job in the hospital canteen and needed to stay a little longer.

'Just a few weeks. She needs to save for a flat, George. She's had a hard time, you know that. And I promise you I'll make it up to you when she goes. We could go away for a weekend, stay somewhere really fancy. My treat. Full on pampering. Go on. She's not that bad, is she?'

He'd rolled his eyes but looked somewhat mollified.

'No, she's fine,' he replied. 'It's just that I miss it being just us, you know?'

I smiled and slipped my arms around his waist, tilting my face up to his, and he sighed then kissed me, his lips soft on mine.

'*You*,' he said. 'You know I can't resist you when you look at me with those big soppy eyes. Oh, go on then. Just for a few weeks though, OK?'

'Just for a few weeks,' I said.

'So – what are you going to do next?' I ask Ella now, as we turn off the river path and head down the winding road that takes us past several other stylish new waterside developments, the first a row of four-storey apartment blocks with a spectacular-looking roof garden atop each. 'About the happenings in Gloucester, I mean? Any new ideas?'

'Not really,' she says. 'I'm back to thinking it's probably someone from my modelling days now, but there are possibly too many options there to narrow it down; I annoyed quite a few people back then. But honestly, it was all silly stuff in the grand scheme of things. I can't think of anything I did bad enough to deserve this level of punishment.'

She grimaces, and I raise an eyebrow. There's a runner approaching us, ruddy-cheeked and sweating heavily, dressed only in short shorts and a racing vest despite the weather, and I wait until he passes then say: 'What sort of thing? I mean, when we lived together you weren't modelling full time, but I suppose you used to be late for jobs sometimes, didn't you, which I know wasn't ideal. Costs money and all that, on a shoot, I assume? But you were quite often late for nights out with me too, *and* with the rent. It was just you. A bit annoying, but not annoying enough for anyone to want to ruin your life, I would have thought. So what else? You never really told me back then. You just used to come home in a mood and say you'd fallen out with someone at work again. Oh, and by the way – you're much better now, as a housemate. A *definite* improvement, I'd say.'

She grins at that.

'I am, aren't I? I was ready for lunch before *you* today. *And* I loaded the dishwasher before we left. Reformed character.'

'You are,' I say.

'And, well…' She starts speaking, hesitates, then says, 'I am sorry, you know. Sorry for how I sometimes behaved back then. Sorry we didn't stay friends. Sorry we lost touch for so long. I think you're amazing, to take me in like this.'

'Ahh, shush.'

I wave a dismissive hand.

'So, go on. What else did you do back then that might be relevant?'

We walk on for a few steps in silence, the rain getting heavier now, and Ella pulls at the drawstrings on her coat hood, tightening it around her face.

'Just more of the same. Typical spoiled brat stuff,' she says. 'All the adulation, the magazine spreads, the ad campaigns … it went to my head I guess. And … well, I suppose for a while I thought I could have anyone I liked too; men, I mean. There were a lot of them around – agents, photographers – and it was quite an incestuous business, you know? Quite small really, and lots of people ended up dating each other, but sometimes I didn't really care if they had girlfriends or not. I wanted them, I took them. Awful, I know. It got to the point where quite a few of the most popular models at the time refused to work with me, and I don't blame them, not now, not one bit. And word got around, I suppose, and…'

She sighs.

'Right,' I say. 'I didn't know that. I mean, I knew you dated quite a bit, but…'

I hesitate, unsure how to continue.

'Well, that wasn't ideal, I suppose,' I say finally. 'But you were young and in that kind of industry … I sort of get it.'

'Yes, but other people managed not to do stuff like that,' she says. 'I messed up. I could have carried on getting the good jobs for ages longer if I'd behaved myself. It didn't even make me happy, you know? And when everyone thinks you're trouble, and you being there's going to cause an atmosphere on set and all that … anyway, maybe one of *them* is behind it. One of the girls I pissed off back then. Some of them are still up there, making the big bucks. So they could probably afford it. It's just ... it doesn't quite fit, in my head. I mean, why wait so long? Years and years? It's odd, isn't it?'

'It is,' I say, as finally, just up ahead, we see our gate, and both automatically start walking even faster. '*Very* odd. But maybe you just need to leave it now. It's happened, it's over, you're getting back on your feet. Is there any real point in pursuing it?'

Her footsteps slow, and I turn to look at her, blinking the raindrops off my lashes. Then, abruptly, she stops walking, her body suddenly rigid.

'Who's that?' she hisses, and squints, nodding her head almost imperceptibly towards the left of the gateway.

I frown and look too, but all I can see is the shadow cast by the high wall in the rapidly darkening late afternoon. There's nothing and nobody there, and I turn back to Ella, puzzled.

'What? I can't see anything,' I whisper, then wonder *why* I'm whispering and say, in a normal voice, 'There's no one there, Ella. What did you think you saw?'

She stares at the spot for a couple of seconds longer, than shakes her head slightly.

'Sorry. Shit, sorry. You're right, it's nothing. I think I'm just paranoid, after everything, you know...'

She rolls her eyes, and I smile reassuringly at her.

'That's OK. It's understandable. But everything's fine now, OK? You're safe here,' I say.

'I know. Sorry, again.'

'No apology needed.'

She nods slowly, then says, 'What were you saying? About me pursuing things, and what the point of it is? I've been starting to think that myself, actually. Seeing Mum yesterday ... I dunno. Life's short, isn't it? I mean, I put all that stupid behaviour behind me a long time ago, but I still deserved to be punished for it, I suppose. So maybe it *is* time to move on now. Start afresh. Tomorrow is the first day of my new life and all that. Do *you* think that's what I should do? You're the sensible one, Harriet.'

I smile and link my arm through hers.

'Come on,' I say. 'Let's get inside. We're getting wet. And to answer your question, yes, I do. I think you should just forget it, and move on. And I also think that when we get in, we should find a really cheesy old movie to watch and open another bottle of wine. And then we can drink to your new life, OK?'

'OK,' she says. 'Deal.'

A grin spreads across her face, the old cheeky Ella suddenly reappearing and then, quite unexpectedly, she turns away from me and starts to run.

'Oi!'

I squeal and run after her, the two of us splashing through puddles and giggling like schoolgirls, all the way to our front door.

Chapter Twenty

HARRIET

I've had a busy but satisfying morning, and as I walk into the staff canteen just before one, immediately scanning the room for Ella, wondering how she's doing on her first day, I'm gasping for a coffee and a brief sit down. I've just waved goodbye to one of my favourite patients, a toddler called Daniel, born with a limb defect which means he has no lower legs. Neonatal medicine is one of my special interests, and I've known Daniel since he was born, seeing him regularly to keep an eye on his general developmental progress. As kids like him often are, he's the most cheerful little chap you can imagine, and is doing so well on his recently fitted prosthetics that he made me laugh out loud as he zoomed into my consulting room, beaming and shouting, 'Hiya, Doctor Hart! Hiya!' at the top of his cute, squeaky voice.

I don't have long before I need to do a ward round, so I queue up at the counter – thankfully, there are only two colleagues ahead of me – then take my coffee and tuna salad to a table over by the window. I've just peeled the lid off the cardboard tub when I see Ella marching through the door from the kitchen, carrying a tray of what look like cupcakes. She puts them into the display cabinet, saying something to the woman on the till with a grin on her face, and the woman – her name is Fiona – laughs. I wave a hand, hoping to catch Ella's eye, and she sees me and waves back cheerfully, then gives me a thumbs-up sign, before turning to reply to a nurse who's pointing at a basket of bread rolls, clearly needing some vital information before making her choice.

Going well, then, I think. *Good.*

I yawn. I'm tired today. Although we both retired to bed early last night, long before George crept in just after 11, that second bottle of wine when we got back from the pub was probably a mistake. I slept badly, waking with a start not long after 3am, panting, my body bathed in sweat, knowing I'd been having a nightmare, the content of which was already drifting away, slipping from my harried mind like water through a sieve. But it unsettled me, and I only dozed fitfully after that, groaning loudly when the alarm went off at six.

I've felt unsettled for days. She's been fine, fun even, to have around, but that wasn't the first nightmare I've had since Ella arrived, although I think I've been hiding my unease quite well from both her and from George. It's all tied up with the *real* reason I don't normally like having women to stay in my house; well, having *anyone* to stay really, but women in particular. The same reason I don't have many close female friends. George thinks it's just that I'm a little antisocial; I like my own space, and he understands that because he's quite similar in many ways. But there's a lot more to it than that. There's a very good reason I am the way I am.

Fran.

The reason is a woman called Fran.

A woman who flitted in and out of my life, only briefly, years ago. Who arrived as just another of those many, ever-changing housemates and became that cliché – the housemate from hell. The housemate who pretty much ruined my life, although even George doesn't know the truth about that. The housemate whose behaviour left me struggling to get along with any other housemate who came after her, who made me wary of female friendship full stop. And now, as I watch Ella disappear back into the kitchen, an image of Fran's face floats unbidden into my head.

She was great when she first moved in. A breath of fresh air. Bubbly, funny, full of energy. And then, slowly, everything began to change. Remember that old 90s film *Single White Female*? The one about the roommate who turns psycho? It was little things at first. I bought a new top for a night out, a floaty Monsoon number with red and white embroidery, and a week later, there was Fran in exactly the same top, expressing surprise when I looked a little affronted.

'Oh!' I remember her saying. 'Gosh, I didn't even notice. I just saw it in the shop and loved it. How funny! We clearly have the same excellent taste.'

I let it go, but next it was the hairstyle. My hair now is long, pulled up into a neat bun for work but flowing midway down my back when I let it loose, but back then I had a blunt, choppy, jaw-length bob. When Fran moved in, her hair was almost waist-length, until she came home one day with a cut so similar to mine that I gaped at her.

'What have you done? *Why?*' I said, and she shrugged, saying something about it being summer and hot and that she'd suddenly got tired of her heavy, thick mane and walked into a salon on impulse.

'Gosh, I suppose it *is* a bit like yours! Whoops!' she giggled, and what could I say? I could hardly accuse her of copying me. It felt like such a *childish* thing to say, like accusing a schoolfriend of copying your homework, and so once more I let it pass. But on it went.

The following week, it was a pair of white denim shorts I'd worn only once before she 'popped into New Look on the way home from work and saw them for half price in the sale, can you believe it? Too good to miss, you don't mind, do you?'

I did mind. I was starting to find it creepy, and a little suffocating. But once again, I laughed it off and let it go, hoping it was a phase that would pass, telling myself I was overreacting, misinterpreting things. Fran was gorgeous, for goodness' sake. Why would she want to look like me? And trends were trends, and fashion was fashion, after all, and didn't we all dress in quite a similar way, women of my age? I told myself I was being too sensitive, and carried on saying nothing, even though inside I was seething every time she appeared in yet another copycat outfit. And, I suppose, because I did nothing, said nothing, it got worse. She started ordering the same food as me in restaurants, the same drinks, sipped by lips wearing exactly the same shade of tomato-red lipstick.

'That sounds yummy. I'll have the same, make it easy for you,' she'd say to the waiter after I'd place an order, and he'd grin and nod, and I'd sit there, squirming. Could nobody else see what I was seeing? It was as if she was trying to *become* me. Sometimes I even thought she was beginning to *sound* like me, to use my turns of phrase, my inflections. But – and this sounds crazy now, given all that was going on – in some ways I couldn't help but still like her. I felt sorry for her, for whatever insecurities must plague her to make her act in such a way, despite the confidence she managed to radiate. She was basically a nice person, and good company, and so I tried to ignore the strangeness of her behaviour, to rationalise it in my head. It wasn't a big deal, not really, was it?

After a while though, people did start to notice, and joke about it.

'Here come the twins,' they'd laugh, as we'd arrive at the pub together with our matching hairstyles, albeit mine dark and hers fair, and our by then embarrassingly similar wardrobes. I'd almost become resigned to it. Decent housemates were hard to find, and I really didn't have the time to go through the process again, or the inclination to have a big row and risk living in a hostile atmosphere. I was too busy, too focused on my medical studies, and I had exams looming. And everyone else just seemed to think it was cute, two friends so close they'd started looking and behaving like sisters.

If only I'd known then what was going to happen next; if I'd known just how far Fran was going to go. I blamed myself for *such* a long time. All the 'what if's. What if I'd nipped it in the bud right at the beginning? What if I'd stopped it, stopped *her*, when it was just clothes and shoes and earrings? What if, what if … how different everything might have been, if only I'd done something, done *anything*…

BZZZZZ.

I jump. I've been lost in thought, and the alarm on my phone has just gone off, my five-minute warning for my ward round. I pick up the phone and cancel the alarm, hesitate for a moment, then tap my email icon, my chest tightening.

Nothing. OK. Good.

I exhale, then look over at the counter and see Ella again, rearranging some dishes. I think about all she's been through recently, losing everything, and my stomach twists with fear. I haven't said a word about this, not to George, not to anyone, but Ella isn't the only person who's been persecuted by some shadowy foe recently.

I have too.

And, in truth, not just recently, but for a long time now. Just online, just via email, nothing in person. Just messages that have messed with my head. Nothing that's actually interfered with my life, nothing that's put anything I have at risk. Nothing like what's happened to Ella. But still...

I refresh my emails once more, just in case.

Nothing. It's OK. Breathe, I tell myself.

And it's not like Ella's, this situation. For a start, I *know* who's behind it. I know exactly who she is, and why she's coming after me. I've blocked her over and over, but she keeps coming back, new accounts, new email providers. I always know it's her though. And what can she really do, other than harass me by email? I have a secure job, a mortgage-free home, a husband who also has a secure job. There *are* things I can lose, but I can't lose everything, not like Ella has, can I? It would be unthinkable, and anyway, the woman hasn't messaged me for over a week now. Eight whole days of nothing, and for a while those vicious emails were coming every single day. Maybe she's given up, finally. Maybe it's all going to be OK after all.

I'm going to be late. I stand up, gathering my belongings, and look for Ella again, but she has her back to me now, heading through the door to the kitchen. I take a deep breath and walk out of the canteen.

Chapter Twenty-One

ELLA

Tuesday afternoon, and I'm shopping. My shift ended at four today, and I need a few bits for this new job. The hospital has provided a uniform of sorts – a black T-shirt with a black and white striped apron to tie on over the top – but they prefer us to wear black jeans or trousers and black shoes or trainers too, neither of which I seem to have. I'm a blue denim girl when it comes to jeans, and I don't really do smart trousers; as for trainers, all mine are white. I'm still trying to make my last wage packet last as long as I can, so I'm not planning to spend much today, but Harriet's kindness has meant my outgoings are minimal right now, and I couldn't be more grateful. With her insistence on me not paying rent, all I really need is money for my phone, bus fares, toiletries and food, and I'm determined to squirrel away as much of each future pay cheque as I possibly can. I can't live with Harriet and George for ever. I just want to get on with my life now.

This new job is OK though; the other canteen workers seem nice, as do the customers, all doctors and nurses and other hospital staff. And Paulette was already singing my praises at the end of day one yesterday, telling me I'm just what the place needs. As for my new temporary accommodation – life in the penthouse is *good*. The light, the space, the tasteful décor, and those *views*. Every morning when I pull back my curtains, I find myself just standing there, staring. In the daylight, I'm enraptured by the sweep of the river, the stark beauty of the tall, modern buildings against the expanse of sky. In the darkness, it's a glittering, light-studded tapestry, no less mesmerising.

One day, I think. *One day, I'll have a place like this. And someone to share it with too.*

Seeing Harriet and George together has begun to make me crave a real connection, a true intimacy. And – I'm not ashamed to admit it – I'm kind of missing the other sort of intimacy too.

Just before the nightmare in Gloucester kicked off, I had a couple of dates with a good-looking PE teacher. He turned out to be quite boring in the end – decent in bed which, casting caution aside along with my knickers, I discovered on our first date – but pretty dull outside of it. After our second hook-up I'd politely told him I'd had a good time, but had realised I was really too busy with the new business to have time for a relationship. But I would like a partner, sometime soon, although I keep telling myself that sort of thing will have to wait. I have more important issues to deal with, and I promised to cook pasta tonight, so now I march into Primark, on a mission. Black jeans and black trainers, for as little cash as possible. Then down to Aldi, for ingredients for tonight's dinner.

Twenty minutes later, I'm back out on the street, clutching a bag containing a decent enough looking pair of black, slightly flared jeans and a second, straight-leg pair, plus some simple black trainers.

That'll do. It's not as if I'm going to be working at the hospital for long, I think, as I scan the map on my phone, checking I'm heading in the right direction for the supermarket. As I turn left and start walking along the busy pavement, the phone still in my hand, I see a woman coming towards me, her face instantly vaguely familiar. I squint at her, trying to place her. Is she one of the medical staff I've served lunch to today or yesterday?

Then I gasp. It can't be … can it?

She's nearly level with me now, and she hasn't looked in my direction, hasn't seen me. I stop dead, causing a man walking behind me to tut loudly and sidestep me, giving me an angry glare, but I ignore him. I'm too busy staring at the woman as she gets closer, and I can feel my heart beginning to pound. Her hair is different: dark and pulled back into a neat ponytail, not blonde as I remember it. Her clothes are different too, no slick business suit or designer coat. She's wearing combat trousers and a green padded jacket; casual, a little scruffy even. But her face? I know that face. I've dreamed about that face. I've had *nightmares* about that face.

It's Lena.

Or the woman who *said* her name was Lena. It's her. She looks different, but it's *bloody* her. I'm sure it is.

She's passing me now, still oblivious to my presence just metres away. I spin around, mouth opening, about to call her name, but she's walking fast, disappearing into the rush hour throng. I hesitate for a second, two, three. *Is* it her? Am I imagining things, seeing her face on a complete stranger? I thought I saw someone lurking in the shadows as Harriet and I walked home from the pub on Sunday, and I was imagining *that*, wasn't I? There was nobody there at all. But this ... this is different. It's broad daylight, and I can *see* her. I feel a rush of anger.

No. It is *you, and you are* not *getting away from me, you witch*, I think. *We're sorting this out*, now.

I stuff my phone into my coat pocket and start to run.

Chapter Twenty-Two

ELLA

'Lena! LENA!'

I bellow her name, and get startled looks from the nearest passersby, but the dark-haired woman is still walking away from me. I push past an elderly man shuffling along with a walking stick, and duck around a gaggle of slow-moving teenagers, and then shout again.

'LENA!'

Still no response, but I'm gaining on her now, and seconds later I'm right behind her. Without thinking about it, I reach out a hand and grab her shoulder, gripping a handful of the khaki fabric of her coat and twisting it between my fingers, and she lets out a cry and whirls around, backing away from me so I lose my hold on her. For a moment, her eyes widen, as if surprised to see me, then she frowns.

'What the hell … can I help you?' she says sharply.

'I … you…' I stutter.

Oh, I think.

Up close, her face is so, *so* Lena. Almost identical. But with her dark hair, this woman looks so much paler than the always lightly tanned Lena *I* know, and *that* Lena was always so beautifully made up too, perfect eye shadow, glossy lips. This version is bare-skinned, not even a slick of mascara. And her voice? Again, so similar, such a familiar tone to it, but the *accent*? Lena had one of those educated, non-specific, southern England accents. This woman sounds northern, Manchester maybe.

'Lena?' I say, hesitantly. 'Is it … is it you?'

Her frown intensifies, a wary look in her eyes, and she backs away from me a little further.

'That's not my name, no,' she says. 'You've got the wrong person. Sorry.'

She runs a hand over the shoulder of her coat, as if to wipe away the impression my grabbing fingers have made, and I stare at her. Even her hands seem weirdly familiar, the neatly shaped nails, one slightly crooked index finger. This *is* Lena, it must be, but I don't understand why she looks and sounds so different, and now she's turning away, and I know I have to try one more time.

'Please,' I say desperately. '*Please.*'

She stops, turns back, opens her mouth as if to reply, then closes it again.

'Lena – or whoever you are – please, just talk to me,' I say. 'Please help me understand. It is you, isn't it? What happened? Why did you do that to me?'

She stands there looking at me with a strange expression for a few seconds, then shrugs.

'As I said, you've got the wrong person,' she says quietly, and there's kindness in her voice now. Sympathy, even. 'I've no idea what you're talking about. I'm sorry, but I need to go.'

Then she turns again, and walks quickly away, not looking back. Seconds later I've lost sight of her among the other pedestrians, and part of me wants to run after her, grab her again, shake her this time, make her admit she *is* the person I think she is. But I can't move. My limbs feel like dead weights, and there's a sinking feeling in the pit of my stomach.

Was *that her?* I think. *Or has all this finally sent me over the edge? She looked at me as if I was crazy. Maybe I am crazy...*

Somehow, I manage to make my way to the supermarket, and buy what I need for tonight. There's a little gardening section, and on impulse I pick up thyme and rosemary plants too; Harriet's huge balcony is still a plant-free zone, and I suddenly have a vague idea of making her a little herb garden out there before I move out, a sort of thank you for everything she's doing for me. I manage to keep it together until I get back to the penthouse, where to my relief there's no sign of Harriet and George; then I put the food away, lock myself in my room, throw myself onto the bed and sob. I don't even really know why I'm crying; maybe because I suddenly feel that today may have been my last chance to get to the bottom of all this, and I let that woman walk away. I didn't trust my own instincts, and I should have. I *should* have. Yes, she looked different, and she acted as if she'd never seen me before in her life. But now, I'm remembering the way her eyes opened wide when she first saw me, before her expression quickly closed down. The strange way she looked at me just before she walked away.

She *did* know me. That *was* her. That *was* Lena, or whoever she really is. And I let her go. I'm doubting myself so much these days that I don't even trust what I can see right there in front of me. And she clearly saw that doubt and ran with it. She took advantage of my confusion, played on it. Made her escape. And what are the chances of me ever just accidentally bumping into her again like that? Zero. A big fat zero.

Fuck. FUCK.

I slam my fist into my pillow, then jump as I hear voices in the hallway outside, Harriet and George arriving home together. They call my name, and I call back to say I'm just freshening up and I'll make a start on dinner as soon as I'm ready.

'Sit down in about forty minutes?' I shout.

'Great! I might have a bath, then – thanks, Ella!' Harriet replies, and through the closed door I hear George saying that in that case, he might pop out for 'a quick 5k'. By the time I've wiped away my tears, cleaned the streaks of mascara from my cheeks and brushed my hair, the apartment is quiet again, other than the distant murmur of some talk radio station that's clearly keeping Harriet company as she bathes. I make a start on dinner, chopping garlic and mixing it with butter, seasoning and a little Parmesan – I've bought the bread, but at least I'm making an effort with the garlic butter – then make a simple salad and tip the pasta into a pan. I've just started sizzling some bacon lardons when Harriet appears, dressed in a hoodie and sweatpants, her hair damp.

'Mmm – smells great! What are we having?' she says, as she sits down at the breakfast bar. 'Good day? I didn't even have time for lunch today so I didn't get to see you.'

'Rigatoni with lemon, bacon, and chilli,' I reply, shaking the frying pan. 'And salad and garlic bread on the side. And, no, not really. I mean, work was fine. But something really weird happened when I went shopping. I *think* I bumped into Lena.'

Harriet looks startled, then frowns.

'You *think* you did?'

'Yep, bit of a peculiar one,' I say.

I tell her the story as I carry on cooking, and just as I'm getting to the end of it George arrives home, pink-cheeked and slightly sweaty after his run, so I have to tell it again.

'Blimey,' he says when I've finished. 'That's mad. So frustrating, if it really was her, and she got away from you. I still can't get my head round any of this, to be honest. People pretending to be other people? People spending so much money to screw someone over? I'm not saying I don't believe you, Ella, I'm just saying ... it's *mad*. And equally mad that there doesn't seem to be anything you can *do* about it. Legally, I mean. I feel so sorry for you, honestly.'

He stands up and reaches out a hand to touch my arm gently, and I smile.

'Thanks. Your support means a lot,' I say quietly.

'Poor you,' says Harriet. 'I mean, that might *not* have been her today, maybe it *was* just someone who looked a bit like her. But I'm not surprised you're confused. They've been so clever, haven't they? *Nasty* clever I mean. Look – if there's anything we can do, Ella ... and at least things are looking up for you a bit now, with the job and everything. Do you feel a bit better – a bit more secure?'

I nod, then turn away to drain the pasta at the sink, grateful for the distraction. I suddenly feel as if I might burst into tears again. Harriet and George sit quietly, watching me, and as I reach for the cream to stir into the rigatoni, I say, 'I do feel better, yes. I was so full of rage, you know? But now ... as we said the other day, I think I really do just need to leave it alone. Seeing Lena – or seeing that woman – gave me hope for a few minutes that I could find out the truth after all. But sod it. Onwards and upwards, right?'

I turn back to face them, and Harriet smiles and slides off her stool.

'Onwards and upwards. I'll drink to that, again. And I do think it's the right decision. But if you ever do decide to carry on pursuing it, talk to us, OK? As I said, if there's *anything* we can do. And thanks for cooking, I'm ravenous. George, can you lay the table? Anyone else want wine?'

'Yes, please,' I say, and as I finish off the pasta I feel a wave of something I can only think must be relief, and realise I'm humming along to the music George has just switched on.

Onwards and upwards. Was today the final turning point? Maybe. Although … I bite my lip.

If I ever see you again, 'Lena', I'll wrestle you to the ground in front of everyone rather than let you get away, I think. *Maybe I won't actively try to find you, or search for answers to all this, not any more. But if you ever cross my path again … watch out, that's all I can say.*

Chapter Twenty-Three

HARRIET

T hursday is always one of my busiest days and by mid-afternoon after a packed out-patients clinic I'm feeling light-headed with hunger. I ate a hurried breakfast at six this morning and all I've had time to ingest since is a few slurps of bad coffee, but now I have a twenty-minute window before my neonatal ward round and I'm in the canteen, a chicken salad sandwich on a paper plate in front of me, a tall white mug of tea at its side. I pick up the sandwich and sink my teeth into the soft white bread – not usually my first choice, but it was all they had left at this time of day – and let out a little groan of surprise and pleasure. It's actually delicious, the bread fresh, the chicken tender and well-seasoned, and maybe it's just because I'm so hungry but, I think, as I chew, swallow and go in for the second mouthful, it might just be one of the best sandwiches I've had in a very long time. Is this Ella's influence? If so, helping her to get this job was *definitely* one of my better decisions of recent times.

Sandwich half eaten, I take a sip of tea and then

automatically reach for my phone, checking my email inbox. Still nothing from her. Eleven days now. Nearly two weeks. Good. This is *really* good. *Has* she given up? Can I relax, finally?

I'm still not sleeping well. I dreamed about Fran again last night, and as I pick up my sandwich again, ready to savour the rest of it, her face floats into my mind and suddenly, there's a sour taste in my mouth.

Regret, that's what it is. Regret – and self-loathing – for my own weakness. Yes, what Fran ultimately did, and the consequences of it, was *her* fault. But also partly mine, because if I'd nipped her behaviour in the bud earlier, if I'd stopped it when it was just the – in retrospect – pretty harmless copycatting, maybe what came next, about eight months after Fran had moved in, would never have happened. *Maybe*.

I was dating a guy called Felix, a primary school teacher I'd met in a bar, and it was going well. And I mean *really* well. We'd used the L-word after we'd been together for just six weeks; after three months, we were talking about moving in together, and in our long, late-night conversations as we lay wrapped around each other in bed, we discussed everything from what sort of dog we wanted to where we'd like to spend our honeymoon and what colour our kitchen should be. And then, about four months into this state of coupled-up bliss, I discovered, with a combination of joy and terror, that I was pregnant.

I'd always wanted kids, always. It was one of the reasons I decided to specialise in paediatrics; that desire to be around tiny humans, to help them through tough times, to watch them grow and thrive. But even I knew the timing wasn't great. I was still working long hours, still training, and although I knew Felix wanted kids too, for him it was at some abstract date in the future, something he talked about only vaguely, only in theory. At that point, he was definitely more interested in dogs, and so when I finally plucked up the courage to tell him, I was already half expecting his reaction to be less than ecstatic. I was right. He was … well, *horrified* I think is an accurate description. Too soon, too young, not ready … the words came like hammer blows, and when he left, saying he needed some space, some time apart from me to think, I sank to my knees on my bedroom floor and howled. Then I packed a bag and headed off to my parents' little cottage in Oxfordshire.

I didn't tell them the truth about why I needed to escape London for a few days; I said it was exam stress, burnout. That I needed to decompress, to breathe some fresh country air, to regroup. And four days later, I actually *did* feel better, and I'd made a decision. I loved Felix, but I didn't *need* him. If he didn't want to do this, I could do it on my own. It wouldn't be easy, but nor would it be impossible. There were hospitals with onsite nurseries, flexible working hours … and even though I was still so early on in my pregnancy, I could *feel* this child, its spirit, its energy. It was already part of me, and there was no way, *no way*, I was going to let it go, just because its father had cold feet. But also, I thought, maybe I wouldn't *have* to go it alone. Maybe the thinking time he'd demanded had led him to a similar conclusion. Maybe we *could* have our happily ever after: our dog and our kitchen and our honeymoon *and* our baby.

And so I travelled back to London with a bubble of excitement in my stomach. I got a late, and hence cheaper, Friday night train to save money, disembarking at Paddington at half past eleven and arriving back at the flat just after midnight. I was expecting Fran to be still out, as she usually was on weekend evenings. But as I walked through the lounge, heading for my bedroom, I heard giggles and squeals, and *two* voices I recognised. Moments later Fran's door burst open and out she ran, wearing nothing but lacy pink underwear, and hotly pursued by a very naked and clearly very excited man. Felix. *My* Felix.

They both stopped dead, and gaped at me, and as I looked from one to the other, as I took in what was happening right in front of me, and what it meant, my little bubble of excitement, of hope and happiness, quietly burst, to be replaced by an almost physical pain, a deep, hollow sensation that made me gasp, made me clutch my belly and stagger into my room, slamming and locking the door behind me.

Felix tapped on it for a while, pleading and apologising, but when I refused to answer him he crept away into the night, to be replaced by Fran. I ignored her too, because by then the pain inside me had become real, a sharp, nagging ache, twisting and curling deep in my core. And then the bleeding began, and I knew.

It was over before it had really begun, or so I thought. Except it wasn't over, and wouldn't be for a long time. I miscarried, obviously, but something went wrong, some tissue left behind, a resultant infection, a D & C, a scarred uterus. A year later, long after Fran had moved out and I'd tried to move on, I was told I was unlikely to ever be able to conceive naturally, my chances of carrying my own child vanishingly small. I told George that, of course, when I met him, when we first began to entertain the idea of spending our lives together, but I never told him the full story. An accidental pregnancy from a one-night stand, and resultant complications, was all I said… The lie was easier, somehow. And as for having children in the future? We've talked about adoption, IVF, surrogates, about other ways of becoming parents, but if I'm being truly honest, deep down I'm not sure I *can* do it in any of those ways. I know those choices work for many, many people, but for me? For me nothing will ever be the same as feeling that child in my belly, conceived naturally, conceived in love. I know too that this makes George sad, but he loved me enough to marry me anyway. I think he hopes that one day I'll change my mind and let medical science help us. Maybe I will. Maybe I won't.

'If it's just us, well, two is still a family, isn't it?' I often say, and he nods and hugs me, and tells me that we still have time, that I'm only thirty-four. That clock is ticking though, I know that, and I often see the bleakness in George's eyes when we pass a playground, or see a child tugging at its father's coat in the supermarket. And yet I still can't go there, can't make a decision, can't decide if I want to put myself through it all. Instead I throw myself into my work, and into the kids like little Daniel, running towards me on his prosthetic legs, face glowing with delight. If I'll never see my own child's face light up like that when it sees me, at least I have this.

What I also have though – and it's something I know I hide very, very well, from everyone – is the anger, still simmering away, just under the surface. Anger that has intensified, if anything, over the years; not fading into a grim acceptance of unchangeable circumstances but more feverish, more visceral now than it ever was back then. And strangely, it's not directed at Felix, not even a little bit. He's a man, after all, and men are weak, and easily tempted. My fury, my rage, is all for Fran.

Fran, who was supposed to be my friend, but who slowly took little bits of my life and made them hers. Who stole not just my hairstyle and my fashion choices but my boyfriend too and, I firmly believe, my chance of motherhood. If she hadn't done what she'd done, if I hadn't come back and found them together that awful night, my pregnancy would not have ended, I'm convinced of that. *Everything* would have been different. She stole my baby, my fertility, my life.

Baby.

'Harriet! I haven't seen you in ages, how are you?'

As if just thinking the word has somehow conjured up a real-life child, suddenly there's a woman standing in front of me, so heavily pregnant that it looks as if the red sweater dress she's wearing is about to rip open across her swollen belly.

'Ava! Hi. I'm OK … how are you? Not long now, I see!'

She's one of the medical secretaries, reaching out a hand now to lean on the back of the chair opposite me and grinning.

'Three weeks. Maternity leave starts tomorrow, thank heavens. I'm bloody knackered lugging this thing around.'

She runs her spare hand across her enormous bump, and I stand up abruptly. Sometimes I'm just fine around expectant mothers, but there are many occasions when I simply can't bear it. Today, it seems, is one of those days. I can feel it now, a wave of bitter jealousy and sorrow beginning to build inside me, and I know I have to get away, now, *fast*. Quickly, I gather my belongings, trying to compose myself, then swallow hard and look at Ava again.

'Well, good luck! And make sure you bring the little one in to see us as soon as you can, OK?' I say, forcing a smile, and she nods and smiles back.

'Of course! Thanks so much, Harriet. See you soon, then!'

'Bye, Ava.'

I can't help myself. I look down her body one more time, at that round, firm bulge, and for a second it's as if I can see through it, through her clothing and her skin, to the tiny life coiled within, warm and protected and safe. I walk swiftly away, my eyes blurring with tears.

Chapter Twenty-Four

HARRIET

A minute of deep breathing and fast walking later – I really should have started my ward round by now – and I'm already feeling a little better. I've grown good at this, over the years; somehow I've trained myself to shift from agonising despair to almost normal again in a matter of moments, and I know I need to focus on work now and put my encounter with Ava out of my mind. But just as I'm about to round the corner into the corridor down to the ward I suddenly hear pounding feet behind me, and then a yell, and I gasp and spin around, my body tensing. Then I laugh with relief as I see my husband, bounding towards me with long, loose strides like an over-energetic puppy.

'George! You nearly gave me a heart attack! What on earth are you doing here?'

We may work in the same hospital, but it's rare we actually bump into each other. George beams at me and grabs me round the waist, pulling me in for a kiss.

'Had a few minutes to spare and felt like some exercise so I ran down to see if I could find you,' he says. 'I haven't had much of you on your own recently, and I knew you'd be somewhere in this vicinity – you've got a ward round about now, haven't you?'

'I have, and I'm late!' I say, wriggling out of his grasp, but unable to stop myself grinning back at him. God, I love this man.

'And shouldn't you be somewhere too? Go, you crazy nutter.'

'On my way. See you later!'

He slaps me playfully on the bottom, then turns and jogs off again before I have time to retaliate, waving a hand in the air as he goes. I shake my head, still smiling, then remember that I really need to get a move on, and as I march down the corridor, I feel a rush of gratitude. I may not have a child, may never have one, but I have George, and he is bloody wonderful. I'm lucky, really, aren't I? And I don't deserve him. I *really* don't deserve him. The sense of well-being fades again.

If he only knew what I'm really like, I think. *Would he still love me then?*

I've kept so many secrets from him. So many, especially recently, that the scale of my deception sometimes makes me feel physically sick. And he's never guessed, ever. When he asks me if I'm OK, on days when I'm struggling to keep up the façade, I just blame the stresses of the job, say I'm tired, and he gives me a hug and tells me he'll cook dinner tonight, or gets up extra early to bring me a cup of tea in bed before I have to leave for the hospital. He's there for me, always. And despite all that, I still can't bring myself to make that decision, to give him the child I know he would love so much…

'Dr Hart! I was wondering where you were.'

I'm at the ward and seconds later I'm back to my professional self again. Doctor Hart, doing her thing. When it's over, I pop back to the canteen to grab a take-out coffee, feeling shattered.

No pregnant women in here this time, thank heavens, I think, as I join the queue at the counter, my eyes scanning the room. *No more freak-outs today, hopefully. One was enough. Because now, more than ever, I cannot lose focus. Just for a little while longer…*

Since Fran stole my chances of motherhood, I've often thought she stole a little of my sanity too, although that's another thing I've grown adept at hiding. I've become an actor, in some ways, I suppose: the outer me professional, accomplished, successful, the inner me a writhing mess of pain and vengeful thoughts. And so while outwardly I moved on from what happened with Fran and Felix, *I* know that for years I was just biding my time, waiting for my chance. Until suddenly, that chance arrived. As if by fate, as if karma was, for once, smiling at me, along came my inheritance, so unexpected, and so very, very welcome. Because not only did it buy me the home of my dreams, it also bought me the chance to get the revenge of my dreams, finally.

Revenge on Fran, or Francesca, to give her her full name. Although she doesn't use that name very often. She hasn't used it at all for a while, in fact. I know that, because I've been keeping tabs on her. Keeping a very close eye on her, in fact.

No, she doesn't use Fran much these days. She goes by her middle name.

Ella.

Francesca Ella Leonard.

There she is now, emerging from the kitchen, cloth and spray bottle in hand, striding towards the nearest table, beginning to wipe it down, giving the two paramedics sitting opposite a bright smile.

We'd met up, at her request, a few weeks after my miscarriage, after I'd kicked her out. She wanted to clear the air, to tell me how terribly, terribly sorry she was, how it had meant absolutely nothing, that Felix had just been a drunken mistake, and weren't we on a break anyway, because that's what he'd said (of course he had). I didn't have the energy to argue. I told her it was fine, that he and I would probably never have worked, that maybe it was all meant to be. She cried, and I even gave her a hug. But I never told her what she'd really done, what the consequences of her 'drunken mistake' had been. I'd spoken to Felix eventually, and he promised he'd told nobody about the baby, and that he'd never share the news I brought him that day, before we walked away from each other for good: the news that I'd terminated the pregnancy. A lie, of course, but he didn't deserve the truth. And so I knew that Fran knew nothing about the baby either, or of what became of it, and when we met I played the game, and played it beautifully, because I knew that although this time *I* might be the loser, one day I was going to *slaughter* this woman. And now that day has come.

I stare at her, and I feel the hatred I've been disguising so beautifully since she stepped into my arms at the door of my apartment last week burning even hotter. Then I smile.

It's been almost a joy, watching her. All that chasing around trying to understand it all, all so futile. Chasing after her mother, after 'Lena'. Me helping her, offering her advice, and then sitting back and watching her run round and round in entirely pointless circles. I may be slightly mad, but at least I'm not stupid like she is. Poor Fran. Poor *Ella*.

She has no idea that everything that's befallen her recently has been down to me. That I masterminded it all. Paid for it, watched from a distance as the plan was executed perfectly. And then – and oh man, what an unexpected little bonus that was! – she called *me* for help, when her life began to fall apart around her. I wasn't expecting that, but why look a gift horse in the mouth? I hadn't intended to carry on, not this long. But hey – *she* came to *me*, right? And just when the hospital canteen had a job vacancy that was perfect for her too. You can't tell me that wasn't a message from the universe, telling me to keep going. I could hardly ignore it, could I? And now if she thinks she's turned a corner, and that her life's back on track, she's very much mistaken.

'Hi, Harriet!'

She's calling across the canteen to me now, moving on to wipe another table, grinning and waving her cloth at me.

I smile back and her grin grows wider. She looks happy.

Oh Ella, I think. *I'll pretend to be your friend, and I'll let you stay in my home, but only until I've finished playing with you. So, be happy today. Make the most of it. Because I promise you, it's not going to last. You think what's happened to you already is bad? You have no idea how bad things are going to get.*

Watch. This. Space.

Chapter Twenty-Five

HARRIET

I deserve an Oscar, really, don't I?

A little smile plays on my lips, and I turn to look out of the bus window, so the man sitting beside me doesn't think I'm smiling at him. I'm on my way home, for another evening of pretending to be sympathetic and supportive, when in reality I'm about to strike again.

Poor Ella. You could almost feel sorry for her, couldn't you? Almost. I don't, though. OK … that's not quite true actually. Since she moved in, since I've seen firsthand that she really is different now, really has changed into a better person than the one I knew, a nicer, kinder, more thoughtful person, well … I *have* had moments of feeling something akin to guilt. Of wondering if I've gone too far, if I'm *continuing* to go too far. Of wondering if I obsessed over her and what she did for so many years that I stopped seeing things clearly. *Is* it time to stop? Has she suffered enough? But no. NO. The person she is now doesn't cancel out who she was back then, or what she did. She deserves everything that's happened to her so far, and everything she's going to get. She *does*. And anyway, it's so nearly over now. Just a little bit longer, and then I'll be done. Done with her for *good*.

It was the money that made it possible. I needed to do to her what she did to me: give her the prospect of a glorious future, and then whip it brutally away, leaving her with nothing. But everything seemed so logistically tricky, and with limited funds I just couldn't make it happen. And then came that joyous, unexpected windfall, and suddenly almost anything was possible. The penthouse purchase took a big chunk of the money, but there was still just over a million pounds left; just over a million pounds which, with proper investment, was more than enough to provide a very nice, secure future for me and George, especially as we were mortgage-free. That was one of the many, many lies I told my husband, about that money; I said the sum remaining was around a hundred grand *less* than it really was, and then I stashed that hundred grand in a new, secret, high-interest bank account. By then, I'd begun to come up with a real plan, a plan that would cost money, but one that I knew – or hoped – would work, and so that money was just for me. My revenge fund. Many might think that to throw away so much cash on getting revenge on someone is outrageous, wasteful, shocking. They'd probably be right. But I don't care. This is something I *needed* to do, something I don't think I'd ever stop thinking about for the rest of my life if I didn't. I *craved* that revenge on Fran. Or Ella, as I soon discovered she now calls herself, when I spent the first couple of thousand on hiring a private detective to track her down. She'd toyed with the name change when we lived together, started telling strangers we met on nights out that her name was Ella, trying it out.

'It's a nicer name, don't you think?' she said. 'And Francesca Leonard was a full-time model. Ella Leonard isn't, not any more. I think that's who I'll be, from now on. A new me. And it is genuinely one of my names, after all.'

Then we'd lost touch, of course, and I wasn't quite sure which name to search for, and although I was almost certain she'd still be living in London, I ended up being unable to find her myself. Unusually for someone who looks like Ella, she's not really a social media user, which didn't help. Back when she was modelling more regularly, she was never off socials, and even when I knew her and the work had slowed down she still posted the occasional sexy, pouting shot when she landed a job. But by the time I started looking for her again, her old social media accounts seemed to be no longer in use, and so in the end I decided the only way to locate her was to get a professional on the job. I got lucky with Dean Dawson, the PI I ended up hiring. He was fast and efficient; he found Ella within twenty-four hours. And as soon as I knew where she was working, in that coffee shop in Kensington, it was game on.

My revenge plot wasn't even that difficult to pull off; everything in life is easier when you have money to throw at it. I'd already found my 'Lena Fox'. Her real name is Katherine Reece, and she's an actor. She's brilliant, in my view; I first came across her in a play I went to at the Greenwich Theatre, and she outshone everyone else on the stage. Then, by complete coincidence, I saw her again two weeks later, busking on Regent Street. I recognised her immediately, and stopped to listen, captivated by her voice and deeply impressed that she could sing as well as she could act. When her song had finished, I went to drop some money in her guitar case and told her I'd seen her on stage only recently. We ended up having a long chat, and it was when she told me how tough her chosen profession was, the decent gigs only coming along now and again, hence the busking, I had a lightbulb moment. I told her I might be able to put some well-paid, if a little unconventional, acting work her way, took her number, then went home to think. By the next morning, every detail of my plan was in place. Find Ella, send Katherine to befriend her … boom.

I'm lost in thought, remembering how surprisingly simple it all was, but the bus is slowing, and I realise it's my stop. I sway down the aisle and jump off, just as my phone pings with an email alert. I glance at the screen, and my heart thuds. *Shit*. I thought she'd stopped. I *hoped* she'd stopped. She *had* stopped. But here she is, my tormentor, back again. Another bloody email. I look at the sender name once more, hoping I've read it wrongly, but I haven't. It's definitely her.

Nisha.

Slowly, I move to the side of the path, out of the way of the people still embarking and disembarking the bus, and tap on the email to open it. As I read the short message my hand flies to my mouth, stifling a gasp. Her emails have always been nasty; I'm used to that. But this … this is different. This is a threat. Specific, detailed.

I've waited long enough, Harriet. I've asked nicely, I've even begged. I've warned you that one day soon your time would run out. Well, that day has come…

There's more, and as I read it again, my head swims.
But she couldn't do that, could she? I think. *There's no way. And*

172

to warn me in advance? That's really *stupid, because now I'll looking out for her. On the alert.*

I inhale deeply, let the air out again, then stuff the phone into my pocket and start walking.

She's just clutching at straws now. Trying to frighten me, I think, as I turn the corner, our apartment block within sight already. A light rain is falling, and I shiver, pulling up the collar of my coat.

This is clearly a last-ditch attempt to bully me into giving her what she wants. But do your worst, Nisha, because it's not going to work. I have more important things to worry about right now than you and your petty demands. So you can try, if you like. But come for me, and I'll be ready for you.

I stop walking, pull out my phone again and, with a firm sweep of my finger, delete the email. I stare at the screen for a moment, then push the phone back into my pocket and head for home.

Chapter Twenty-Six

HARRIET

T hank goodness it's Friday.

I didn't sleep well last night, fidgeting and sighing so much that at 3am an exhausted George finally muttered: 'OK, I give up!' and jumped out of bed, spending the rest of the night in our second spare bedroom. When he asked me this morning why I'd been so restless, I muttered something vague about a super-busy day ahead and a couple of tricky cases, and he nodded sympathetically as usual and gave me a hug, then rushed out of the door to start his own busy day, clutching a flask of coffee and shouting, 'See you tonight! Roll on the weekend, eh?'

Another lie, of course. Work isn't the reason I didn't sleep well. Despite my bravado in deleting Nisha's email yesterday, today I feel panicky every time I think about it. *Can* she somehow get to me, and carry out her threat? I don't know, but I'm trying to convince myself that all I need to do is stay vigilant.

If she tries anything, I'll see it coming a mile away, I think, as I swallow the last of my tea, then quickly gather my belongings. As I pass Ella's bedroom door, I pause, listening. Silence. She's still asleep. Good. I smile as I quietly let myself out of the door of the apartment. If there's the smallest chance that I'm going down – that Nisha's going to take away some of the best bits of my life, as her email threatened – then it won't be without a fight. And it won't be before I finish what I've started with Ella. So, last night, I began the next stage. She's been lulled into a false sense of security over the past week or so; nice little new job, rent-free living accommodation. Time to rip that away from her too.

It's worked so well up until now. Shockingly well, although when it began, once I knew where Ella was, it did take a while to convince my new actor friend Katherine to take on the job. As I'd hoped, the money won her over in the end. I assured her she absolutely wasn't getting involved in anything criminal, nothing that would get her in any trouble with the law, and stressed, without giving her full details, that Ella was not a victim, but a bad, bad person. That she deserved to be played with a little. Katherine is a *good* person, and she hesitated for quite a while. But she was struggling financially, and it was a *lot* of cash for the little she actually had to do; twenty-five grand to play a high-flying businesswoman for a handful of hours a week for a few months? To sit in a fancy London coffee shop and chat, make a few trips to Gloucester, take and make a few phone calls? I did insist she sign a non-disclosure agreement though, just for a little added protection, just in case. It's pretty easy to do, even without involving a solicitor; there are free templates online, and again, it took a little time to persuade her, but she signed in the end. I think she finally realised it was the easiest money she'd ever make, and so, once she'd finally come on board, she threw herself into the role with aplomb.

I think we both sort of began to enjoy it. We went shopping together, and I bought her a selection of designer coats, suits and handbags so she looked the part, and a beautifully realistic blonde wig. Being reasonably tech savvy, I built a basic website detailing all 'Lena's' imaginary business interests and opened a new email account for her. I even bought her an iPhone, with a new phone number. And then I sent the glamorous, successful Lena Fox to Ella's workplace, and she played a blinder. Within days, she was reporting back to me that Ella was already opening up to her; not too long after that, my dumb little ex-housemate had accepted a job offer from her new 'friend' and was making plans to leave London. That had been the bit I'd been most worried about. Ella had always been impulsive, never reading modelling job contracts properly, never checking out new photographers who offered to work with her. Had she changed in the years since I'd known her, I wondered? Was she more switched on now when it came to her career? But, to my relief, it seemed not. If she did check out Lena online – I told Katherine to send her the link to the website – it appeared that what she saw was enough to convince her. And Lena had already told her she didn't use social media; I doubt Ella even bothered to look any further anyway. It worked like a dream.

It took a bit of time to set everything up at the Gloucester end, but Katherine was between acting jobs, other than mine, and so she helped me out. We registered a new pop-up food business with the local authority and the environmental health office, got all the proper paperwork, sorted insurance – the premises had previously been a food vendor, which helped – and it was a steep learning curve for a doctor and an actor but

Katherine was great, and soon we were ready. We decided to let Ella take over and source suppliers and everything else she needed herself once she was in situ, but I was pretty pleased with what we had in place. A short-term rental on the premises in Gloucester – we got a great rate too, because the place had been empty for a while – fully kitted out with café equipment also on short-term lease, and a cash payment to Ella to get her started, no bank account in Lena's name required. I worried a bit about her somehow tracing the business back to me after I closed it down, but I figured if she *did* start searching online, it would be Lena Fox's business interests she'd be looking for, and of course they didn't actually exist, not outside the fake website. I *did* have to open a bank account for Mug & Meadow, for the takings, and that was a little risky; I had to use my real name and personal details to get it set up, but the name on the actual account was the café name, and Ella could only pay money in, not withdraw funds or access the account in any other way, and so I figured that was safe enough. She'd been told to forward all bills and expenses to Lena to pay, and she was more than happy to hand over that responsibility; she was busy enough with running the place. It meant too that when I eventually closed the account again, the bank wouldn't give *her* any details.

To be honest, when the café opened I was a little surprised by how *much* money started coming in to that account; amazed to see how quickly she made a success of Mug & Meadow. Amazed and, reluctantly, a tiny bit impressed. Ella had more about her than I initially thought, which meant I was making back some of the money I'd spent. And so on we went, Lena taking Ella's phone calls and replying to her WhatsApp messages, me dealing with any emails she sent. On my instructions, Lena cheered her on, told her repeatedly how brilliantly she was doing, got her all excited about her future. I let it carry on for five weeks, and then, again a little nervous about how easy it would be to pull off, I put the second part of my plan into action. We were comfortable that the security camera situation would work in our favour, and I'd had Dean, my PI, follow Ella about a bit, checking out her routine, so I was as sure as I could be that she never returned to the industrial estate at weekends, locking up late on Friday afternoons and not returning until early on Monday mornings. Just in case, I got Lena to call Ella on the Friday before we struck, telling her to stress again how brilliantly the café was doing and to tell her to make sure she had a restful weekend away from it. Dean had also reported that most of the other businesses on the estate operated in a similar way, closing at weekends, and that the place was generally almost deserted on Saturdays and Sundays. And so, that first weekend of February, the next phase of my plot began.

Along with a couple of other out-of-work actor friends, who were happy to ask no questions in return for hefty pay cheques from me, Lena hired a van and, using her spare key, swiftly cleared out Mug & Meadow early on the Sunday morning, changed the door lock so Ella wouldn't be able to get in again and dropped off the new keys with the letting agent, making up a story about the lock having been accidentally broken. I'd done my research thoroughly beforehand, trying to ensure that everything we'd done, everything I'd orchestrated, was unlikely to result in any legal action, but I still held my breath on the Monday, expecting Ella to call the police as soon as she arrived for work and realised what had happened. Dean made sure he was there though, joining a little throng of perplexed café customers and hanging around as Ella tried to explain her plight to what he described as two rather bemused-looking officers.

'Nothing they can do, that's what they told her,' he reported back, and my shoulders dropped with relief.

Doing a superb impression of Ella's voice – she tried it on me over the phone, and its accuracy made me shiver – Lena (I'd totally stopped thinking of her as Katherine at that point; she was Lena, end of) had already called the café's main supplier a few days earlier to cancel the next order; I told her to leave the rest of the orders as they were, just to add to Ella's confusion. I knew it would also take her a while to track down the property's owners or landlords; Lena had dealt with all of that stuff and, true to form, Ella had never asked her for any details.

Then it was just a simple matter of gradually closing everything down. The bank account, the email account, the phone number, the website. Everything had existed for such a short time that after a couple of days, nothing was coming up on Google searches for Lena Fox or Foxy Eats Ltd, and I smiled as I imagined Ella's frustration and dismay as every trace of her new employer evaporated. Two days later, it was time for the next step – her flat.

And now, she's in mine. Still sound asleep. Already very late for work.

Thank you, little drug.

That's why she's still asleep in her cosy bed right now. It's just after seven, and she should be at work in the hospital canteen, on the breakfast shift today. But she's not, and that's going to get her in big trouble with Paulette, especially when it happens repeatedly over the next couple of weeks, which it will. I'll be making sure of that, all thanks to a particular type of antihistamine. It's not hard to get hold of; you can buy it in any pharmacy, under various brand names, and on the wards we use it for things like eczema, hives caused by food allergies or chickenpox, reactions to insect bites and stings. I could have just popped into Boots or Superdrug and bought some on my way home from work, but I thought carefully about that and, strange as it may sound, I thought it might be safer to 'liberate' some from the drugs cupboard at work instead. A purchase from a high street pharmacy would show up on my bank statement, unless I used cash, which, like most people, I never carry any more, plus all the shops have CCTV cameras. And although I'm pretty sure Ella will never work out I've been drugging her, I'd prefer there to be no record at all of me being in possession of antihistamines right now. It *shouldn't* be easier to steal them from the hospital, but it is. The drugs room has a secure door with an access code, which I, of course, have; once inside it, there are no cameras to observe what we do, just a book to sign to log which drug we've taken out and the quantity. It should work, but things do go missing; people are in and out all the time, people in a hurry, people who urgently need drugs for a patient and forget to note them down. And it's not as if an antihistamine is a *controlled* drug within the hospital; those are kept in a separate cupboard, a cupboard which requires a key. I could access that too, if I wanted to, but I don't. Not yet, anyway.

Do no harm.

It's from the original version of the Hippocratic Oath, written almost 2,500 years ago.

'First, do no harm.'

Some medical schools don't even bother making students

swear it any more, but I still like those words. And 'harm' is open to interpretation, right? Short-term inconvenience isn't really *harm*. I cooked dinner for Ella and George last night, a spicy butter chicken, perfect to disguise the mild taste of the pills I crushed into her portion. Then, as alcohol hugely amplifies the already fast-acting effects, I made sure she had several glasses of the good cabernet I opened, then watched her, closely but discreetly. To my delight, she crashed quickly, starting to yawn widely, blinking her eyes and expressing surprise at how knackered she suddenly felt.

'You work hard. You're on your feet all day, and you have all of us demanding medics to deal with!' I said. 'I'm not surprised you're exhausted. Go on, have an early night.'

She'd nodded and stumbled off to bed, George raising an eyebrow.

'One too many there, I reckon,' he muttered, as he stood up to clear the plates.

I agreed, feeling a little pang of concern, but I reassured myself that in the spirit of 'do no harm', I'd carefully calculated the overdose. She'd sleep badly, but find it hard to wake up; when she did drag herself out of bed, no doubt in a state about being so late for work, she'd feel rough, maybe a little nauseous, her heart rate faster than usual. She might feel nervous and restless, her head heavy. Rather like a hangover, in fact. It was kind of perfect, given she'd knocked back three large glasses in quick succession. She wouldn't suspect a thing, and even if she ever did, how could she prove it? It would be fine.

My morning flies by, two cases of croup and a toddler with painful cellulitis taking up most of my time, but just after midday I swing by the canteen, eager to see what's happening with Ella. I spot her immediately when I walk through the door; she's wiping tables over by the windows, and as I head towards her she looks up and grimaces. She looks awful, her eyes red-rimmed, her skin simultaneously pale and blotchy.

'Oh shit, Harriet. I really screwed up this morning. Did you not realise I was still in bed when you left?' she hisses.

I feign surprise.

'What? No, I didn't! Were you? The place was so quiet, I just assumed you'd already gone. Did you sleep in or something?'

She sighs and rolls her eyes.

'Yep. Very unlike me. I must have had too much to drink last night and forgot to set my alarm. I didn't wake up until gone eight so I was nearly two hours late. Paulette was *not* happy. Gave me a verbal warning. Just an informal one, luckily, but I need to be careful it doesn't happen again. And I feel rough as a dog now. That'll teach me. Your wine stash is too good, that's the problem.'

She smiles weakly, and I smile back, then say in a sympathetic tone, 'That's crap. I'm sorry. Look, I have to run, but I'll see you later, OK? I just popped in to grab a coffee. Hope you get through the rest of the day all right. It's never fun working with a hangover.'

'Tell me about it,' she groans, and I squeeze her arm then turn and walk away, feeling a little swell of satisfaction.

Perfect, I think. *She's still on probation. Paulette is fair, she'll give her a couple of chances, but if she screws up too many times – bye, bye, Ella.*

George and I are heading off to a wedding down in Somerset tomorrow morning, one of his old childhood friends.

Ella will have the weekend to herself, a nice quiet one. And then, when we get back on Sunday evening…

I grin widely as I thank the man at the counter for the coffee he's just handed me. Nothing from Nisha so far today, either. No emails, no further threats. Maybe she expected a panicked reply from me, and because I've ignored her yet again, she's not sure what her next move should be after all. This might just turn out to be a very good day. I glance over at Ella, still wandering listlessly from table to table, then head out of the canteen and back to work.

Chapter Twenty-Seven

ELLA

I *feel so rough. What's wrong with me?* I think, as I shuffle down the street towards the bus stop, then pause as I reach Zara.

Sod it, I need cheering up. I'm going in.

As I wander slowly around the shop, picking up sweatshirts and jumpers from tables and putting them down again, not seeing anything I really like, I sigh. I used to be able to drink with the best of them, back in the day. Now, my body seems to have developed an aversion to alcohol pretty much overnight. That debacle on Friday morning, when I slept in and got a tongue-lashing from Paulette was bad enough. I mean, it wasn't as if I even had that much to drink on Thursday night, just a few glasses, although to be fair they *were* on the large side. But for it to happen *again*, this morning...

I'm passing a full-length mirror, and I stop walking and stare at my reflection. I look as bad as I feel, my eyes blood-shot, my hair greasy. I didn't have time to wash it today; when I opened my eyes, my head pounding, to discover to my horror that it was already after 9am, I leapt out of bed so quickly that spots danced before my eyes, and I had to lean on the bathroom door for a few seconds until the light-headedness ebbed away.

I'd felt fine all weekend, that was the weird thing. Harriet, George and I had a couple of gin and tonics on Friday night, with a Thai takeaway; I probably shouldn't have drunk anything after the night before, but I needed a hair of the dog and George does make a damn good G & T. And the two I drank hit the spot; I slept like a happy baby, and woke up on Saturday feeling fresh and full of energy. I waved Harriet and George off – they were heading to some old friend's wedding and staying away for the night – with a promise that I'd clean the apartment while they were away, and as soon as they'd driven off, I began with gusto. The fact they don't have a cleaner is one thing that slightly surprised me about this very well-off pair, but as Harriet told me, it's usually only the two of them there, and they work such long hours the place barely gets dirty at all some weeks.

'I just feel it's one area I don't need to spend money on,' she said. 'We do a proper clean once a fortnight or so, the two of us together, and it only takes a couple of hours. The rest of the time we just try and keep on top of it, you know? So if you could just make sure your own bedroom and bathroom are kept in order, that's fine, don't worry about the rest of it.'

It's the least I can do, though, to do a bit more cleaning, if Harriet won't accept rent, and she didn't object too strongly when I suggested taking the job on while they were away.

'It *would* be nice to come back to a clean apartment. Thanks, Ella. You're a star,' she said, with a smile.

And so that was my Saturday morning, happily pottering

around the beautiful, bright rooms with duster and vacuum cleaner, fantasising that the place was mine. I must admit I spent a little more time than I should have in Harriet's walk-in wardrobe. George uses the two large closets in their bedroom, leaving Harriet as the sole occupant of the beautifully organised adjoining dressing room. She doesn't have as many clothes as I'd have, given her income, but she's still managed to *almost* fill the rails and drawers with her understated but elegant pieces. I flicked through the rows of jeans and blazers, shift dresses and simple, stylish knitwear, checking the labels. It's mostly high-end high street, with some bits from the more affordable stores I shop in, plus a few designer items. A Mulberry tote bag, a Marc Jacobs clutch, a pair of Dior aviator sunglasses. I always admired her dress sense, back when I first met her. *Neither* of us had much money in those days, but she always managed to *look* more expensive, more chic. My taste was more showy, more tight-fitting, more try-hard. I think, looking back, that even though *I* was the model, the one who worked in the fashion business, I actually sometimes envied her effortless sophistication, maybe even tried to imitate it a little. While we lived together, I remember now and again buying clothes that were very similar to hers, or even the same, almost without realising it. I sometimes wondered if Harriet minded, but I don't think she did; she never really complained about it, and it's a compliment, isn't it, after all, if someone wants to emulate your style? I envied her a lot, in retrospect. She's only two years older than me, but somehow she seemed to have it all together, even back then, while I was still drifting. Her career, her boyfriend, her plans for the future; I didn't *mean* to mess anything up for her, but somehow, I did it again, the thing I did way too many times back in the day. 'Borrowed' her boyfriend, a guy called Felix, just once. I mean, they were technically on a break, but even so. I should *never* have gone there. Why did I do it? I've asked myself that a thousand times since, and I've never been able to work it out. I was drunk, I remember that, but that's a pretty pathetic excuse. I think maybe I was just in need of some comfort that night, in need of someone to tell me I was beautiful, even if it was very much the *wrong* someone. Again, a worthless excuse though, and it was bad, the outcome of that evening, even for me. I've been far, far too scared to bring it up since I moved back in with Harriet – it makes me feel ill, when I look back and remember the shock and pain on her face when she walked into the apartment and found us together – and she hasn't mentioned it either thankfully, but shit, it was rough. They split up, Harriet and Felix, and I had to move out, of course. And yet we did meet up a while later, and to my immense surprise I *think* she'd forgiven me. She said they'd never have worked out long term, and that it was all fine, no hard feelings. I'm not sure I could have been quite so generous, if it had been the other way round. I don't think I'd have taken her in if she fell on hard times later on either. And yet, that's what she's done for me. She's pretty incredible, really. And she got a really good man, in the end. George is way, way better than Felix was. So, maybe I did her a favour of sorts, with my sleazy behaviour. Maybe it was meant to be. I still feel awful about it, even after all these years, but there's no point in raking it all up again now. If she's not going to mention it, I'm *certainly* not.

I stayed in on Saturday night, raided the fridge to cook myself a simple dinner – an omelette with ham and asparagus, washed down with some sparkling elderflower – watched TV and went to bed early. Yesterday I wrapped up warm and went for a long walk along the river, pausing now and again to snap a photo of an elegant swan or the curve of a bridge, enjoying the simple pleasure of moving my body, the crisp winter air, the nods from passers-by also enjoying a Sunday stroll. When I left the riverside path to head for home, though, I thought briefly that, once again, I saw somebody lurking just outside my field of vision, watching me, and a horrible sense of dread swept over me, every muscle tensing. But when I whirled round to look, I could see nobody and, when I'd managed to calm myself down again, I eventually dismissed it as residual paranoia.

Maybe I'm actually suffering from a mild form of post-traumatic stress disorder, I pondered, as I settled down on the sofa in the apartment. *Drinking too much, seeing people who aren't there … could what happened in Gloucester be enough to trigger PTSD?*

I decided to look it up, then promptly forgot because seconds later the door opened and Harriet and George piled in, weary and slightly hungover after the wedding.

'*I* need a hair of the dog today,' Harriet groaned, staggering into the kitchen and heading straight for the fridge. She waved a bottle of white wine at me.

'Join me, Ella, come on.'

I hesitated for a moment, then shrugged. I didn't have to have a lot, did I? She flopped onto the sofa beside me and I accepted the glass she was proffering, and … well, I'm not quite sure what happened then. I must have drunk too much, *again*, because this morning … let's just say it was like Groundhog Day, except worse, because this time Paulette just stood and stared at me as I stumbled into the canteen hours after I should have arrived, and shook her head sadly.

'It's a good job *I* was opening up today, and we weren't

relying on you,' she said stiffly. 'What's going on, Ella? It all started so well. I warned you last week…'

She sighed heavily.

'Look, you know you're still on probation, right? This is your final warning. I don't want to lose you but…'

She shrugged, and I apologised profusely, just as I did on Friday, but I don't think it made much difference, and that made me feel even worse. I *can't* lose another job, not so soon after the nightmare of Gloucester. But as the hours ticked by, and I tried to ignore how ill I felt and get on with my duties, my thoughts kept returning to how odd it was for me to have two such severe hangovers so close together.

Do I have PTSD? Does that make your response to alcohol change? I'm just going to have to drink less from now on … maybe I'll have to stop drinking altogether for a while, if it's affecting me like this. Or – could it be a hormone thing or something? A liver problem? Am I sick? Do I need to see a doctor?

Then I had a stern word with myself, because clearly I'm turning not only into a lush but also a raving hypochondriac.

Stop making excuses. You got drunk, you're paying the price. It's not like you've never had a hangover before, is it? Shut up and stop whining. Put it all behind you, get your act together and MOVE. ON.

Now, in Zara, I pause in front of a row of striped shirts, with kimono-style sleeves and neat white buttons. While I'm still in my trial month, the job pays weekly, and my first week's pay cheque appeared in my account on Friday evening. I shouldn't be spending any of it on clothes, should only be buying the bare essentials right now and saving like a demon, but it's been a bad day and…

My fingers run over the cool, soft cotton, first the red and white, then the blue. As I touch the green, I hesitate, then pick it up and, not giving myself any more time to think about it, walk quickly to the checkout counter. For once, there's no queue, and two minutes later I'm back out on the street, my heart beating a little too fast, the new shirt in my bag.

When I get back to the penthouse, it's empty, George and Harriet not due back from the hospital for a couple of hours yet and, feeling wiped out, I dump my bags on the kitchen island and head into my bedroom. I only intend to lie down for a few minutes but I must have fallen asleep as soon as I shut my eyes, because when I wake with a start and look at the clock on my bedside table, I'm shocked to see it's after seven. I can hear the sound of saucepans clanging in the kitchen, and when I drag myself out of bed and walk in, Harriet turns to me with a surprised expression.

'Have you been asleep? Are you OK?'

I nod, then sigh.

'I'm not sure, to be honest. I slept in *again* this morning. I've been feeling dodgy all day. Just too much wine again, I suppose. It's my own fault. But Paulette is going to fire me at this rate. She was *not* happy today. I had to buy a top in Zara on the way home to cheer myself up.'

I gesture at the bag still lying on the countertop next to my handbag, then walk over and pick it up, pulling the shirt out.

'Nice, eh?' I say.

Harriet's eyes widen.

'It … yes, it *is* nice,' she says slowly. 'I have the exact same one, actually.'

'Oh!' I look at the shirt in my hands, then back at her. 'Have you? How weird! I didn't realise. I haven't seen you wear it? I'm sorry…'

Harriet shrugs.

'No, I probably haven't worn it since you arrived, to be fair.'

She pauses, looking at me with a curious expression, then smiles.

'It's fine, don't worry about it. It'll suit you. Green is great on you, with your eyes.'

I smile back, but my stomach flips.

Did *I know she had this shirt, though?* I think. *Did I see it in her wardrobe on Saturday, when I was poking about? And now I've gone and bought the same one? I don't know, I can't remember. Shit, what's wrong with me? My head still feels so fuzzy…*

I swallow hard, forcing myself to speak normally.

'OK. Great minds think alike, and all that, I suppose! Can I help you with dinner?'

'No, you're fine, I'm just … oh, hi, darling.'

George has walked in, and he grins at his wife then looks at me.

'OK, Ella?'

'Not bad, thanks,' I say. 'Except I got in trouble at work today for being late again and then I accidentally bought a top identical to one Harriet has on my way home. So, you know … winning!'

He laughs. 'Whoops!'

'It's fine, I don't mind,' Harriet says. 'Now why don't you two clear out of my way and I'll make dinner? Go on, scoot.'

She waves a wooden spoon at us and George winks at me.

'Come on, Ella. Can I get you a drink while we wait for the chef to work her magic?'

He heads for the fridge, as I raise an eyebrow.

'George, that's very kind of you, but no, thanks. Not tonight. Just water for me this evening.'

He laughs again.

'OK. One water, coming right up.'

'Great. I'll be back in a mo – just going to put this stuff away,' I reply.

I look down at the shirt still crumpled between my fingers, and stuff it back into its bag, then glance at Harriet, who's stirring something on the hob now, humming quietly to herself.

It's fine. You're fine, everything's fine, I tell myself, as I pick up my handbag and head for my room. But suddenly, for no reason that I can pinpoint, it's back, that creeping feeling of dread. The feeling that even though I can't see them, someone *is* still watching me. And that actually, this *thing*, whatever it is, might just be on a break, a bit like Felix and Harriet were way back then.

That it might not be over at all.

Chapter Twenty-Eight

HARRIET

Ella stuck to water last night. If she's really cutting down on booze, this is going to be tricky. Because she'll get very suspicious, won't she, if she's still feeling groggy and hungover in the morning without any alcohol? Maybe I need to change tack now, but to what...?

I consider the problem as I sit on the bus, heading for home, my head resting against the cold window, rain hammering the glass, the pedestrians and streetlights outside a watercolour blur. It's after eight already, and I feel exhausted. Sometimes, despite the constant swaying and bumping, the endless slowing down and speeding up of a commuter bus, I nod off on these journeys home, although somehow, miraculously, my eyes always snap open again just before I reach our stop. But tonight, I'm too wired. I *need* to make sure Ella loses her canteen job; suddenly, I'm getting tired of all this. I want her out of my hospital, and out of my home too. She's getting too comfortable in it, not that I blame her for that. Who wouldn't?

My thoughts drift back to Gloucester. Even though it's

vastly different to Ella's current accommodation, I knew she'd like that little flat that came with her new 'job'. I actually own it too; poor George doesn't know this either, but I didn't sell *all* the properties I inherited. I kept just that one small apartment, giving me as it did an excellent location well away from home to carry out my plans for Ella. My friend Farah loved the Cotswolds, but was also a townie through and through, and the Gloucester place was, apparently, her compromise; a little bolthole close to glorious countryside but with all the amenities of a regional city. It was perfect for Ella, and when Lena told me how utterly thrilled Ella was to finally have her own little place, I felt my first twinge of conscience, a pang of sympathy. I have so much, and she, despite her undeniable physical assets and, it now appears, sharp business acumen, still has so little. Then I remembered what she took from me, and hardened my heart again.

Evicting her was so easy. With PI Dean still keeping an eye on Ella's comings and goings, I had Lena and her two friends standing by in their van around the corner from the apartment until he gave them the all clear. I knew the security camera arrangement in the block suited us as well as it had on the industrial estate, so when Ella went out that morning my little team swooped in, swiftly boxing up her relatively few belongings and once again changing her door lock. Now that she was both jobless and homeless, I wondered if she'd go back to the police, so I kept Dean on her tail. She did, but again it appeared there was no help to be found; he told me she'd first checked into a guesthouse and then had begun sleeping in her car. She woke up as he peered in at her when she was asleep in a layby on the first night, but he told me he wasn't too worried about that; he'd dressed so only his eyes were visible, so she'd be unlikely to recognise him again, and with a number of vehicles at his disposal he simply switched cars the next day, following her in a blue Audi instead of the Volvo he'd used the night in the layby. He said she seemed more on guard after that though; he thought she might have been aware of his presence outside the leisure centre she was using to shower and change in, and again when he followed her back to the industrial estate. None of this bothered me too much. If Ella was twitchy and paranoid about someone following her, it was fine by me.

I knew she couldn't have much money left, and I also hoped she still lived by the 'no credit, ever' rule she'd always stuck to when I knew her; it seemed she did, but I slightly underestimated her, because, to my disappointment, she landed herself a new job pretty quickly. I made sure it didn't last long though. I took a day off work, telling George I was going to visit an old friend who was ill, and travelled to Gloucester myself to break into Ella's car in the yard behind her new workplace. I didn't want to involve anyone else in what, on that occasion, was definitely a criminal act, but I was pretty sure I wouldn't get caught, because I was almost certain she wouldn't report the incident. Dean had been keeping very close tabs on her and had somehow been able to find out that her car insurance had expired. If she'd reported her car being broken into, she'd just get herself in trouble, and anyway she was living in the thing, so it wasn't something she could risk losing. He'd also told me the yard was deserted during the day and had no cameras, but warned me about the ones out on the street, so I dressed to hide my appearance as much as possible and then, my nerves jangling, I went for it in the middle of the afternoon.

I managed to bypass her car alarm because – and I'm half shocked at my own behaviour and half a little proud of myself for this – I'd managed to clone her car key. It's amazing the sort of services having large amounts of money at your disposal can give you access to. Dean – who I'd gradually discovered flitted around on the edges of the law at times – put me in touch with someone at the car wash he discovered Ella used every couple of weeks while she still lived in London, based in the car park of her local supermarket. Her habit was to leave the car and the keys while she shopped, and it was, apparently, quite simple therefore for the unscrupulous car washer to copy the unique code from her key onto a blank key with some sort of dodgy cloning device, then hand her key back to her with her shiny, clean vehicle. I broke a window of her car anyway after I'd opened it though, just for fun. What a cow I've turned into. What a cow *she* turned me into.

I roped in one of Katherine's male actor friends again to try and get her fired. I paid him another generous sum to mix a couple of household cleaning chemicals in the teashop toilets and then play the part of an irate, coughing customer. And, of course, to my astonishment, I didn't have to wait long to find out just how beautifully *that* worked. Because that day, the day everything finally became too much for Ella to handle alone, was the day she called me. *Me*. The 'friend' she hadn't seen for years. And, as I said, I deserve an Oscar, I think, for all my super-convincing hugs and sympathy. The hours of listening to her banging on and on about it all. Listening to her trying to work out who's been treating her so badly, biting my tongue when she made her sordid little confession about shagging other models' boyfriends back in the day. I hadn't known that, but it hadn't really surprised me.

Didn't just do that at work, did you? I thought viciously.

I'm on my own now though, for this final stage. Lena – back to Katherine again – told me that although she's very grateful for the money, she's glad it's all over. She admitted she'd actually grown rather fond of Ella and had started to feel a little bad about how much we were screwing up her life. When they ran into each other on the street on Tuesday – flipping hell, what were the chances of that? – she called me immediately afterwards to warn me and to tell me she was pretty sure that by playing dumb, she'd got away with it. But she also said again that she felt sorry for Ella now, and that she hoped the 'games' I was playing were over. I get it, her fondness for Ella. I really do. It's why we did become friends, for a while, back then. Why even over the past week, every now and again, just for a few seconds, I've genuinely laughed at or felt touched by something she's said or done. There's something about her, something irritatingly endearing. Vulnerability and charm and stunning looks are a powerful combination. And she hasn't had it easy, not always. I think that's why I've had those moments of guilt, of self-doubt, of wondering what the hell's wrong with me to treat another human like this. But then I remember. She stole my *child*. She ruined my life. And so it's not over. Not yet. Especially not now, when I have her exactly where I want her.

I do want her gone soon though – I mean, she's even started her old tricks again. Last night, with the shirt? I *haven't* worn mine since she arrived, I know I haven't. So *was* it just a coincidence, or has she been snooping? Wandering into our bedroom, my dressing room, while we're at work? While we were away at the weekend, maybe? At the thought, I feel a flash of fury. How *dare* she?

And then, just as quickly, the feeling dissipates, to be replaced with a warm glow of satisfaction.

But still … she has no idea, has she? No clue whatsoever. She genuinely thinks I'm her saviour. She thinks I'm the one who's helped pull her out of the massive hole she found herself in. And one day, one day very soon, I'm going to tell her the truth, and I can't wait to see the look on her face then. The shock in her eyes. The horror in her expression when she realises it was me. All me. All of it…

I shift in my seat, my elbow knocking that of the man sitting next to me, and I murmur an apology, which he ignores. Got to love London commuters. Then Ella's face floats back into my head, and there it is again. The *guilt*. That little gnawing feeling in the pit of my stomach. It infuriates me. Why does it keep coming back?

I'm not a bad person, I'm really not. But I am doing bad things, aren't I? Messing with someone's life, her livelihood, her career. Even her personal safety, at times. I put Ella in danger when I took away her home and her income, I know that. Anything could have happened to her while she was sleeping in her car, and what sort of woman does something like that to another woman?

I blink hard, trying to focus on what's outside the rain-splattered window, checking where we are on the route. Not far to go now. She'll be home already, cosy in my apartment, safe and secure, good food on the table. Will I feel yet *more* guilt, when she loses that too? I've been thinking a lot about it recently, the whole issue of guilt and morality. When somebody's done something so terrible to you, and your actions are about exacting revenge, is the guilt justifiable? Is it worth it? *Will* it be worth it? I've planned this for so long, for so many years, that it's something I probably *shouldn't* think about too deeply. Because – what if it's *not* worth it? What if, when all this is finally over, the emptiness remains? What if the satisfaction I feel now at seeing her suffer fades, to be replaced by … nothing? Will I regret it? Will I wish I'd never done it, any of it?

I take in a shuddery breath.

No, I tell myself fiercely. *No. She deserves this*. You *deserve this. So no weakness, no regrets. Keep. Going.*

Nearly at our stop.

'Excuse me … sorry! This is me,' I say to the man beside me, and he looks up from the phone he's been staring at since he got on and nods, twisting his body so I can slide out past him. Clutching my bag, I make my way carefully towards the door as the bus lurches and creaks to a standstill. But as I jump off the step onto the pavement, a woman who's standing at the bus stop waiting to climb on moves at the same time and suddenly we collide, hard, her bulky body slamming into mine, knocking my bag from my arm, a surprised-sounding 'Ooof! Shit, I'm so sorry!' coming from her as she staggers backwards, clutching at my sleeve in an attempt to steady herself.

'Oh! It's OK, don't worry, probably just as much my fault,' I say, and I bend to pick up my bag, which has tipped onto its side. She's already crouching, still apologising, picking up my wallet, my hairbrush, handing them to me.

'I think that's everything,' she says breathlessly. 'Really sorry, I'm such a klutz.'

She smiles ruefully, a flustered-looking face under a black woolly hat, a woman around my own age, and I shake my head.

'No problem,' I reply.

She nods, then turns quickly and jumps onto the bus, the doors closing behind her almost immediately, the bus trundling off into the night. I wipe my bag, wet from the rain-soaked ground, with my coat sleeve, then zip the top closed and walk quickly home. It's only when I get in that I realise my phone has gone. I search the bag three times, increasingly frantic, checking every pocket, but it's not there, and so I tell George and Ella, who are on the sofa watching some vintage comedy, that I'm going out again, that I've somehow dropped my phone, that I need to check if it might still be there, on the pavement at the bus stop. George offers to come with me, but I tell him not to be silly, that there's no point in two of us getting soaked, that I can be there and back in ten minutes anyway.

'If you're sure,' he says. 'Dinner will be ready for when you get in, OK?'

The phone's not there, of course. If it *had* been, someone would no doubt have spotted it by now, pocketed it. This is London, after all. I *could* try asking at the nearest police station, if I could find one open, just in case someone has handed it in. But my gut's telling me that would be pointless. My gut's telling me that my phone was never here on the ground at the bus stop. I knew it even as I sprinted back to look, the sudden realisation hitting me of what really happened when I was least expecting it, making my stomach churn. Every instinct is screaming at me now, telling me that *she* took it. That woman. That hard, precise collision. She was down on the ground, scrabbling for my belongings, before I'd even had time to register what had happened. Slick. Professional even.

Nisha is all I can think, as I trudge home again, feeling

numb, and not just from the biting wind that's now partnered with the unrelenting rain.

Nisha.

That wasn't her, not in person. I know what she looks like. But that woman – Nisha sent her. I have absolutely no doubt about that.

Not empty threats after all, then, I think. *Is she finally going for it? Has she finally decided to try to take what she wants, to get from me what I've refused to give her? Because I don't know what she's going to do with my phone, but it's her. I know it is.*

And so it begins. And so it begins.

Chapter Twenty-Nine

HARRIET

'Dr Hart! Wait up, got something for you!'

The strident voice of the security guard makes me turn around, surprised. Ian normally just grunts a 'good morning' as I walk into the hospital; sometimes I don't even get the 'good' bit, just a muttered 'morning'. Our post is normally delivered to the department, so I can't imagine what he has for me, and I'm a couple of minutes late and still livid and upset about my phone being stolen last night, so I take the few steps back to Ian's desk reluctantly.

'What is it? Sorry, I'm running a bit late, I don't have much time…'

My voice tails off as I see what he's holding out to me.

Is that…? How…?

'This yours?' he asks. 'Some woman dropped it in earlier. Said you lost it on the bus last night? She recognised you 'cos you'd treated one of her kids or something. She said you'd got off the bus and it had driven off again before she had a chance to pick it up and hand it back to you.'

Slowly, I reach for the familiar-looking phone in his hand and tap the screen. There it is, the screensaver, the photo of me and George next to Lake Windermere, taken last summer. It *is* my phone. Wow.

'Yes,' I reply. 'It's mine. That's amazing, how kind of her. Thanks so much, Ian.'

He taps his forehead in a kind of mock salute.

'No problem, Have a good day, doc.'

As I make my way upstairs, my thoughts run wild.

That story whoever returned it told can't be true. I didn't drop my phone on the bus. She took it. But … why return it, just a few hours later? Have I got this wrong? Could I have dropped it without noticing? Is there a chance this was nothing to do with Nisha after all? The woman seemed nice. Flustered, apologetic. Maybe she didn't steal my phone. Maybe it was all in my head, just an innocent accident, and my fears conjured it into something sinister. Maybe Nisha's threats are just threats. Maybe...

I look down at my phone, safely back with me, undamaged, and feel a rush of relief.

It's OK. Everything's fine. Don't. Get. Paranoid.

For the next few hours I manage to almost forget about it. It's a busy morning, as always, and by midday I'm gasping for a coffee and, finding myself with ten minutes to spare, decide that's just enough time to run to the canteen. I've only taken a few steps down the corridor though when, for the second time, today, a raised voice stops me in my tracks.

'Harriet? I need a word, please.'

It's Susan Blair, the hospital's Clinical Director, a dark-haired, normally smiley Glaswegian, but today she's not smiling. Quite the opposite. Her mouth is set in a grim line and she has a steely look in her eyes. Suddenly, I have a feeling of dread, my chest starting to tingle.

'Susan! Erm ... well, I was just going to grab a coffee, I'm due in a meeting in a few minutes. What can I do for you?'

She gestures down the corridor behind her.

'Sorry, but I need you to come into my office, if you don't mind. I'll be as quick as I can.'

She turns and marches swiftly away, clearly expecting me to follow, and I hesitate for a moment then do. When we're in her room, she closes the door and points at the chair in front of her desk.

'Take a seat,' she says. She sits down in her own chair across from me, then sighs.

'I'll get straight to the point,' she says. 'We've had a complaint about you. Nothing to do with your work, I hasten to add. But ... well, it's about your behaviour *outside* of the hospital.'

'My ... my *behaviour*? What are you talking about?'

For a moment, I feel flummoxed, and then a shiver runs through me. Oh, God. Could this ... could this be Ella? Could she have worked it out? Does she know what I've been doing to her? And now she's told the hospital? But she couldn't know, could she? Nobody knows, expect Katherine ... 'Lena' ... but the NDA, the money, she wouldn't, would she? But what if...

'It was something which happened yesterday. On the bus, on your journey home from work, I believe,' Susan is saying.

I drag my attention back to her, trying to focus. What did she just say?

'On the ... on the *bus*?' I stutter. So, not Ella then. Of course, it couldn't be Ella. But what then? The fricking bus, *again*?

'Yes. It's a bit of an unexpected one, actually. I'm not quite sure what to make of it. That's why I thought I'd just have a quick chat with you first, and didn't ask you if wanted to bring anyone with you. You know, a union rep or someone.'

Susan fingers a piece of paper that's lying on the desk in front of her, a neatly typed complaints form.

'OK,' I say, frowning. 'I mean, the only unusual thing that happened on the bus last night was that I bumped into a woman as I got off and dropped my bag and then she helped me pick everything up again. But I honestly think it was more her fault than mine. I think *she* thought that too, she kept apologising. Is it her? Is she trying to claim she was injured or something? Because I can assure you…'

Susan is shaking her head.

'No, no, it's nothing like that. OK – a woman phoned this morning. She basically said you sat next to her husband on the bus last night, and that you … this sounds so bizarre … she says there was some inappropriate behaviour…'

'What? Are you … *what*?'

I gape at her, stunned, and she holds up a hand.

'She gave details, hang on. She says that first of all, he noticed you had the camera on your phone on and that you seemed to be … erm, well, filming his *crotch* area.'

She pauses, clears her throat and continues, which is fortunate, as my mouth has now actually dropped open and I'm not sure I can speak even if she asks me to.

'And then, as you got off the bus, you had to push past him and you "brushed against him in an intimate manner". Those were her exact words. Her husband told her all about it as soon as he got home, and she says he was quite shocked by the whole thing. He didn't challenge you about the filming thing because he said he couldn't be entirely sure, but he said there was no doubt that you "pressed your body against his legs very deliberately" – her words again – when there was no need for any physical contact because he'd moved aside to let you get past. Hold on, just let me finish…'

I realise I've just muttered something incoherent, but Susan's holding up her hand again.

'The only thing is, she's refusing to give her name. She says her husband recognised you immediately, because you once treated their son here, but he didn't say hello when he sat down next to you because he didn't like to intrude. And she's actually said they don't want to take it any further, but they just thought it was something we should know about. They want it "logged", she said, in case it happens again. So…'

She shrugs.

'So – do you have any response?' she asks. 'Obviously, this would be classed as misconduct outside of the workplace, but as I'm sure you know, it could still mean disciplinary action as, if proven, it could affect your suitability for employment and bring the Trust into disrepute and … well, I don't need to go on about that now. Talk to me.'

'Susan, this is *ridiculous*.'

I run a hand through my hair, trying to think.

'I mean, I *was* sitting next to a man on the bus, but I didn't even really look at him, I was staring out the window most of the way home. And as for *filming* him – that's just rubbish. I don't remember even taking my phone out of my bag. And why would I film someone's *crotch*?'

It's almost laughable, but Susan isn't smiling, so I shrug and carry on.

'And as for rubbing against him or whatever she said I did

as I got off – bollocks, again. I clearly remember him moving his legs to the side so I could get out from the window seat. I mean, maybe my coat brushed against him or something but there was definitely no prolonged contact. I don't get it, this is such a crazy accusation. Come on, Susan, you know me. Surely you don't believe there's any truth in this nonsense?'

She shakes her head slowly.

'It does seem very unlikely…'

'*Totally* unlikely,' I say. 'Look – do you want to see the recent videos on my phone? Because I promise you, there are no crotch shots in here!'

I risk a smile, and to my relief she smiles back.

'Shit, I am sorry about this, Harriet,' she says, leaning back in her chair. 'But you know, any sort of complaint, we're obliged to investigate, so…'

'I know, I know,' I say, as I pull my phone from my pocket and tap in the security code, at the same time thinking about the story this caller has told: that I once treated her son here. The same story told by whoever dropped my phone off at reception earlier. But *she* said nothing about me filming or touching her husband. She just told Ian I dropped my phone on the bus and she was returning it. I don't understand…

I'm tapping on the photos icon now, scrolling down to the most recent pictures and video clips. Some shots from the weekend, at the wedding in Somerset, me and George and some of our friends, glasses of champagne in hand, smiling. And then … I frown. What's that?

Slowly, reluctantly, I move my finger to the last image on the screen, a ten-second video clip, and tap it. As it starts to play, I gasp.

'No way! No … WAY!'

It is, quite clearly, and just as in the allegation Susan has described, a video of a man's crotch area. Dark denim jeans, a noticeable bulge, the camera zooming in. I stare at it, unable to take in what I'm seeing, and then become aware that Susan is standing up and leaning across her desk, eyes focused on the small screen too.

'Ha–Harriet!' she stutters, but I drop the phone onto the desk and leap to my feet.

'This was *not* me,' I say, so loudly I'm almost shouting. 'This is some sort of set-up, I don't know why or by whom but … look, Susan, go and ask Ian on security. I lost my phone on the bus last night, or it was stolen, or … or something, I don't really know. But some woman returned it this morning, so she must have … *they* must have…'

Panic-stricken, I gesture at my mobile.

'It's an iPhone. Anyone can take photos or video on anyone's iPhone, you don't even need the code, you just swipe the screen to access the camera, everyone knows that. I have no idea why they'd make a video like that, but that's clearly what's happened. Look, go and ask Ian. He'll tell you my phone was handed in this morning. There'll be security camera footage from reception too, we should be able to see *who*…'

'OK, OK, calm down.'

Susan has moved around her desk and now she's reaching out to me, gently gripping both of my wrists.

'I believe you, I do. I just don't get why anyone would do something so peculiar, but people are strange, so … I'll go and see Ian, just to tick the box. The caller, that woman, she said she didn't want to take it any further anyway, so … it's OK, Harriet. It's OK.'

And it is OK, sort of, anyway. An hour later, I'm back in the paediatric unit, desperately trying to catch up on the time I've missed, although I still feel sick and shaky.

It's all right, it's over, I keep telling myself, but my stomach is doing somersaults. Susan wouldn't let me go down to security with her, but clearly Ian backed up everything I'd said about my phone being handed in. When she'd asked him about camera footage, he'd apparently looked doubtful though, and when Susan had asked to see it anyway, she'd realised why.

'She was all bundled up in a big coat, a scarf that covered half her face and a baseball cap, pulled right down,' she told me when she arrived back in her office, where she'd asked me to wait.

'I mean, it's February and it's cold in the early morning, but it did look a bit like she was trying to make sure nobody would recognise her. No idea what she looks like at all, I'm afraid. Maybe you're right, maybe she did steal your phone, or maybe you dropped it and she thought about keeping it, then had second thoughts. I really don't understand the video clip and the phone call, though. It's like she's deliberately trying to make trouble for you. I wonder if her fingerprints might be on your phone? If you wanted to go to the police, maybe? But...'

She frowned, looking at my mobile which was lying on the desk in front of me.

'I suppose they'd be all messed up now. I mean, Ian's handled it, you've handled it...her DNA though, maybe? That could still be there.'

'What's the crime though?' I asked, a little more sharply than I intended to. 'Handing in a mobile phone she claimed to have found? Making a silly video on it before she gave it back?

212

The police are swamped with *serious* crime, Susan. They wouldn't be remotely interested.'

She frowned.

'I suppose. But there's still that phone call. So who is she? Is there someone you've accidentally upset recently, maybe? A parent with a grudge? I haven't heard about anything, but do you have any ideas?'

I shook my head.

'Just leave it. It's over now, forget it,' I muttered, and Susan looked at me curiously and then let it go.

'Fine. It's up to you. I've noted it, but we'll leave it at that, if that's what you want,' she said. 'Strange one though.'

Christ, I'm getting good at lying. Of *course* I know who's behind this, but I can't tell Susan that. That brief feeling of 'maybe it was all an innocent accident after all' has left the building now. When Nisha emailed me, this is what she threatened. My career. She told me that if I didn't give her what she wants, she'd come for my career. Make sure I lost my job, make sure I'll never be employed in the medical profession again. Is this how she's going to do it then? Make out I'm some sort of – I don't know – *sex addict* or something? Seriously? But now I'm even more freaked out than I was last night, because she's obviously not working alone. This *was* Nisha, and she *does* have people helping her. But how did she do this?

I think about the woman I bumped into at my bus stop. I don't get the same bus home every day, so was she just standing there in the cold for hours, waiting for me to appear? Or is someone watching me here at work, waiting for me to leave, noting which bus I board so they know exactly when to accost me at the other end? I haven't noticed anyone, but that doesn't mean they're not there, and I feel a chill on the back of my neck, as if a cold, dead hand has just touched it. Maybe there *was* someone lurking around outside the apartment complex, that day Ella thought she saw a figure in the shadows. Maybe it was me they were watching.

And then that man on the bus. Was that *his* crotch? When the woman got hold of my phone, and jumped back onto the bus, did she go and sit next to him, to make that video? I shiver as I imagine the two of them giggling as she aimed the camera at his groin. I've tried to remember more about him, but I barely glanced at him, wrapped up as always in my own thoughts as I endured my commute. And who looks at anyone, really, on public transport in London? Nobody looks, nobody speaks. Headphones, mobile phones; we're all locked in our own little bubbles, physically close on crowded tube trains and buses but mentally a million miles apart. He was at the bus stop near the hospital, I remember that; he got onto the bus just behind me, and when I grabbed the first empty seat I saw, he slid in next to me. But that's normal, nothing out of the ordinary. Why didn't I look at him? Why wasn't I more careful with my phone? *Peabrain.*

I inhale slowly, then blow the air out again. I have work to do, and I need to concentrate on my patients. I run a hand over my hair, smoothing it down, tucking a loose tendril into the band securing my ponytail.

It's all good, I tell myself again. *I'm OK. Nisha* tried *to get me in trouble, but she's failed this time. An amateur attempt, really. And now I'm* really *on guard. Next time, I'll be ready for her.*

Part III

NISHA, HARRIET AND ELLA

Chapter Thirty

NISHA

She wasn't suspended, then. Damn it. Just leaving work at her usual time, looking quite happy.

From a safe distance, I watch as Harriet Hart walks out of the main door of MediWest Hospital, chatting animatedly to a colleague, then smiles, waves and turns left, heading, I presume, to the bus stop to go home. Ugh. Boring as hell, that woman. Rarely goes out for drinks after work, or anywhere else either. Just scuttles off home to her equally boring husband and their fuck-off big fancy apartment. The apartment she bought with *my* money. The money she *stole* from me. *Bitch*.

I'd hoped what I'd just done might have made *some* difference, but clearly she's somehow wormed her way out of it like the slimy little sneak she is. So, if inappropriate moves on a man on public transport wasn't enough to shake up her cosy little world, it's time to step it up a bit. And I have just the thing. Get out of the *next* one, *Doctor* Hart.

She's out of sight now, so I turn and start walking in the opposite direction. I'll call in on Letisha on the way home, tell her it's game on. Polly and Jake did well on the bus; it's not their fault it didn't work. But what Letisha's going to do…

I grin. It'll cost me, getting my mates involved. They may be friends, but they'll still want paying. But I'll have money soon, so that won't be a problem. She's resisted until now, ignored my emails. But she won't be able to ignore me much longer. She'll be *begging* me to take her money … *my* money. She'll be throwing it at me. And the silly thing is, she could have avoided all the crap I'm about to chuck at her, if only she'd seen sense and played ball in the first place. If only she hadn't been so freaking *greedy*.

OK, so I'm the first to admit I wasn't the best daughter. In the three years before Mum died, I saw her maybe twice. Well, once or twice. But that was just how it was with me and Mum. Never saw eye to eye, even when I was a teenager. *Especially* when I was a teenager. She was the only daughter of Malaysian immigrants; Dad, aka Martin Cartwright, a bricklayer from Birmingham, buggered off when I was a baby. I don't blame him, being married to Farah can't have been easy. She was always off doing her fancy-schmancy interior design stuff, poncing around with her 'creative' mates, while I was left with nannies. By the time I was old enough not to need watching any more Mum and I barely knew each other. She'd always just assumed I'd go to university, get what she called a 'good solid career', make my own money like she did. But when it came to A-Level time, my attitude was why bother? I'd lost count of how many properties she owned by then, but surely she had enough money for both of us? Why should I kill myself studying and slogging away at some shitty uni when I could just be living a nice life with my inheritance? I told her that, and she blew up at me like a fucking volcano.

I'd turned eighteen a few days earlier, and I'd been dumped by my first serious girlfriend *on my birthday*, although my mother didn't know that. Never asked, didn't seem to care. The row was the final straw. I'd had enough of her never being around, but still trying to control my life, and when she told me there'd be no money from her until I could present a 'serious career plan', I was out of there. It was her own fault. She'd made a big mistake on my birthday. I'd had a monthly allowance for years – not much, not enough, but something at least – but on my eighteenth she'd given me my first credit card, a card with a 20K limit but with strict instructions it was only to be used in emergencies. Well, it *was* an emergency, in my view, and so I took that card and used it to take out the maximum amount of cash it allowed – £500 – every day for the next three and a half weeks, figuring it would be a month before the first statement arrived and she'd find out what I'd done. Then, with over twelve grand stashed in my backpack, I wrote my mother a note, waved goodbye to London and flew off to Spain.

I'd intended to spend just a few months what I called 'luxury backpacking' before telling her how 'terribly sorry' I was and heading back again, but it didn't really work out like that. I knew she'd be pissed off, but I somewhat underestimated the situation. She was *livid*. *Furious*. When I rang, she fumed at me so viciously I honestly thought the line might burst into flames.

'Don't bother coming home. That money won't last forever, and when it runs out, don't think you can come crawling back to me for another handout. You've made your bed, now lie in it, for good,' she spat, before I dropped the payphone I was using, in a booth in the reception area of a sweet little Valencia hotel, back into its cradle and stared at it, a bit shellshocked.

Fine. I could manage without her. And it wouldn't be forever, would it? The old cow would die someday, and then it would all be mine. I was her only child; who else would she leave everything to?

Well, I got that wrong, didn't I?

Oblivious though, I spent the next five years bumming around Europe. When the credit card money ran out, I worked a series of jobs in bars and restaurants, until an encounter with a glamorous, slightly older woman in the south of France led me to the world of house- and pet-sitting. She ran an agency providing the service to wealthy clients, and I fell into the role – and her bed, from time to time – with gusto. People I sometimes struggle with, but animals – well, they're the best, right? I bloody love dogs and cats, and to get paid to live in a beautiful villa or a stunning rooftop apartment for weeks at a time, with little to do except walk and feed a dog a couple of times a day and make sure all the windows are locked was right up my street. Before I knew it, another year had passed and then another, and by the time Lucia and I decided to go our separate ways and I decided it was time I flew back to London for a visit I was twenty-five and hadn't seen my mother for over seven years. I'd contacted her briefly every now and again over the time I'd been away, short messages to let her know I was still alive, to check *she* was, but we hadn't had a face-to-face conversation since I was a teenager. That first meeting did *not* go well.

'Still no apology, for stealing all that money and running out on me?' she snapped, and although I could see the pain in her eyes, I just couldn't bring myself to tell her I was sorry.

'Still no apology, *Farah*, for neglecting me for years while you built your empire, and trying to make me into something I never wanted to be?' I snarled, and when she flinched, and I saw the sheen of tears in her eyes, all I felt was satisfaction.

I went away again, found myself another house-sitting agency, in Italy this time, and didn't return to London for another five years. By then, I'd had enough of the peripatetic life, and although I missed the sunshine, I knew this was where I needed to be, for a while at least. My mother was getting older, and I hoped at some point to be able to build some bridges. Was that for purely selfish reasons, to safeguard my inheritance? Maybe. Maybe not. Sometimes, not often but sometimes, it actually made me cry, this complete lack of any relationship with my only known relative. Mum's parents both died young – I barely remember my grandparents – and she had no siblings. Just us, except there *was* no us. But how to improve the situation, I had no idea, and so my visits remained sporadic, and barely civil. And then, quite unexpectedly in the end, she died. A massive stroke, in the middle of a Saturday night, and that was it.

It was only afterwards that I found out about Harriet. A young doctor, who'd moved in next door at some point, and who'd become Mum's friend. Who'd cooked for her, and kept her company, and made her laugh. Who'd done all the things a daughter should have done. All the things *I* should have done. And then I discovered that Doctor Harriet Hart had not just replaced me in Mum's life, but had been handed my future too.

There was no actual 'reading of the will'; that, apparently, only happens in movies. People sitting in a solicitor's office, gasping as the deceased's wishes are revealed. There was no confrontation, no drama. Just an email from their end, followed up by a panicked but, in the end, entirely fruitless telephone call from mine.

'I'm afraid that yes, I can confirm that your mother has left you … well, nothing. Nothing at all,' the solicitor said.

My inheritance. All of it. Property worth millions. All signed over to *her*. My mother didn't even leave me one poxy little flat to live in; she cut me out, entirely.

I think I was in shock for a while, actual real shock. I'd always just assumed that, despite our non-existent relationship, Farah still cared enough about me to make sure I was provided for. That even if we never healed the rift between us, her will would still favour me, largely because there *was* nobody else, or so I thought. But there was.

Harriet bloody Hart.

And now, it's time to take it back. I've waited long enough, been reasonable and patient long enough. It's time for direct action.

You'll be sorry you ignored me, Hart, I think, then realise that, lost in thought, I've just walked straight past Letisha's flat. I double back, and as I press the doorbell and wait for her to appear, I'm smiling.

Chapter Thirty-One

HARRIET

I'm struggling to get on top of my anxiety today. When I'm at work, I'm normally too busy for it to get a grip, but today, even though things are as frenzied as usual, the thoughts keep creeping in, nibbling at the edges of my brain. I can't seem to get Nisha out of my head.

I keep telling myself I'll be ready for her if she tries anything else, but it's making me so paranoid I'm looking over my shoulder every thirty seconds. Is she going to send someone new to mess with me today? Tomorrow? Is it time I offered her *something*, to leave me alone? Would that even work at this point, or is it too late? And yet … I'm not a victim; I refuse to be a victim. I was Ella's victim once, but now I'm in control, and I can win this Nisha thing too. I just have to stay strong and not let her get to me. But what if she does something worse, something *really* damaging…?

The arguments and counterarguments go round and round in circles in my head until I feel dizzy.

Thank *heavens* it's Friday and I have this full weekend off. I haven't told anyone about the bus thing, obviously, and it's weighing heavily on me. Twice last night George asked me what was wrong, and although I told him I was just exhausted, I could tell by his face he suspected there was more to it. He let it go, but I'm going to have to get on top of this or he's really going to start asking questions. I'm pretty sure neither he nor Ella will find out about what happened via anyone here at the hospital. My chat with Susan Blair, like conversations about all employment issues, will be bound by strict confidentiality rules. So there's no gossip, nothing like that, but I need a break, need to be away from this place for a couple of days, need to be at home where it's safe, where nobody can get to me. And I need, even more urgently now, to crack on with my Ella campaign. To get our home, my sanctuary, back. Just me and George, that's all I want. A nice, quiet life. I'm becoming quite obviously irritable, both at work and at home, and I hate it. Yesterday when Ella came in I noticed she'd painted her nails a pale baby pink, almost exactly the same barely-there shade I wear, and after the Zara shirt incident on Monday I instantly felt my blood begin to boil.

'Oh. That's the same colour as mine,' I found myself saying, far too snappily. She looked at me with a surprised expression.

'Is it? I've had it for ages … I didn't realise,' she said, and I saw George giving me a look, one of those husband–wife looks that says: 'What is *wrong* with you?'

Later, he told me I'd been quite rude.

'I thought you were enjoying having Ella here,' he said. 'Why did you speak to her like that? It was only nail varnish.'

'I know. I'm just tired. I'll apologise,' I said. I didn't say sorry to Ella though. I don't believe she's had that nail colour for ages, any more than I believe she bought that stripy shirt accidentally on Monday, but I can't explain any of that to George, can I? Because that would open a whole can of giant Ella-and-Felix-shaped worms from the past, and there's no way I'm going there. So, onwards. She'll be gone very soon now, if I can just keep it together. I look furtively over my shoulder yet again. Nobody in sight. It's just before 4pm and I'm outside the door of the staff canteen in what's grandly called 'the cloakroom', an alcove off the corridor where we can dump coats and bags and umbrellas while we eat. We have lockers elsewhere in the hospital, but sometimes we go to grab food on the way in or on the way home, when we have our stuff with us, so it's handy to have somewhere to stash it. And now, it's about to serve another purpose for me too. There aren't any security cameras here, I've checked; probably because it's a private area of the building, open only to staff, no members of the public wandering through. I look around one more time, then move quickly towards the rail at the back, where I've already spotted Ella's black tweed coat. I slip my hand into my bag and pull out the pepper mill I secreted there earlier, discreetly liberated from my table in the canteen when I popped in for a lunchtime salad. It's one of those trendy acrylic ones, with a ceramic grinder in the base, and it probably didn't even cost that much, but that's not the point. I drop it into one of the big patch pockets on Ella's coat, then pick the coat up and leave the cloakroom. I'm just in time; no more than ten seconds later, the canteen door opens and Ella and Paulette walk out together.

'Hey!' I say brightly. 'Just in time. I grabbed your coat for you, here you go.'

I'd messaged Ella earlier to say I was finishing at four, the same time as her today, and suggested we treat ourselves to a cocktail in the bar on the corner before heading home – a rare Friday evening diversion – and she'd sounded delighted. I also knew that both she and Paulette were on duty this afternoon, and that they'd be handing over to the night shift team before – I very much hoped – leaving together. And here they are. Perfect.

Now Ella grins and reaches out to take her coat from me. I've folded it in half, and as I hand it over I deliberately tip it so the pocket opening is pointing downwards. A moment later, there's a crash as the pepper mill slips out and bounces on the tiled floor.

'What's that? Oh … I…'

Ella's staring down at it, and as Paulette follows her gaze, she frowns.

'Ella? Is that…? That's one of ours. What's it doing in your pocket?'

'I … I have no idea. I … I mean, I didn't … why would I take a pepper grinder?' Ella stutters.

'I have no idea,' Paulette says drily, and Ella stares at the pepper mill on the floor, her face flushing, then looks desperately at me.

'Oh, someone probably put it in her pocket as a joke, Paulette,' I say breezily. 'Why would Ella take something like that? She's staying with me at the moment and we have plenty of condiment dispensers, she doesn't need to provide her own!'

I laugh lightly, and Ella gives me a grateful smile, then turns to Paulette.

'Exactly,' she says. 'It was probably Chen and Jaden, they're always taking the piss … sorry, I mean they're always teasing me and trying to wind me up. They probably thought it would be hilarious for me to find that thing in my pocket halfway home.'

'Good shout,' I say. 'Those two are notorious.'

Chen and Jaden are two of the paramedics, joined at the hip and big fans of practical jokes. If this hadn't been down to me, it might well have been the sort of thing they'd do, but I'm watching Paulette's face carefully and I'm not sure she's convinced. She's looking at Ella with a sceptical expression.

'Hmm. First repeated lateness and now canteen property in your pocket,' she says, raising an eyebrow. 'I'll give you the benefit of the doubt this time, Ella. But…'

She shrugs and sighs.

'Anyway, I'm off. I'm in all weekend and I'm shattered already. Can you put that thing back before you leave? Have a good one.'

She turns and walks quickly away from us, and Ella groans quietly.

'Bloody hell,' she says, as she bends down to retrieve the pepper mill. 'Harriet, this wasn't me, OK? Why would I? And what if it wasn't Chen and Jaden?'

She straightens up again and looks at me.

'I haven't said anything, because I've been trying to get on top of it, but I've started to … I don't know … I've started to feel really scared again over the past few days. I've just got a weird feeling this thing isn't over, and I don't know why. What if *this* is them again, whoever they are?'

She waves the pepper mill at me.

'Maybe they're still following me … shit, I did think *again* last weekend that someone was hanging around, when I was coming back from my walk, but nobody except hospital staff could have got into the canteen to do *this*, could they? So that doesn't fit, because nobody here can have been involved in Gloucester…'

The words are spilling out of her, her eyes wide and frightened now, and I reach out and grasp her left wrist.

'Ella. Ella, calm down. It'll just be a joke, OK? You're right, this can't be connected to Gloucester. It probably was just those jackass paramedics. Forget it. Go on, put that thing back where it belongs and we'll go and get that cocktail. My treat.'

She takes a breath.

'You're right, sorry. I'm overreacting. I'm just so worried Paulette's going to sack me, you know? I've started thinking the past few weeks might have given me PTSD, honestly. I'm really not myself at the moment. Right, just give me a minute.'

She heads back into the canteen and I stand there, thinking, feeling a little uneasy. I wanted to get Ella into trouble with Paulette, and I think that's *sort* of worked. Another little nail in her coffin, anyway. But I need to be careful. I really don't want her to start thinking someone working here is responsible for what happened in the Midlands. If she starts suspecting me even a little bit…

'Done!'

She's back.

'Great,' I say with a smile, and force my worries to the back of my mind. I'll think about it later. For now, I definitely need that drink, and maybe it will calm Ella down too, stop her obsessing. I loop my arm through hers and point down the corridor.

'Let the weekend begin!' I say.

Chapter Thirty-Two

ELLA

'Good weekend, Ella?'

Lola, one of the other canteen staff, waves cheerily at me across the counter, then grabs a tray of cutlery.

'Ooof!' she says. 'I swear these things get heavier every day.'

'Ahh, you know, just a quiet one,' I say, and she grins.

'Me too. Perfect, it was. Back to it now, though,' she replies, then grimaces again at the weight of her burden and staggers across the room to the long table from which customers help themselves to knives, forks and napkins, dropping the heavily loaded tray onto it with a crash.

I sigh and head into the kitchen. It *was* a quiet weekend, but I wouldn't call mine perfect. I've felt even more on edge since that stupid pepper mill fell out of my coat pocket on Friday. *Was* it just a joke, some colleagues messing around? Or was it the start of a fresh wave of 'happenings'? As I arrived at work this morning, I passed Chen and Jaden's ambulance, the two of them sitting in it, and I challenged them about Friday evening, with resultant blank faces and a flat denial of any involvement. I mean, they probably *would* deny it anyway, even if they had done it. But the way they reacted seemed genuine to me; they looked as if they really did have no idea what I was talking about. So, if not them, who? I simply don't know, and my imagination is working overtime.

After our cocktail on Friday evening – well, it ended up being three, which was probably foolish, although weirdly, it didn't seem to affect me this time – Harriet and I picked up fish and chips for us and George on the way home, and shortly after we'd finished eating I excused myself and went to bed. I feel like a spare part sometimes, when the three of us are sitting there in the evening; I'd rather go and watch TV in my room. They're a couple after all, and they need their privacy, and Harriet's seemed a bit tetchy, on and off, this week. The thing about the nail varnish ... shit. I told her I'd had that colour for ages, but I lied, and I don't even know why. I saw it on her, and thought it looked lovely, and when she was touching up her nails in front of the TV one evening I made a mental note of the shade and then popped into Boots on my way back from work and bought myself a bottle. But after the Zara shirt thing, how could I tell her I'd deliberately copied her nail colour? I still don't know what happened with the shirt, not really. But the nail polish ... what's wrong with me? I seem to be slipping back into how I was when we first met, imitating her style almost without meaning to. I know it's not a big deal, not really – I mean, a pale pink polish is a pale pink polish, loads of people wear it – but she was definitely annoyed about it, and that's the last thing I want to do, to annoy Harriet. So, a Friday night alone in my room it was, not that it's a hardship in a room like that.

On Saturday, happily hangover-free but feeling restless and jittery, I went for a walk in the morning to try to clear my head, and arrived back at the apartment to find only George there, Harriet having been called in to the hospital to cover a colleague who'd gone sick. She'd suggested we didn't tell him about the pepper mill incident ('He worries, you know? And he has some pretty complicated cases on his hands at the moment. I don't want to add to his stress levels by telling him about something which was probably just a silly prank,' she said), and so we hadn't mentioned it, which was fine by me. I'm pretty sure George is getting a little tired of me being around – I sometimes sense a shift in the atmosphere when I come into the room – and I don't want anything to make him want me here even less. But on Saturday he seemed to pick up on the fact I was feeling a little down and made an effort to chat.

'I've never been a big fan of tattoos, but I'm kind of intrigued by yours,' he said, as we sat at the kitchen breakfast bar, mugs of tea in hand. Harriet had nipped out to the local bakery first thing, returning with a loaf of sourdough bread for the weekend, plus a box of delicious-looking dark chocolate muffins. George offered me one, and I smiled and accepted, picking a chunk of chocolate off the top and popping it into my mouth, savouring the melting sweetness on my tongue.

'Intrigued how?' I said. 'Why, do you fancy getting one all of a sudden? Mid-life crisis?'

He laughed.

'No! Hey, it looks great on you, but I'm far too much of a coward. How much did that hurt? And how long did it take? It's amazing, when you look closely at it. It's like a black and white photograph, isn't it?'

I was wearing a T-shirt, despite the chilly February day – oh, the joys of a well-heated apartment, where you can strip off jumpers and layers as soon as you walk in! – and I looked at my right arm, at the black and white roses winding their way down to my wrist.

'It's called a realism tattoo,' I told him. 'And they do take longer than a traditional one. Worth it though. This took about thirty hours, I guess.'

'THIRTY?' George spluttered into his tea. 'Christ on a bike.'

I grinned.

'Not all at once. I think it was done in about five sittings, so about six hours each time. It does hurt, but I reckon my pain threshold is quite high. It wasn't too bad. Cost a bit though. I had it done when I was still living at home and didn't have any rent to pay. Money's a bit tighter nowadays.'

George nodded.

'You'll be back on your feet soon, don't worry. And money isn't everything. I swear Harriet was happier before she inherited all that dosh.'

'Really?' I looked around me, at the sleek kitchen units, the expanse of polished wood flooring, the magnificent views from the picture window opposite, and wondered how on earth anyone could be unhappy with a lifestyle like this.

'I mean, you know her better than me, but she always *seems* pretty happy. You *both* seem so happy – as a couple, I mean. This place, your life … I'd kill for it, to be honest.'

George smiled briefly, then pushed his hair back off his forehead and sighed.

'Ahh, appearances can be deceptive. It's not all about *stuff*, you know? And … I mean, yes, we are happy, I suppose. We were, anyway. But, recently, the past few months … I don't know. Harriet's been different. I can't really put my finger on it but … oh, ignore me. Maybe I'm imagining it. Or maybe it's just work stuff. That's what she says it is. But she just doesn't seem herself to me any more. I try to carry on as normal but she's always kind of … *preoccupied*. Not entirely present. And it's been worse over the past couple of weeks. Or maybe it's just that we've been married for a while … I guess all couples go through patches like this now and again?'

Then he grimaced.

'Gosh, I'm so sorry, Ella. I didn't mean to burden you with this. I'm sure it'll pass, forget I said anything.'

'No, no, it's fine,' I said quickly. 'If you want to talk…'

He looked at me silently for a few seconds, then sighed.

'I shouldn't … but, oh, I don't know. Has she mentioned kids at all? As in, us having a baby at some point? I'd love one, you know, but she's … well, she's still on the fence. I'm wondering if that's part of it – the way she's been recently, I mean. I *try* not to put pressure on her, but she just won't talk about it and … oh bugger, Ella. Sorry, again. I really shouldn't be talking to you about this, if she hasn't. Please don't say anything?'

'Of course I won't. And she hasn't, by the way. Mentioned anything about babies, I mean. I didn't realise it was even on the cards, to be honest. You both seem so career minded…'

'Forget it, honestly,' he said. 'It's fine, everything's fine. Forget this conversation even happened.'

'OK, no problem. Look, I'll get out of your hair,' I said. And then, trying to lighten the mood, added: 'Although you have so much of it that I could probably quite easily curl up in there and you wouldn't even notice.'

He laughed.

'Haha!' he retorted. 'I'm having a haircut next week, for your information. It has got a bit long recently, I admit it. And don't leave on my account. I'm going out in a bit anyway. I've got a squash game and a few beers lined up with one of the lads. What are your plans for today?'

'Not a lot,' I said, relieved that the silly remark had lifted his mood.

Maybe me being here isn't a problem for him after all, I thought, and felt *my* mood lifting too.

'I'm going to have a look through the property rental sites, just to keep an eye on what's out there while I save. And then I was just going to watch a movie or something. Nothing that costs any money!'

I grinned, and he smiled back.

'Well, Harriet's now doing a double shift today so she won't be back until late. I'll treat us to a takeaway for dinner, OK? Your choice.'

'Amazing, thanks! I'll have a think. Probably be Indian though, I love a madras.'

'Fine by me. See you later.'

As we went off to enjoy our afternoons I felt weirdly better than I had in days. It felt nice that he'd confided in me – *I definitely won't jeopardise this little improvement in our relationship by mentioning our conversation to Harriet*, I thought – and the encounter made me feel calmer, less jumpy. It didn't last though. Now, back at work, I find myself looking suspiciously at everyone around me, and it isn't until I see Paulette glaring at me when I'm so focused on watching two nurses leave the canteen that I walk straight into a table and drop the tray of empty glasses I'm carrying that I have a stern word with myself.

Come on, I think fiercely. *Pull yourself together.*

But as the day drags on, in every quiet moment the thoughts hound me.

Maybe I gave up too easily.

Maybe I should still be moving heaven and earth to find out who did this to me.

Because Friday wasn't a joke, I just know it wasn't.

It's still *happening. It's* not *over. And I simply have no idea what to do next.*

Chapter Thirty-Three

NISHA

'Brilliant. Ace. Just let me know when it's done, OK? I'll buy you both lunch. And I'll make it properly worth your while as soon as I can, mate, I promise.'

My heart is beating fast as I end the call. Letisha, whom I've known since school, is primed and ready. She's even told Toby to start pretending to feel ill during lessons today, so it won't come as a surprise to anyone there when she calls his teacher first thing tomorrow to tell her he's sick again. And he's a proper little actor, Toby. Like dogs and cats, kids are up there for me, and he's been great so far, faking the stomach pain and other symptoms. He was totally excellent in his school play last year, and he's going to smash this too. They both are.

I might actually call in sick myself tomorrow too. I don't want to end up with a last-minute viewing to do or something like that, and miss the call from Letisha. Yes, I'll do that. I'll do a Toby and start moaning about a headache or a stomach ache mid-afternoon, then call in at eight in the morning and tell them I'm feeling dreadful. It's going to be a big day tomorrow; I need to be around, ready to celebrate at lunchtime.

I pick up my phone to check my appointments for the rest of today. I'm an estate agent now, in Clapham, and I need to leave in about twenty minutes to show a young couple around a cute two-bed. It's the sort of house I'd like to buy, when I get my money back. I put the phone down and call up the property details on my computer screen. It's in a gated mews not far from Clapham Common, and it's not badly priced at £750,000. Arranged over three floors, open-plan kitchen/reception, big double and full bathroom on the first floor, second double with ensuite shower on the second. Off-street parking too, not that I have a car right now. I'll get one though, soon. I'll be able to have anything I want soon.

I challenged it, of course, when Harriet inherited all my money. When I discovered, to my horror, that a parent, under UK law, has no legal obligation at all to leave *any* inheritance to their children, I looked into grounds for contesting the will, and settled on 'undue influence or coercion', because surely the Hart woman must have put pressure on my mother to change her will? Surely I must, at some point, have been the sole beneficiary? The problem was, it turned out, that my mother had been very specific that nothing should be left to me, citing a complete breakdown in the mother/daughter relationship. The other problem, of course, was that contesting a will can take months – sometimes years – and that costs money. And while by then I did already have this job and wasn't doing too badly at it at all (maybe some of my mother's skills with property rubbed off on me somehow), I simply didn't have enough cash to fund a prolonged legal battle. And – problem number three – even if I *had* managed to find the money, the solicitor I consulted warned me I had little to no chance of winning anyway.

'Your mother was very clear in her wishes,' he said. 'I'm afraid my best advice to you would be *not* to throw any more money at it. I rather fear you'd end up even worse off than you are now, unfortunately.'

I took the advice – I didn't have much choice – and instead I tried to appeal to Harriet Hart's sense of fairness and justice, although, typical me, I may not have gone about it in *exactly* the right way. I wrote her what, in retrospect, was a pretty nasty first letter, accusing her of manipulating her way into my mother's life with the sole aim of nabbing a share of her fortune, and demanding that she return the money to me, as the rightful heir. She did reply, but informed me she'd had absolutely no idea about 'her friend and neighbour' Farah's wealth until after her death, and that she'd been utterly astounded when contacted by Farah's solicitor and told about the will. She went on to say that she had, however, had many long chats with my mother about me, and about how sad Farah was that we were estranged. She added:

I know that she was in perfectly sound mind, right to the end. If she decided to omit you from her will, that was entirely her decision and I, for one, fully respect that. I'm sorry, but I can be of no further assistance to you on this matter.

I bet you fucking fully respect it, I thought. *You and your bulging bank account, you money-grabbing slag.*

The thing about doctors, though, is that they're easy to keep tabs on. A quick Google and I easily found out where she works, and exactly what she looks like. She's striking; it wasn't

JACKIE KABLER

hard to spot her walking in and out of the hospital, not hard either to follow her around a bit, get the lie of the land. But the day I followed her home to her shiny new penthouse apartment was the day I knew I had to do something. When I looked it up online and saw the sale price, I nearly choked on my wine.

I should be living in a place like that, I thought viciously, eyes narrowing as I looked around me at the in-need-of-fresh-paint walls and small, viewless windows of my one-bed rental flat. That's when I stepped things up. I'd been sending her the occasional email for ages, reminding her I was still around, telling her I hadn't given up, that I expected her one day to do the right thing and give me back what was rightfully mine. But the next day, I started a new email campaign, bombarding her for a week or so, stopping for a bit, then starting again. Telling her I knew how recklessly she was spending my money, threatening the legal action I knew I couldn't afford, telling her she had a short window to see sense and settle this amicably before I'd take her for everything she had. When she continued to ignore me, making me apoplectic, I hit pause again and began to think.

What would make her give in to me? What's important to her?

As far as I could see, she only had three things in her life: her job, her home and her husband. And of these, I could see by the hours she put in that her career was clearly streets ahead of anything else in her priority list. And that's when the plan began to form, and soon I knew exactly what I had to do. I sent another email, and this time I told her I was coming after her career. That I was going to make sure she lost her job, her reputation, all of it. I wrote:

*I've waited long enough, Harriet. I've asked nicely, I've even
begged. I've warned you that one day soon your time would
run out. Well, that day has come…*

What happened on the bus was just a little taster. There's
no way she'll get out of what I'm going to do next. And she's
not even that bright, for a doctor. She's never noticed me
following her about, for a start, I'm pretty sure of that.
Although she's got someone staying with her now, some friend
who also appears to be working at the hospital, and she's a lot
more switched on. I'm pretty sure she's spotted me lurking
around near the apartment development at least once, so I
need to be careful there. She's street smart, that one. Or maybe
just more paranoid. Whatever. I don't need to follow Harriet
around any more anyway. I know her routines now, the times
she goes to and from work, the different clinics she runs when
she's there.

I have everything I need to step this up. To get what I want,
what I deserve, finally. I look around the office. It's quiet, just
Gav over there tapping on his keyboard, chewing gum a little
bit too loudly in that irritating way of his. Everyone else is out.
My eyes drift to the street outside, cars and people passing in a
never-ending stream, just like every day in this busy part of
southwest London, and I think about Harriet, who'll be at
work today too, doing her thing with the poorly kids. And
then, quite suddenly, I feel a sharp pang of remorse.

Shit.

I want to hurt Harriet, I have to, as a means to an end. But
for some reason it's only just dawned on me that what I'm
about to do will very likely have an impact on some sick
children too. As I said, I like kids. Like them much better than

most adults I know. And if one of their doctors is taken out of action, suspended, sacked, whatever, there's bound to be collateral damage, isn't there? Kids who'll have to wait longer for diagnosis or treatment. Kids who might suffer, because of *me*.

I pick up the mug of coffee that's slowly cooling on my desk and take a sip, thinking.

Do I give her one more chance? Just one? Send her one final email before I do this? Tell her she has until midnight to respond, or face the consequences?

Yes. That's what I'll do. It probably won't make any difference, but at least I'll know I tried. Tried for the kids. If she still ignores me, then that's not my fault, is it? On her head be it. She'll be the one to feel guilty, not me. She's the one in the wrong here. She's the thief. But I'm not a bad person. I've given her *so* many chances to do this the easy way. And now she'll have one final chance, and if she still doesn't take it, well…

I smile. If she doesn't get back to me tonight, tomorrow is going to be one of the worst days of her life. I pick up my phone and begin to type the email.

Chapter Thirty-Four

HARRIET

I drugged Ella again last night.

'I know it's only Monday, but it's been a long day and it's miserable outside, that's my excuse. Join me?' I said, waving a bottle of red at her. She looked at the bottle, hesitated briefly and then said, 'Well, I suppose I was OK after the cocktails on Friday, wasn't I? Go on then! Just one, though.'

But of course one turned into two and then three and … well, same old, same old. She staggered off to bed and she was still there, out for the count, when I poked my head into her room just before I left for work. I look up at the clock on the wall. Just after nine-fifteen. She could still be there now, for all I know, slumbering away. I hope so. And I hope when she finally does drag herself into the canteen, Paulette fires her on the spot. She can, if she wants to, because of the trial period thing. No full disciplinary procedure required. Her contract can be terminated just like that, and I reckon this will be one transgression too many. And once she's lost this job, I might just tell her that sadly, she's going to have to find accommodation elsewhere too. That it's becoming tricky to persuade George to let her stay much longer, especially if she's jobless again, and so that much further away from being able to save enough money for a place of her own. I'll blame *him*. It won't be *entirely* a lie, either; he really did ask me last night if she'd be staying much longer, as he watched her stumble out of the kitchen, one shoulder of her slouchy jumper slipping down her arm, her bra strap on show, her hair tousled. She looked a mess. She *is* a mess.

I told him it would only be another few days, maybe a week, and he looked surprised.

'Oh – really?' he said. 'She didn't say anything to me. OK, well ... good.'

And it *is* good, I keep telling myself. Just as I planned, Ella had a shiny, bright future – or so she thought – and I gave it to her and stole it away again, and now she has nothing. It's not quite as satisfying in the end as I thought it would be, actually. It's taken away *some* of the anger, *some* of the pain, but ... oh, maybe I'll feel better when she goes. When her life is in ruins, again. Maybe. I bloody hope so.

Nisha, though. What to do about *goddamned* Nisha. I had another email from her yesterday, another threat, this time with a deadline. She wanted a serious commitment from me, by midnight, to enter into talks about giving her what she described as 'a substantial portion' of her mother's money back. Otherwise, she said, I'd regret it.

I'm coming for you. And this time, you're going to be in real trouble.

I've thought about going to the police about Nisha and her

threats more than once, but I've never gone through with it, for a number of reasons. The fact that George doesn't know she even exists. The fact that I have that secret bank account, the one I used to fund my revenge on Ella. Because if I set the police on her, Nisha is definitely going to fight back. And then George will find out that Farah had a daughter, whom I probably *should* have shared the money with. And if the real figures start being bandied around, the true sum I inherited, he'll realise I hid some money away too, and there'll be questions, awkward questions, and maybe the police will also have questions. Maybe I'll be forced to disclose what I spent that extra money on, and everything I've done to Ella might come out, and then George might wonder who on earth he married. He might even leave me. Or maybe none of that might happen; maybe I'm just catastrophising, as I often do. But I can't risk it. And also, when I read that email last night, it just sounded a bit desperate. I mean, she's had long enough now, and all she's managed is that pathetic little stunt on the bus. I honestly don't think she has the intelligence or imagination to do anything more effective.

I could give her a few tips there, I think, with a wry smile. And so I ignored her little deadline – midnight, the drama of it all! – and deleted her email with an irritated swipe of my finger. This morning though, I'm suddenly so weary of it all. I just don't think she's going to give up, and I'm not sure how much longer I can take it. Back then, I justified keeping the money because I told myself that's what Farah wanted. She really *had* spoken to me many times about her estranged daughter – that wasn't a lie. She told me how Nisha stole thousands of pounds from her and skipped the country, how they rarely spoke, how cold and distant Nisha was when they did. And although now

I do have a well-paid job, I had so little growing up, my parents scrimping and saving for every little thing. I wanted a better life, a more comfortable one. And I'd lost so much already; maybe the inheritance was the universe giving me something back, I reasoned. Maybe that money came my way so that, if I ever *do* decide to go down that very expensive IVF route, paying for it won't be an issue. But now it all feels so exhausting. I just want Nisha's relentless bombardment of me to *stop*; I just want to be left alone.

So – *do* I give her something? Make a token gesture? I have money left in my secret Ella account, around thirty grand, I think, nicely topped up by the surprisingly good income from Mug & Meadow. If I offer her that, will it be enough? It might be, if I tell her in no uncertain terms that it's a one-off, that it's all she's going to get. Thirty grand is a decent amount, after all. It's a deposit on a flat, or a new car. Not to be sneezed at. I glance at the clock again. I have a clinic starting in about ten minutes. If I do this now, and she accepts and buggers off, and Ella loses her job this morning and I can get rid of her too, well … what a day this could turn out to be.

I'm doing it. I grab my phone and type the email. Thirty thousand pounds, in her account by the end of the week, if she agrees in writing to stop all this, to never contact me again. I read it through and then, before I can change my mind again, hit send.

There, done. I sit back in my chair and exhale, feeling a strange sense of lightness, letting my thoughts settle. And then I sigh and get to my feet. Clinic is calling, and I have a full list, so Nisha and whatever she decides to respond with will have to wait. My first few cases are pretty straightforward, sweet kids, nice parents, and I find myself relaxing, enjoying myself, taking extra pleasure today from this job that I love so much, this job that I'm *good* at. I make a difference, I know I do, and that really is a joy.

'Ms Perez? And this must be Toby. Come in, have a seat.'

My next appointment is here, a tall, dark-haired woman with a tense expression on her face, and a teenage boy, who gives me a little smile. I glance down at my notes, refreshing my memory. Toby Perez, fifteen years old. Referred by his GP after suffering regular bouts of diarrhoea and severe stomach pain, with no obvious cause. He looks well enough today, his eyes bright, his skin clear, but that means nothing, and as they both sit down my mind is already racing, running through possible diagnoses. I make a little small talk, trying to put the mother, in particular, at ease, then ask Toby a series of questions. When I'm done, I ask him if he minds hopping up on the bed behind me so I can do a quick examination. He nods, and stands up, then hesitates.

'Mum,' he says. 'Could I … erm, could I…'

She looks up at him expectantly.

'What is it, love?'

'It's just…'

He pauses, looking uncomfortable, his weight shifting from one foot to the other.

'Well, could I just speak to the doctor on my own for a minute? Would you mind?'

Ms Perez frowns, looking from her son to me and back again, then shrugs.

'Well – I suppose so. I don't know what can't be said in front of me though. But … OK, whatever.'

She looks at me again, as if for permission to leave the room, and I smile and nod.

'We'll be fine,' I say reassuringly. 'You can wait just outside. I'll call you back in when we're done.'

'Thanks, Mum,' Toby says, sounding grateful, and his mother gives him another look, eyebrows slightly raised, then leaves the room, closing the door firmly behind her. Toby is already sitting on the examination couch, swinging his legs up onto it. He lies down and pulls up his sweatshirt, revealing his olive-skinned, still hairless torso.

'OK, so let's chat as I have a little feel of your tummy,' I say, crossing to the sink in the corner of the room. 'Is there something in particular you want to tell me, or ask me?'

He says nothing as I wash and then dry my hands, and it isn't until I've walked back to the bed and am standing next to him that he says quietly, 'Well, it's a bit embarrassing really. Erm, you see…'

He stops talking, staring at the ceiling, then swallows and says, 'Can you just give me a minute?'

'Of course,' I say gently. 'No hurry. Let's have a little look at you first.'

I start to gently palpate his stomach area, feeling carefully for any lumps or areas of tenderness.

'Shout if there's pain or discomfort, OK?' I say, and he nods, still staring at the ceiling. I move my fingers upwards, pressing lightly, then jump violently as Toby suddenly screams.

'Oi! No! Stop it!'

'Wha–what is it?'

Shocked at the ferocity of his reaction, I take a step back, hands in the air, and he yells again, jumping from the bed, his top still up around his armpits.

'You can't touch me like that!' he screeches.

'Did that hurt? I'm so sorry…' I stutter, then whirl around as the door is flung open and Ms Perez rushes in.

'Toby! What's wrong, what's happened?' she says, then turns to me, her expression a mix of distress and confusion.

'I … I'm not sure,' I say. 'I was just examining his tummy and I must have touched a tender spot. Toby, can you lie down again, just so I can check? I'm so sorry that hurt, but we need to see where that pain's coming from. I'll be extra gentle, I promise.'

'No way,' Toby says. He's pulling his sweatshirt down now, shaking his head, his eyes wide. 'You're not touching me again, you … you pervert.'

'Excuse me … pardon?' I say, stunned, but he's walking across to his mother now, still talking.

'Paedophile, that's what you are. I didn't even know women *could* be paedophiles,' he's saying, and my mouth drops open.

'Mum, she touched me. Down there.'

He gestures towards the groin area of his black jeans, and his mother gasps.

'She did *what*?'

'She touched me. She ran her hand over it. She shouldn't have done that, should she? I have *stomach* pain. There's nothing wrong with … with *that*. Why did she do that? *Pervert. Paedophile.*'

He turns to me as he spits out the last two words, a cold, angry look on his face, and his mother gasps again.

'Darling, are you serious?'

She grabs his arm, pulling him protectively towards her, then spins around and glares at me.

'What's *happened* in here?' she says angrily. 'No, don't even answer that. We're leaving, immediately. Come on, Toby. Let's go and report this so-called *doctor*. How dare you molest my child? How dare you?'

'But … I didn't … There's been some kind of misunderstanding, I would *never*…' I stammer, but she's not listening; she's marching across the room now, towing her son behind her, and moments later the door slams and they're gone.

'Oh my God.'

I whisper the words as I lower myself onto my chair, a sick, hollow feeling in my chest. I didn't touch him, not there, not even by accident, I know I didn't. He's lying. And I am *stupid*. So, *so* stupid. Why did I let his mother leave the room? Or if he insisted, why didn't I bring in a chaperone? Why did I leave myself open to this? This … this *farce*. This *nightmare*, because that's what it's about to be. A shitstorm. Suspension, an investigation … and after what happened on the bus too…

'Oh my God!'

I sob the words this time, tears suddenly rolling down my cheeks.

Too late.

I was too late with my offer to Nisha. Too cocky when I ignored her midnight deadline, too sure she could never do anything that could cause me any real harm. Well, I was wrong about that, wasn't I? Because this is her, again, I have no doubt at all about that. I don't know who the two people are who've just left this room, but Nisha is behind it, I know she is. Fuck. *Fuck.*

I'm not sure how long I've been sitting here, my head resting on the smooth wood of my desktop, my shoulders heaving. Then I hear it.

BRRRRRR.

My desk phone has started ringing. I turn to look at it and see an internal number flashing on its little .LED screen. Already. They didn't hang about, did they? Slowly, I reach out a hand and pull a tissue from the box next to my computer monitor, then dab at my face, wiping away the tears. The phone continues to ring, shrill and urgent in the quiet room. I throw the tissue into the wastepaper bin and then, bracing myself for what's about to happen, I pick up the receiver, mildly surprised to see that my hand is steady, no sign of the tremor I can now feel running through my entire body. I clear my throat.

'Dr Hart speaking,' I say softly.

Chapter Thirty-Five

ELLA

I feel so sick as I reach the front door of the apartment that I have to lean on it for a few moments before I put the key in the lock, breathing deeply, trying not to actually throw up. When I finally get into the hall, I'm surprised to hear voices coming from the kitchen. I knew George was off today but Harriet should be at work. Does he have someone else here with him? But no; as I walk in, I see that it's indeed George and Harriet, sitting together at the breakfast bar. He's holding her hand, and she's crying.

'Harriet! What is it? What's happened?'

I'm so shocked to see her like this that I momentarily forget my own misery, and rush across the room towards her, dumping my bag unceremoniously in the middle of the floor. They turn towards me, looking startled.

'Ella! Why aren't you at work?' asks George.

I hesitate, looking at Harriet's tear-streaked face, but there's no point in putting it off. I just need to tell them.

'I've been fired,' I say. 'Totally my own fault. This *stupid* issue I seem to have with alcohol … I obviously had too much last night *again*, and I just didn't wake up this morning. I slept right through my alarm, just like before. Paulette told me it was once too often, and she sacked me on the spot. I'm so, so sorry, and I'm going to get another job as soon as I can, I promise. I'm quitting drinking too, I mean it this time. But … never mind about me. Harriet, what's wrong? You look awful.'

'Thanks, mate,' she says, with a loud sniff, and I clap a hand to my mouth.

'Oh bugger, sorry, I didn't mean it like that. I mean – what's happened? Why are *you* home in the middle of the day? Are you sick?'

Harriet shakes her head, and her tears, which had stopped briefly, fill her eyes again. Her mascara is all over the place, her face pink and puffy.

'I've been suspended,' she says.

'*What*? You've … what? Why on earth…?'

She sinks her head into her hands, and George pulls her into his arms, murmuring softly.

'It's OK, babe. It's going to be OK.'

He looks up at me and rolls his eyes.

'It's some ridiculous misunderstanding,' he says. 'She hasn't told me the full details yet, she's too upset. Something about a complaint, the mother of a teenage patient who obviously misinterpreted something she said or did. I'm not quite sure why she's been suspended though, must be pretty serious. Harriet … hey, darling. Come on, talk to me, please.'

He puts a hand under her chin and gently tilts her face up towards his, and she lets out a little sob.

'Oh George … it's just … I don't know *what* happened. I was just examining this kid's tummy and suddenly he's yelling and jumping off the bed … he'd asked his mother to step out for a minute because he wanted to tell me something, but then he didn't say anything, and … then he said I'd *touched* him. His penis. He called me a *paedophile*, George. It's a *nightmare*…'

George gapes at her.

'He said you did *what*? And there was no chaperone in the room? *Harriet*…'

She runs a hand across her face, looking distraught.

'I know, I know. I was distracted, you know? My mind was on other things, there's a lot going on at the moment, and I know that's no excuse, but the kid said he needed to speak to me in private, and it wasn't an intimate examination, and his mother was just outside the door and she seemed fine with it so I took that as consent, but, you're right, I know … oh, *God*. What a mess.'

'But *why*?' I say, looking from Harriet to George and then back again. 'Why would he say that? Why lie? What's the point? Is he after compensation or something? Is that even a thing?'

George is running both hands through his hair, his eyes wide.

'Who knows why? But yes, he could get damages if the case was proven … it'll be his word against hers though. Harriet, are you *sure* you didn't touch him accidentally or something? I'm sorry to ask, but…'

'I'm sure. I'm positive. This is just … I don't know. I don't know anything any more.'

She's slouched in her seat now, her voice barely a whisper. She looks broken, defeated, as if she's already given up.

'Fuck,' says George.

I feel a wave of nausea sweep over me, and swallow hard,

then take the few steps to the nearest seat on suddenly weak legs and drop down onto it. For a few moments, there's silence, all of us staring blankly and miserably into space. Then I reach out to Harriet and take her hand.

'Looks like we're both in the shit then,' I say.

'Looks like we are,' she says.

Chapter Thirty-Six

NISHA

W ell, that went rather well, didn't it? My face actually hurts, I've been smiling so much for the past twenty-four hours. As soon as it was done – as soon as Letisha and Toby finally got away from the hospital yesterday, massive fuss made and formal complaint lodged – Letisha was on the phone to me, *buzzing*.

'We did it!' she shrieked. 'Toby smashed it, and I did pretty bloody brilliantly too, if I do say so myself. We'll all be rich any day now, you'll see, Nish!'

Harriet sent me an email just before Toby and Letisha arrived at the hospital. I didn't see it until later on – after all, she'd missed her midnight deadline by many hours, so I wasn't exactly glued to my phone – but it wouldn't have made any difference. She offered me thirty grand. THIRTY. What a fucking insult. I didn't even dignify it with a response, simply deleted the email.

Let her stew for a bit first, I thought, *before I contact her again*.

I'd planned to take us all out for lunch to celebrate, but I asked Letisha if she'd mind if we made it dinner instead. I had a sudden urge to go and hang around outside the hospital, to see if there was any sign of Harriet, to see if I could work out what was going on. My plan now is to message her again in a day or two and tell her I'll get Toby to withdraw the complaint, to say he got it wrong, but only if she pays me properly. Pays me BIG TIME. Because she will, now, won't she? There's no way she's going to let her career go tits up over this. I think I know her well enough, even from a distance, to be pretty sure about that. This thing is nearly over, finally. I can feel it.

I didn't have long to wait at the hospital either. A few minutes after I arrived, there she was, leaving through the main entrance, her eyes red, her head down. Going home, hours before the end of her shift. Definitely suspended this time, I reckon. I mean, two alleged offences in a week? That's a bit of a coincidence, Dr Hart, isn't it? Taken up sexual molestation as a new hobby, have you?

I was so amused by it all I actually snorted with laughter just after she'd passed me, and had to hide behind a bush in case she turned back. She didn't though. She just shuffled off towards the bus stop, looking absolutely miserable.

Jeez, Toby played a blinder. He totally deserves the new smartphone and PlayStation he's been promised for his part in this. They were both a bit dubious about it at first, but when I explained how Harriet's basically an evil witch who ripped me off and stole my inheritance, and has point-blank refused to even talk about giving any of it back, they got it. The ten grand I promised to pay Letisha helped, of course. I owe Polly and Jake a grand each for the bus thing too, so this had better damn work. But it will, I know it will. Toby is *such* a good little actor. He had to make several GP appointments, complaining of crippling stomach pain and diarrhoea, *and* fake being ill at school a few times too, to make it convincing, and he was ace. The poor GP couldn't find anything wrong with him – surprise, surprise, as he's as fit as a flea – so we got the paediatrician referral we wanted and, good old NHS, we were able to choose our preferred consultant. It all worked like magic.

I pick up the bottle of water on my desk and take a long swig. I have a headache today – Letisha and I caned the Prosecco last night at our celebration dinner – but it's worth it. Although now the initial excitement is fading, my conscience is bothering me again, just a little, which is annoying.

I've caused a doctor to be suspended, I think. *A doctor who looks after kids. No matter what she's done, that's not ideal, is it…?*

I worry about that for a minute, then pull myself together.

It's not really going to ruin her career, is it? Because she'll be back at work soon. As soon as she realises that if she gives me what I want the complaint will be withdrawn and all of this will go away, she'll pay up. And then all will be well again.

No, I refuse to beat myself up over this. And I need to stop thinking about it now anyway, because I have work to do and houses to sell. But first – coffee. Hot and strong. Maybe a couple of paracetamol too. That'll sort me out.

I've just arrived back at my desk, mug in hand, when I hear the ping from my phone. An email. *Another* email from *Harriet*. Wow. I thought *I'd* have to chase *her*, even now, but she's not stupid, is she? She's worked out this was all me. So what's she going to do about it?

I open the email, and as I read it a smile creeps across my face. Yes. *Yes*, finally.

Nisha, I'm sorry. What you've done to me is unforgivable, but now I've realised the depth of your feelings about this, and I'm truly sorry you've been driven to such lengths. So please – can we talk? I'm willing to pay you more than I originally offered you – £100,000 – if you can make this go away, and leave me to get on with my life. Here's my number. I'll be waiting for your call.

Chapter Thirty-Seven

HARRIET

I feel as if I've been living in fog for the past few days, barely keeping it together. The more I think about what happened on Tuesday, the more terrified I feel. An accusation of sexually inappropriate conduct is about as serious as it gets; if I'm found guilty, I'm likely to be struck off the medical register, I'd never be able to practise again. The police have been informed. That means this could result in a criminal conviction too; every time I think about that, I break out into a cold sweat. Yesterday, accompanied by a solicitor provided by the Medical Defence Union, I was interviewed under caution, and even though the officers I spoke to were pleasant enough, I can't seem to stop myself from shaking, my mind in turmoil. At the hospital, of course, things began with my interim suspension, followed by me being asked to provide a written statement giving my side of what happened in my consulting room. Even if the police decide there's no evidence of any wrongdoing on my part, there'll still have to be a General

Medical Council investigation of the complaint, and that could take months.

And all of it, *all* of it, is my own fault. Not just my foolishness in being so distracted by everything that's going on I examined a teenage boy without insisting a chaperone be present, but everything that led up to it. If I'd shared some of the money with Nisha earlier, if I hadn't underestimated her so hugely. Now, this woman who clearly hates me enough to attempt to completely ruin my life is the only one who can save me, and all I can do is wait for her to decide if that's something she's willing to do. When I emailed her on Wednesday – apologising, offering her more money, asking her if we could please talk – she replied only briefly, telling me she'd think about it and get back to me by the end of the week. Now, it's Friday, and I'm still waiting, unable to settle or concentrate on anything, frightened to leave the apartment for reasons I can't really put my finger on, even though I know that even a short walk in the fresh air would help to calm me, to quell the sense of foreboding that tightens my chest and makes my heart race. I offered Nisha 100 grand in the end. I have the thirty that's left in my secret bank account, plus another twenty in an old Post Office savings account; the remaining fifty I'll have to liberate from other investments, and just hope George won't notice, for a while at least. I'll come up with some sort of story to cover it eventually.

I groan out loud. I'm standing by the bedroom window, and after a drizzly start to the day the sun has just come out, the river below glistening as the golden rays dance across it, but I'm too stressed to appreciate the beauty of the view today. Shit. *George.* I *had* to tell him what had happened, when I arrived home on Tuesday. I was so distraught I'm not sure I would have been able to hide it anyway, although if he'd worked elsewhere, and not in the same hospital as I do, I might have given it a go. But even though disciplinary proceedings are supposed to be confidential, people always talk, and the suspension of a consultant is always going to be noticed and speculated upon. What else could I do? This is too big, too serious, not to share it with my husband. He was great initially, but as the day went on, I could tell that in reality he was struggling to get his head around it, and the potential implications of what I was being accused of. Then, on Wednesday, everything got worse, if that's even possible. He came home from work with a face like thunder, and asked me why I'd never mentioned the previous incident on the bus. So, not so confidential after all. I've no idea who's been gossiping – Susan? Ian on security? – but it's all round the building now, apparently.

'What the fuck, Harriet?' my husband exploded. 'First this kid accusing you, and now I hear some bloke says you filmed his dick on a bus? Why didn't you tell me?'

Ella was in the room at the time, and her mouth dropped open. I explained as best I could, obviously without mentioning Nisha; I told them it was just some stupid made-up accusation, that someone stole my phone and obviously thought it would be funny to film a silly video and then send the phone back to me, to call the hospital and make up a story to go with it. But I could tell they were both bemused.

'But … why?' Ella asked. 'Who would do that? It doesn't make sense.'

'No sense at all,' glowered George.

'I know, tell me about it,' I said helplessly.

'I still don't understand why you didn't tell *me* about it?

Tell *us* about it?' George snapped, gesturing at Ella, and I just shrugged and told them it hadn't seemed like a big deal at the time, at which they both looked a little dumbfounded.

Then, of course, Ella's mind began working overtime again.

'What if this is all tied up with me and Gloucester? What if they've moved on to *you* now, because you're my friend? Because you've been helping me? Shit, Harriet. Maybe this is all *my* fault? I couldn't bear it if it is. Do you think it could be?'

All I could do was shrug again, and tell her I had no idea *what* was going on. Lie upon lie upon lie. It's becoming second nature to me now; it's not even difficult. Who even am I? The irony of all this is not lost on me; I tried to ruin Ella's life and now the same thing has happened to me, but even worse. Ella's been through hell, but at least she will, one day, be able to come back from this. She still has a potential career, no criminal proceedings hanging over *her*. The unfairness of it all makes me want to scream.

George had calmed down again by yesterday morning, telling me we can get through this, that even though he can't understand why two such similar accusations would suddenly be made against me, that of *course* he believes me, of *course* he'll stand by me, no matter what. But I know him well enough to see that he's still having a hard time processing it all, and last night, when Ella had gone to bed, leaving us alone together in front of the TV, he finally told me something he's never told me before, something he said he's wanted to share in the past but never really found the right time. Something he said he's never told *anyone* before.

'I had a bad experience, with a dentist. I was six, and I was having a check-up. Mum was with me, but she had to leave the room because my brother Henry was just a baby and he'd started screaming the place down. I remember the dentist getting a bit stroppy about it and saying he couldn't concentrate. He more or less ordered her to take Henry outside and leave us in peace, which, looking back, was obviously just a ploy. Then, as soon as she'd gone...'

He swallowed hard, staring down at his hands. He was clenching them together so hard his nails were digging into his skin.

'Oh George...' I whispered. 'You don't have to...,' but he shook his head, his mouth set in a grim line.

'I'm OK,' he said. 'I want to tell you. As soon as she'd gone, he told me my teeth looked great, and that as a reward he was going to show me something hardly anyone got to see. I remember sitting up in the chair feeling all excited, you know? Wondering what he was going to show me. Then of course the bastard unzips his trousers and grabs my hand and makes me touch him...'

He blew out some air, closing his eyes for a few seconds, then opened them again.

'It didn't last long,' he continued. 'And then he's doing the classic "this is our little secret" thing and telling me that if I breathed a word, next time I came in he'd use the drill on me and it would "really hurt". He even switched it on and waved it in my face. And of course, me being the timid and obedient little chap that I was, I never said a thing. Not to anyone. And luckily, when it was time for my next check-up, it was a female dentist. I never saw him again. I don't know if he retired, or if what he'd done to me wasn't a one-off and he got done for it or what. I never asked where he'd gone. I was just so relieved he wasn't there. After that, I sort of put it out of my mind – he didn't touch *me*, after all. Just put my hand on his ... But I thought about it every time I saw a dentist. And this … this stuff with you, Harriet. It's brought it all back for some reason. Maybe I thought I was OK, and all the time I haven't been, not really, I don't know…'

I wrapped my arms around him then, and after a moment's hesitation he put his head on my shoulder, and we sat there for a long time, him tense and silent, me murmuring soothingly in his ear. I might not have done the things I'm accused of, but I suddenly felt overwhelmed with shame for what I *have* done, the things I can't tell George about, the things that have led to all this. When we went to bed, I snuggled up close, but after a minute he gently pushed me away.

'I need some space, Harriet. I love you, but it's just … I'm finding this strangely difficult,' he said.

This morning he was out of bed before I woke up, and this distance I'm feeling between us is adding to my misery. George and I never fall out, *ever*. And although we're not *rowing*, not exactly, I feel as though we are, and it's horrible.

I turn away from the window and walk out of the bedroom. It's nearly lunchtime, and I don't remember eating breakfast this morning, but I have no appetite, my stomach constantly churning, my phone practically glued to my hand as I wait for some form of contact from Nisha.

This is my punishment, isn't it, for what I've done to Ella? And now, with George the only one working, I'm rattling around the apartment with her most of the time, because I couldn't tell her to move out after all, could I, not now? George already thinks badly of me for not being honest about what's been going on at work. How could I kick my newly unemployed 'friend' out on the streets too? He'd think I was cruel as well as a liar. And so I'm stuck with her, for another while at least. To her credit, she's been job hunting online pretty much all day every day, trawling the websites, firing off applications, lining up interviews. As I reach the kitchen, I see she's still at it, tapping away at her laptop, a look of grim determination on her face. She looks up and smiles.

'Hey. How are you feeling? Fancy a walk? It looks lovely out there and I think I've done all I can for today. I've got three interviews on Monday though. I'm chuffed about that – I mean, they're nothing special, but they're jobs. Anyway – walk?'

I shake my head, and walk over to the counter to switch on the kettle.

'No, sorry, Ella. I just don't feel like going out.'

'I'll go for a wander with you, Ella.'

I turn to see George walking in. He's been at The Club, a squash game before his late shift at the hospital, and he must have showered there instead of coming back and doing it here as he usually does, because he's dressed in a clean grey sweatshirt and jeans, his hair damp and slicked back from his face.

'Oh! OK – great,' Ella says, and I take a breath and force a smile.

'Good idea,' I say.

George and I stand there, looking at each other, for a few seconds, and Ella, obviously sensing some sort of uneasy atmosphere, closes the laptop and jumps off her stool.

'I'll just go for a wee and grab my jacket,' she says. 'See you in the hall in a couple of minutes, George.'

He nods, watching her leave the room. He waits until she's gone, and we hear the sound of her bedroom door closing behind her, then he turns back to me.

'Look, I'm sorry about last night,' he said. 'I didn't mean to push you away. I know you're going through shit, and I do trust you, honestly. I'm just finding this hard – the memories it's brought back. Come here.'

He holds out his arms, and I feel a sob rising in my throat as I step into them. After hugging me tightly for a few seconds, he steps back and gives me a little smile.

'Sure you won't come with us?' he asks. 'I wouldn't normally choose to hang out with just our lodger but I really could do with a bit of fresh air before work, it's going to be a long one this evening. And it *is* a lovely day.'

'Nah, I'm OK,' I say. Suddenly, I wouldn't mind a walk, but I can't risk it, I realise. If Nisha phones, I need to be somewhere private. That will *not* be a conversation I want anyone else to listen in on.

'Suit yourself. See you in a bit then,' he says.

'See you later. Love you,' I call after him as he walks away, and without looking back he raises a hand in the air in response. I watch him go, feeling an unexpected wave of sadness, then make myself a cup of tea, and carry on with my waiting game.

Chapter Thirty-Eight

NISHA

I think I've kept her in suspense long enough. I just wanted her to fret a little longer, to worry that I wasn't going to reply. That way, she'll be so relieved when I *do* call her that hopefully she'll be more amenable to my new request. Request, demand, whatever you want to call it. I'll do it in a few minutes. I'll just get myself a coffee first, get my head together.

I've had a busy morning, and I've just got back into the office after showing a woman around a fabulous apartment just a few minutes' drive away. Fifth floor in a newly built block. Concierge facilities, nice balcony, open-plan layout, communal rooftop garden with breathtaking views. One bedroom, but it's big. It reminded me a little of Harriet's place. A scaled-down version, obviously. Just under half a million. I'd be happy in a place like that though. Her offer of one hundred grand is just rude; clearly there's no way I'm accepting such a paltry amount. I need more, a lot more. I feel a flutter of nerves as I sit back down at my desk. I'm the only one here right now, but I can see from the shared calendar that two of the others will be back within the next half an hour. So, let's do this. I swallow a mouthful of coffee, take a deep, slow breath, then another, and dial the number she sent me.

'Hello, Harriet Hart speaking.'

She answers on the second ring.

'Hey. It's Nisha. How's your day going, Harriet?'

There's a pause on the line, then she says, 'Not great. I'm glad you called though. I was scared that … anyway, have you had enough time to think about my offer? What are your thoughts?'

My heart has started to pound.

'My thoughts?' I say, trying to keep my tone cool and calm. 'My thoughts are that one hundred grand is a bit of an insult, to be honest. My thoughts are that your career is on the line, and I can make all your problems go away, but that's a big ask, and one hundred grand simply doesn't cover it. You're going to have to do a lot better than that, I'm afraid.'

I hear a little gasp from Harriet, and then her voice again, higher pitched than before, a note of hysteria in it.

'But … Nisha, that's all I can easily get my hands on. I can't … look, one hundred grand is a lot of money, come on! And you *know* it's legally mine, and you *know* it's what your mother wanted, for me to have it. I'm offering you a reasonable compromise here. And it's *not* a big job, is it? For you to sort this mess out. It's one phone call, one letter from whoever that woman really was. One letter to say that her son lied, or that it was a misunderstanding, whatever. That I didn't touch him. One letter to withdraw the complaint and apologise for the trouble it caused. One hundred grand, for that? That's easy money, you know it is.'

I wait, patiently, until she finishes her little rant, rolling my eyes. Then I say:

'That's not the point, Harriet, and you know it. I'm not messing around any more, and I'm not waiting any longer either. I want one and a half million. One point five million, and I'll sort everything out for you at work and then leave you in peace. It's only a fraction of what I should have inherited, but it is what it is now. One point five million pounds. And I'm not negotiating. Take it or leave it.'

I can hear her breathing. She's practically panting now.

'One point five *million* pounds? Are you insane? I'd have to sell the apartment, and I *can't* … Nisha, *please*. Maybe I could get a bit more … look, there's one property I didn't sell, in Gloucester. It's just a little one-bedroom flat, nothing fancy, but I reckon it's worth around a hundred and sixty, something like that. If you could wait? I could put it on the market straightaway, I'm sure it would sell quickly. You can have all of it, whatever I get for that. Plus the hundred I've already offered you. That would be over a quarter of a million…'

'Not. Enough.'

I interrupt her.

She still has a flat in Gloucester, as well as the London apartment? I should have demanded more, *I think. But hey-ho…*

'I told you, no negotiations,' I say sharply. 'Sell the flat, *and* your penthouse. Whatever it takes. You don't have a choice, Harriet. If I don't get my money … I mean, you think things are bad for you now? You have no idea how much worse it could get. I know plenty of people who'd quite happily come forward and accuse you of things on my say-so. Your bosses might have let the first one go, and maybe you'll wiggle out of this one with Toby too. But if there are *more* accusations? No smoke without fire, eh? Think about it. Your career, your reputation … it's up to you. Your call.'

I'm feeling a little breathless myself now. It's a lie, what I just said about knowing lots of people who'd help me out with more false allegations. I've probably gone as far as I can, to be honest, but she doesn't know that. She's crying now, I realise, and it's not a nice sound, but I harden my heart. I can't go soft now, not when I'm so close. And I am, I can sense it.

'OK. OK, you win.'

It's barely a whisper, but my heart leaps.

'Good. We're agreed then? One point five million? By when? I need a date,' I say.

'I … I don't know. I need a bit of time, obviously. It's a lot of money. Erm…'

She hesitates, and I grin and silently punch the air. I've done it. I've freaking done it. A million and a half quid, on its way to my bank account…

'…three or four months?' she's saying. 'I'll get the Gloucester place on the market immediately, so you can have the money for that as soon as possible, like a sort of down payment? And I might be able to free up some more, from investments. It's just this place might take a bit longer to sell, and I'll have to clear it with my husband, and find somewhere else to live, and … can you wait, say four months?'

I stay silent for a few seconds before answering, just to make her think I'm considering her plea, but in reality I'd wait a year, if I had to.

'Fine. Four months,' I say. 'It's the seventh of March today, so let's settle on'—I scan the calendar on my desk—'the fourth of July. It's a Friday.'

'Friday, fourth of July. OK, deal,' she says. 'And in the meantime you'll…?'

'I need proof that you're serious about this first, then I'll make the call to the hospital,' I say. 'You can send me that 100K you offered for a start. And you'd better get that Gloucester place on the market pronto.'

'Right. I'll do it straightaway,' she says quietly. 'So … well, bye for now, then.'

'Bye, Harriet. Keep in touch,' I reply, and a moment later the line goes dead. I drop my phone onto my desk and stare at it for a moment, then let out a whoop.

Yessssssss!

I jump to my feet and boogie around the office, not even caring that people walking past outside can see me through the huge window. It's an estate agent's, isn't it? They'll just think I'm celebrating a big sale or something. Except what I'm actually celebrating is a lot bigger than that.

One point five million. I can buy somewhere outright, live rent and mortgage-free. Buy a car, have a holiday, invest some cash for my future. And it's all going to happen in the next four months. Yes! YES!

I sit down again, feeling a little breathless and remembering that two of my colleagues could walk in at any moment now, but I'm smiling so widely my cheeks ache.

The fourth of July. Independence Day in the US. And now my Independence Day too.

I cannot bloody wait.

Chapter Thirty-Nine

ELLA

S tay calm. Interviews are no big deal, just be charming and professional. You've got this.

I've been giving myself a little pep talk for the past five minutes, and as I emerge from the tube station and stop to check the map on my phone, I've almost convinced myself that today is going to go brilliantly and I'll return to Harriet's this evening with the news that I have a new job already. *Almost.* I'm probably over-qualified for all the roles I have interviews for today, so my experience isn't going to be an issue. It's just the little matter of explaining away the past few months. I can't exactly say I was conned into taking a job in Gloucester which then basically disappeared into thin air, and then moved to a job here in London and got fired within two weeks for repeatedly getting pissed and being too hungover to make it in on time. I've settled on a story which might just work; I'm going to say that my mother is terminally ill with cancer (true), and that I've had to take the past four months off work to help care for her (obviously not true, but I doubt they'll check). I've been thinking about my mother a lot over the past few days, and every time I do I want to cry.

Would she let me visit her again, I wonder? I just suddenly feel that I want to try, one more time, but...

I sigh and try to push her out of my head. A lie that involves my dying mum does not feel good, but I don't know what else to say, and as long as I don't get flustered, or start blushing, I should get away with it. But I'm definitely not feeling my usual confident self this morning, and as I traipse down the busy street towards my first appointment, at a small tapas bar that opens at midday for lunch and carries on until late, my thoughts drift back to the hospital and Harriet. I'm not really surprised *my* employment was terminated – all my own fault after all. But what's happened to her is just crazy. The kid claiming she touched him up is mad enough, but that other thing on the bus? I really can't imagine anyone less likely to start videoing a man's nether regions than Harriet; it's laughable. I still don't really get why she didn't tell me or George about it though, and I can understand why he was pretty peed off about that. But what's worrying me more now is who's doing this to her, because it certainly seems like someone has a bit of a vendetta. And who could hate Harriet enough to do something like that? Nobody, that's who. It's all down to me, I'm certain of that, and that's what's adding to my nerves today, adding to my desperation to get a new job as quickly as possible, so I can get out of her hair. She's been so good to me, and if me staying in her home really has brought this nightmare to her door, and they're targeting her now because she's a mate of mine, I'm not sure how I'm going to forgive myself. She could lose her *career*, for pity's sake.

I've relaxed too much recently, I realise now. I let my guard down far, far too soon. I even dismissed those couple of times I thought I saw someone hanging around, watching or maybe following me, putting it down to my overactive imagination, not letting it worry me. And now look what's happened. Harriet's in the shit. George is unhappy. It's such a mess. I've brought misery to their door, and now I need to leave again, as soon as I can. Once I'm out on my own, maybe I can finally get to the bottom of all this, but it's the last time I'm going to involve anyone else, I just *can't*…

I stop walking, spotting the tapas bar just across the road, and look down at the phone in my hand, checking the time. I'm two minutes early. Perfect.

OK, forget everything else for now. Focus. You've got this, I think, pausing for a few seconds to compose myself. Then I look right and left and march across the street.

Fifteen minutes later, I'm walking back to the tube station feeling rather less sprightly. That did *not* go well; the manager seemed to think my lack of bar and cocktail-making experience was a deal-breaker, even though I stressed what a quick learner I am and that every other element of the job was perfect for me.

'I'm sorry. I need someone who can hit the ground running,' she said. 'I simply don't have time to train someone with no bartending skills, and you really should have pointed out that you don't have any in your application.'

Well, if you'd actually read *my CV, you'd have known, and not wasted both our mornings*, I felt like saying, but I managed to stop myself.

So – on to the next, an Italian deli and coffee shop two tube stops away. This sounds ideal for me, and I have high hopes as I push the door open. The place is adorable: a charming Italian grandmother behind a counter groaning with delicious-looking salami and chorizo, red and white checked tablecloths, traditional music playing on the sound system. Unfortunately for me, the job applicant who arrived for interview an hour before me was apparently equally charmed by what she saw and also so suitable for the position that she was offered it on the spot.

'I'm *so* sorry! I was just looking for your number to call you, but I seem to have lost it. Here, have some pepperoni and garlic bread, on the house, as an apology,' the grandmother gushed, pushing a neatly wrapped paper parcel into my hands.

Free food aside, it really is *not* my day. Interview three is no better, but at least this time it's me who decides it's a big fat no. What had sounded like a cool, modern diner in the job ad turned out to be a grubby little café with grease-stained laminated menus and a man slouched over a table in one corner, snoring loudly.

'Don't mind Frank. He has a couple of pints for breakfast and then sleeps it off before lunch. He'll soon wake up when he sees you though, love. You'll get him going,' the owner told me, leering at me through smeared spectacles then making a hand gesture that seemed to imply that my presence would get Frank going in an area of his body I really didn't want to think about. I made my excuses and left, pronto.

Shit, I think now, nibbling disconsolately on a pepperoni stick as I stare blankly out of the tube window. While I waited on the platform, in desperation I sent an email to one of my old modelling agencies, the one I had the least serious falling out with, the one which still got me very occasional bookings while I worked on my catering career. I told them I was hoping that after a long break I might be able to resurrect my career in front of the camera, and asked if they'd consider representing me again. I'm not holding out much hope; it's been ages since my last gig, and that was just a very low-budget catalogue shoot: two hours being shot from the waist down in a series of increasingly ugly pairs of patterned leggings. Still, beggars can't be choosers, as the rather unpleasant old saying goes. I'd been so hoping I'd be able to go back to Harriet with some good news about today. She seemed so low all weekend, cooped up in her bedroom most of the time. Once or twice George tried half-heartedly to get her to come and join us in the living room, but she wasn't having it and he actually seemed quite relieved that she said no. They are *definitely* going through a sticky patch. I feel *so* sorry for her, and almost as sorry for him. I saw a softer side to George when he opened up to me about wanting a baby so much; now his relationship with Harriet seems to be under even more strain. And today I'm going to have to go back and tell them that I'm still unemployed, still a burden. It's crap. *Everything* is just crap.

The tube is slowing, my stop approaching. Feeling despondent, I stand up and make my way to the doors, suddenly feeling like bursting into tears.

Chapter Forty

HARRIET

I'm on a train from London Victoria, heading for Brighton. I haven't told anyone I'm leaving the city; I haven't even left a note. This morning, after George left for work and Ella for her day of job interviews, I paced the apartment like a caged tiger until suddenly, I couldn't bear it a moment longer. I *had* to get out of there, had to get away from everyone and everything. Had to go somewhere I could be alone, somewhere I could breathe, somewhere I could *think*. I love the sea, I always have, and Brighton may be just an hour away, but every time I go there it feels like a *world* away from my normal life in London. Regency squares and crescents, the iconic pier, the quirky little shops in The Lanes and, of course, the seafront with its pebbled shore and multi-coloured beach huts. It's a cool, bright day, and as the train picks up speed, I yearn to be on that beach so much I can almost smell the salty air and feel the breeze in my hair.

I *will* tell George where I am, later. I'll send him a message, tell him I just needed to get away for a night to clear my head, tell him not to worry. When I think about George, I feel an actual, physical ache. That story he told me, about the dentist … my *God*. I know he says he believes me, that he says he trusts I'm telling the truth about the accusations against me. But what if, somewhere deep down, he's not a hundred per cent sure? What if he's doubting me? What if he thinks, even a tiny bit, that he might be married to someone who has something in common with that monstrous figure from his past? And yet, as much as that's tearing me apart, I can't focus on it right now. I have a more pressing concern, that I can't share with George. Can't share with anyone, although I may be about to change my mind on that one. Nisha, and her staggering demand.

One and a half million pounds. One and a half *million*.

I agreed to it, but only because I had to. What choice did I have? I was in a spin, terrified. I'd have agreed to anything. But now that a few days have passed, I'm starting to think a little more clearly, and that's what this trip is all about. I intend to go home with a *plan*. Yes, I'll have to give her *some* money, and that's fine. The secret account cash and post office savings are available immediately, and to make up the rest of that initial hundred grand I just need to get to my bank. There's a branch in Brighton, I've already checked; I have some fixed rate ISAs, and the only way to access the cash in them now, before the end of their fixed terms, is to close my accounts, which they won't let me do online. Once that's done, first thing in the morning, I'll get on another train, and travel to Gloucester. Over the weekend, telling George and Ella I was exhausted and didn't feel like being sociable, I hid away in the bedroom and managed to fix up an appointment with a local estate agent, who's going to meet me at the flat there early afternoon. It took a while to find one who could act so quickly, and who would agree to come and value the property and take pictures for the sales page of their website all on the same day. But eventually, after stressing how urgent it was, and how busy I am as a 'top doctor in a London hospital', I found someone who said they could get the place online with a basic listing by Thursday.

'The floor plan and the EPC – you know, the Energy Performance Certificate – will take an extra couple of days to sort out but we can add those later,' he said. His name is Trent, and he sounded young and enthusiastic on the phone. 'Apartments like that sell super-fast, so I don't think you'll have a problem. I reckon we'll get an offer on the table within a week.'

I told him that sounded good to me, then dug out the two sets of keys I have for the flat and slipped them into my travel bag so I wouldn't forget them. Once Nisha sees the property listed for sale online, and has one hundred grand in her bank account, surely that will be enough to show my commitment? But if she really thinks she's getting a massive payday here, she can think again.

No. Frigging. Way.

If she honestly believes I'm going to hand over one point five million quid, if she thinks I'm going to move out of my beautiful home, she must need her head examined. And tonight, I'm going to apply myself to this little problem and find a solution to it. I'm already part of the way there; by the morning, I intend to have it all pinned down.

Brighton is as much of a joy as it always is. I'd booked a sea-view room in a boutique hotel, a converted, four-storey Georgian townhouse, and to my delight my room is on the top floor and has a tiny, sheltered balcony. There's white linen and a soft woollen throw on the bed and a big, comfortable armchair and it's *perfect*. I check in, then go for a long walk on the beach, letting the thoughts tumble through my brain, then slowly reorganise themselves. Then I wander into The Lanes and take a break in a little coffee shop, where I nab a window seat, nibble on an iced bun and make notes in a small leather-covered notebook. Back at the hotel I sit on a velvet sofa in the bar, quiet on this Monday evening, and sip a glass of merlot, then take another glass up to my room and order room service, a grilled squid starter followed by beef casserole and a lemon tart for dessert. By nine o'clock, I feel calm, resolute and exhausted, and I climb into the king-sized bed and sleep better than I have in weeks.

This morning I'm up early; after a quick tea and croissant in the breakfast room, the closing of my ISA accounts goes smoothly, and soon I'm on the train to Gloucester. Trent is as bright and helpful as he sounded on the phone, and takes details of the flat and supervises the photography cheerfully and efficiently, telling me again he thinks the place will sell quickly – that he already, in fact, has two potential buyers lined up – and as I board the train for the return journey to London, I feel my spirits lifting.

It's all coming together. I have a plan of action, and there's only one more hurdle to jump before I can start to implement it. One person whom I have to persuade to help me.

Ella.

Yes. I'm bringing Ella in on this now. She'll help me, because she won't have a choice, I'll make sure of that. And then I'm going to kill two birds with one stone. Get rid of both of them, for good.

Chapter Forty-One

ELLA

'So what's all this about? You're making me nervous, Harriet.'

I've just sat down opposite her at the kitchen breakfast bar. We're on our own in the apartment; George has gone to work, and I was just dressing after my shower when Harriet tapped on my bedroom door and asked me if I had a few minutes for a chat. She looked serious and, I thought, a little nervous. I immediately felt my stomach lurch. I'm pretty sure she's about to ask me to move out, and the prospect of having to sleep in my car again is making me feel sick. She's made me a coffee, and there's a plate of fresh, warm pastries and a pot of honey on the table. She must have been out to the bakery as soon as it opened again; she knows how I love to drizzle honey across a croissant, so she's clearly paving the way for a difficult conversation, and what else can it be?

I pick up my coffee and meet her eye, bracing myself. She went away on Monday without telling me or George in advance; she messaged later in the day, saying she'd gone to

Brighton for the night, needing a bit of space and a break after everything that's happened recently. George was upset, and a bit annoyed, but when she arrived home last night they seemed to make it up, although she went to bed early, looking tired and drained. Now, she still looks on edge, taking sips of her tea and poking at the Danish on her plate, but I can't wait any longer. If this is going to happen today, I need to get it over with.

'Go on then, shoot,' I say.

She puts her mug down and sighs.

'I need to tell you something,' she says. 'And, well, I think you might be a bit shocked.'

She pauses, takes a breath, exhales, then leans back in her chair.

'But I think you'll understand, when I tell you the reason.'

'The reason? The reason for what?' I ask, but in my head I'm saying: *I know, I know, you need me to move out...*

'The reason I've been doing what I've been doing for the past six months,' she says. 'Because, you see...'

Another pause.

'...everything that's happened to you – Lena Fox, Mug & Meadow, you losing the Cloisters job, and the job at the hospital, all of it – that was me, Ella. I did it all. I planned it, I orchestrated it. It was all me. Not your mum, not someone you used to work with. Me. It was me.'

I stare at her for a moment, then laugh.

'Oh, fuck off! Don't be ridiculous. Why are you saying that?'

She shrugs.

'I'm not joking, Ella. It was me. But I had a very good reason, trust me.'

I laugh again.

'But ... it can't have been. Seriously, Harriet, stop this, you're freaking me out. It wasn't you, don't piss about. You're the one who *saved* me from it all. Why would you ... Harriet, come on...'

She's not laughing though. Not even smiling, and bewilderment is beginning to numb my brain now, my heart starting to thud. Why would she say such a thing? And yet ... the way she's looking at me, the expression on her face ... she's telling the truth, isn't she? Oh my God, she's telling the truth...

'But ... how? *Why*? *Fuck*! Do you have any idea what I went through? I gave up everything ... I had to sleep in my *car*, for fuck's sake! I was so scared ... why? WHY?'

I leap from my seat, and as I shout the last word at her I thump the breakfast bar so hard that my mug quivers, sloshing coffee over the rim. She sits there calmly, just watching me. Then she says:

'I'll tell you why. As I said, I think you'll understand. And then I have a proposition for you. Do you want to sit down again? This might take a while.'

'For *fuck's* sake...'

I can't seem to stop swearing. I shake my head, hands on my hips, breathing heavily, glaring at her, but she simply gestures at my chair, clearly waiting for me to sit again before she speaks, and so, still muttering expletives under my breath, I do.

'Go on then. I literally can't even *imagine*...'

'You don't have to imagine. I'm going to tell you,' she says. 'And please, just let me speak. Just let me get through it. If you have questions, I'll answer them afterwards.'

And so she tells me. She starts right back when we were

housemates, saying something about me 'copying her' all the time, which confused me a bit (did I do that? *All* the time? Maybe a little, almost accidentally, just like I've done again recently, but not so anyone would notice, surely?) before getting to the meat of the matter: the night she was away at her parents and I slept with Felix, and she came back unexpectedly and caught us at it. I almost interrupt her at that point – *all of this, because I slept with a stupid man years ago?* – but she raises a hand, and carries on, and then she tells me what it's really been all about, and my blood turns to ice. A pregnancy, a baby, a miscarriage. Her resulting infertility. Her heartbreak. Her future crumbling in front of her. *What?*

'Harriet … oh, Harriet … I didn't know…' I whisper, but she shakes her head and carries on, as I sit there, listening, feeling numb, horrified. She tells me how it was all my fault. How she planned my punishment in her head for years, how the money she inherited finally made it possible. And then the astonishing details of how she did it, from hiring an actor (Lena Fox is an *actor*! No wonder I couldn't find her … no wonder she looked so different when I saw her in the street … Lena doesn't *exist*) to everything that's happened since. By the time she's finished I feel weak, wrung out, utterly bereft. I can't, just *can't*, take this in. I actually thought she was still my friend, despite that little glitch back in our house-sharing days. I'd genuinely thought she'd forgiven me. But it clearly wasn't just a little glitch, was it? It was the beginning of the end, the beginning of something I could never have imagined in my worst nightmares.

All of this was *Harriet. All* of it. She sent someone to mix chemicals in a toilet to make sure I lost my second job in Gloucester. She broke into my car. She *drugged* me, for Christ's

sake. Lost me another job. Made me think I was ill. And …
fuck … she even let me go and throw accusations at my mother.
My mother, who actually *is* ill, terminally ill. How *could* she?

'How *could* you?' I say, when I can finally speak. 'This is …
this is *insane*. You're crazy. OK, I shagged your boyfriend, and I
am so, so sorry about the baby, and everything else but …
Harriet, that wasn't my fault. I know seeing me and Felix
together upset you, but you can't know that was what caused
your miscarriage! It could have happened anyway, these things
happen to women all the time, and I know it's tragic, but …
come on! To try to ruin my life, so many years later. *Seriously*?
And why take me in? Why let me come and stay with you
when I rang you? Why help me? If you really wanted to
destroy me, you could have just left me out there on the streets.
I don't get it. And … George? Does George know about all
this?'

'No. George knows nothing. He knows I miscarried and
ended up with complications, but not about any of the rest of
it. Not about you, or what I've been doing. And he can't know,
Ella, OK? He *can't* know.'

Her tone is fierce, and I wonder why on earth she thinks I
will ever agree to keep this a secret from her husband, but I let
her carry on.

'And as for you moving in here, it wasn't planned,' she
says. 'Well, obviously it wasn't; the last thing I expected was
for you to call *me*. I was just going to leave you to get on with
things, after the Cloisters thing. I thought I'd done enough, and
that even though you'd never know it was me who'd done it
all, I had the satisfaction of knowing I'd messed up your life.
Nothing like what you did to me of course – and by the way,
that *was* down to you, Ella. I don't care what you think. I know

that baby would have lived if it hadn't been for what you did that night. But anyway. When you phoned, telling me you needed help, it was like … I don't know, like the icing on the cake or something. As if the universe was saying, "Go on, keep going. You've got a chance here to screw her over even more, why not take it?" And I just thought how much easier it would be, with you right here, instead of trying to do it at a distance. So I decided to carry on for a bit. And here we are.'

She raises her eyebrows, a little half smile on her face, and I gape at her, astounded.

'So here we are?' I repeat, sarcasm dripping from my tone. 'And where are we, exactly, Harriet? Because I'm not really a lot worse off than I was when I arrived here, to be honest. But you – look at you. You're the one in trouble now, you're the one whose big fancy career's heading down the toilet. Looks a lot like karma to me.'

I'm the one with a sneering smile on my face now. Inside, I'm still reeling – it's going to take a long time to process all this, and I'm still struggling with the enormity of it – but surely she must see how pointless it's all been? Then I remember what she said before she told me all this – what was that about a proposition?

Her smile has faded, and she's regarding me coldly.

'You said you had a proposition for me,' I say. 'What's all that about then?'

She rests her chin on her hands and closes her eyes for a second, then opens them again.

'It's about what's been happening to *me*,' she says. 'Because it's not karma, Ella. It's not just bad luck. I've been persecuted by someone too. And that's what I want your help with, because…'

'My help? *My. Help*? Are you mad?' I spit the words at her, suddenly furious, but she ignores me and carries on talking.

'...because you're right. You've been through some not-so-nice stuff, but you're actually not that much worse off than you were before. You can find another job, and rebuild. But that will take time, Ella, and lots of hard work, and yes, I know you're not afraid of hard work. I was actually seriously impressed with what you did with Mug & Meadow and how quickly you made a success of it...'

'Wow,' I interrupt her again, and to my surprise I suddenly feel my fury begin to dissipate. A compliment now? This *woman*...

'Thanks. I really loved it,' I say quietly. 'It was a great business idea. It could really have gone places.'

She nods slowly.

'Probably. Too late now though. But back to what I was saying: I've been persecuted by someone too. I'll tell you all about it in a minute, but what I'm proposing is this. I need someone to help me stop her. This person who's behind what's been happening to *me*. The one who's behind my suspension. And if you agree to help, I'll pay you one hundred and fifty grand, on the understanding that you never tell anyone what I've done to you, and you move away and don't come back. Abroad, ideally. No more contact. Do the job, take the money and go. We'll be quits, forever.'

My eyes widen. I've never felt less inclined to help anyone in my life but ... one hundred and fifty grand? *Shit*. That's ... that's a pretty life-changing sum for someone in my position. Enough to start my own Mug & Meadow, or something similar... Is she for real?

'What would I have to do?' I ask. 'And who is she, this mysterious person? What's her beef with you?'

She picks up her mug, looks into it and grimaces.

'Cold. Shall we get another drink first? Actually, do you want a glass of wine? I think I need a drink.'

'It's not even 10am, Harriet,' I reply. Then, 'Oh, sod it. Today's screwed anyway now. My head is mashed. Go on. Try not to drug it though, if you don't mind.'

She looks at me askance for a moment, then, to my great surprise, emits a little snort of laughter.

'I'll try to resist,' she says, and even though I try to stop it, I feel a grin spreading across my face. Almost immediately, the atmosphere in the room changes.

Is this a good *thing, what's just happened?* I think, as Harriet walks to the drinks cabinet, stands there scrutinising it for a few moments, then selects a bottle of something red. I realise that my anger is now being rapidly replaced by … *relief.* I feel *hugely* relieved, in fact. Because now I *know.* Suddenly, no longer is my persecutor a shadowy, unknown figure from my past. It's Harriet, and she's right here in front of me, and all the fear and confusion have vanished, just like that. I'm still *shocked*; I still think her actions have been utterly bonkers, the scale of her revenge plot against me astonishing. And although I'm desperately sorry about the pain she must have felt, I still *don't* feel responsible for her losing her child, because how can we ever really know what caused that? But I did take her boyfriend, and she wasn't the only woman I did something like that to, back in the day, so maybe I *did* deserve to be punished in some way. But now I know exactly what's been going on. And now I have a chance to walk away from this with a fat lump sum in my pocket. Is it too good to be true, though? What will I have to do, before I can move on?

She's back now, two glasses of red wine in her hands. I take one, then peer exaggeratedly into its depths and sniff it theatrically, and she laughs again and gestures towards the big sofa in the living area.

'Shall we sit somewhere more comfortable?' she asks.

We sit, and each take a sip of wine, and for a few moments there's silence. Outside it's sunny, dust mites dancing in a shaft of bright light coming in through the vast window, the polished floor gleaming.

'Right. Let me tell you about Nisha Cartwright,' she says.

And off she goes again. The tale of her elderly next-door neighbour Farah, and her wayward daughter Nisha, cut out of her will. Nisha's attempts to get back what she feels is rightfully hers, and what she's now done to Harriet after she refused to play ball.

'Wow. She's as sneaky and conniving as you. Well, almost,' I say, when she's finished, and she smiles. It almost feels as if we've reached an uneasy truce.

'Almost,' she agrees. 'So now, I've agreed to pay her one point five million pounds, to bugger off and leave me alone, even though it's definitely not what Farah would have wanted...'

'One point five *million*? What the...?' I splutter, but she shakes her head.

'No, no, don't worry. I have no intention of actually giving it to her. I'd have to sell this place, for a start, and there's no way I'm going to do that. And, like everything else, George doesn't know about any of *this* either, Ella, and I have no plans to tell him, OK? So, Nisha. I'm about to hand over one hundred grand that I've managed to release from savings accounts, just to keep her quiet for now. And I've put the Gloucester flat – your flat – on the market. I've told her she can have the proceeds from that too. But that's not what's going to happen. That's where the money I'm going to pay *you* will come from. George doesn't know the place even exists, so I can easily get away with that. Nisha's not getting a penny more. And that's where you come in.'

I raise an eyebrow.

'Go on,' I say.

'I have a plan,' she says. 'A plan to get rid of her once and for all. Giving her the hundred grand will buy us time, and we have until the beginning of July anyway; that's when I've agreed to hand over the full amount. But I can't do this on my own, so I need your help. You can carry on living here in the meantime; I'll pay your way until it's done. And then you get your money, and you go. And you never breathe a word. To George, or to anyone. Do we have a deal?'

I pick up my glass and take another slug of wine.

'That depends. What are we going to do? How are we going to get rid of her, as you put it? She doesn't sound like someone who's going to go away easily?'

Harriet picks up her own glass, and raises it in the air.

'We're going to kill her,' she says.

Chapter Forty-Two

HARRIET

I t's been a bit of a mad twenty-four hours, but this afternoon I feel more together, more in control, than I have in a while. True to his word, my jolly little estate agent Trent managed to get the Gloucester flat on the market first thing this morning, and the listing looks good. I sent the link to Nisha, as proof I'm moving things along; ten minutes ago, I also transferred the one hundred thousand pounds to her bank account. She replied almost immediately, telling me it had arrived, and actually thanked me. She's welcome to it; it's the last money she's ever going to receive from me, so I hope she enjoys it.

In more good news, after thinking about it all day yesterday, Ella told me earlier that she's willing to do it: she's going to help me get rid of Nisha. I wasn't entirely sure she'd go for it; after all, deciding to help someone commit murder is a pretty massive thing to agree to. But I kind of had a feeling that, with that sort of money on the table, she might be tempted, and I was right. Plus, I threw in a little threat, just to help her decision-making process.

'It's up to you,' I said. 'But if you don't help me, not only will you leave here penniless, but I might just go to the police and tell them I caught you stealing from us. That money has started going missing, and that it only started happening when you moved in…'

'But I didn't … I would *never*…' she spluttered, and then she got it, and shook her head slowly.

'You absolute cow,' she said.

I shrugged.

'I mean, who are they going to believe, two doctors or a homeless, unemployed loser?' I said bitchily. 'And trust me, I can manufacture evidence. Look at what I've done to you already. It wouldn't be hard. Enough evidence to send you to prison, I reckon. But as I said, up to you.'

She didn't really have a choice, did she?

'You win,' she said, eventually. 'Fine. Whatever. Let's just get it over with and then we'll never have to see each other again.'

She seems to have accepted it now. A done deal. We're even getting on quite well, on the surface anyway. A lull in the hostilities. Putting on a good show for George and anyone else who happens to be around. The thing is, of course, that we're not actually going to kill Nisha at all. Can you even imagine? I would never, *ever*, no matter what she did to me. I'm a doctor; I *save* lives, not deliberately end them. But I just need Ella to *think* that we're going to kill her. It's all part of my grand plan, and if it works, which I believe it will, I'll be free of both of them, and what a joy that will be. For now though, I just need to keep my wits about me, and carry on as if everything is proceeding nicely. I need Nisha to keep thinking I'm gradually getting her money together, and Ella to believe we're putting a plan together to eliminate Nisha. So, onwards.

We have the apartment to ourselves again this afternoon, and Ella has just come in from a walk, her cheeks flushed, her hair scraped back in a tight ponytail.

'Is this a good time?' I say, and she looks at me questioningly. She's pulling her jacket off and she's just wearing a short-sleeved blouse underneath, black and white, like her tattoo. It's been raining today, but it's mild outside, the official start of spring only about a week away now.

'To have a chat about what we're going to do,' I clarify. 'You know, when we…'

I leave the sentence unfinished, and she hesitates for a moment, then nods.

'Sure,' she says. 'I'll just go and put my coat away.'

When she returns, we sit down together at the small round table by the kitchen's floor-to-ceiling window. I have my notebook on the table in front of me and I pick up my pen and wave it at her.

'So,' I say. 'There are obviously a few things we need to decide. We know the date – fourth of July. I'm going to say there's some paperwork I need Nisha to sign before I can transfer the money; I don't think it will be hard to get her to meet up with me in person if she thinks she's about to become a millionaire. And obviously she'll have to get the hospital complaint withdrawn in advance of that too. Plus I'm going to tell her before we meet up that you'll be with me. I'll just say I'm bringing a friend I trust, because I'm anxious at being on my own with her or something.'

'OK. That should work. Where are we going to meet though? At her place?' Ella asks.

'No, I'm thinking somewhere on neutral ground. A hotel room, maybe. Leave that with me for a bit. It's *how* we're going to do the deed I've been focusing on for now. I've had a good think, and I reckon something she can drink is going to be the easiest.'

'So you're going to drug her? Like you did me?'

Ella looks at me quizzically.

'Well, not quite like I did with you. You're still alive. And I am sorry about that, you know. That was…'

I look down at the table, trying to choose my words carefully. She did seem particularly shocked when she found out about me slipping medication into her drinks, so I need to tread carefully here. I still need to keep her on side as much as possible.

'…that was a step too far,' I say. 'But what I gave you – well, it might not have been very pleasant in the short term…'

'It wasn't,' she says darkly. 'I don't think I've ever felt so ill in my life. Well, other than that time when we lived together and I got so drunk on margaritas at that Mexican bar in Soho that I fell asleep on the bus home and then woke up and vomited all over my skirt, do you remember?'

I smile.

'How could I forget?' I reply. 'And I think that was actually *my* skirt. I lent it to you for the evening. I don't think I was ever able to wear it again after that. Anyway … I'm sorry I made you feel ill. But there'll be no long-term damage, I promise. It was just a bit too much antihistamine. Whereas what I'm planning to serve to Nisha is going to be … well, let's say the effects will be more long-lasting. Permanent, in fact.'

Ella looks down and starts picking at one of her cuticles.

'This is a lot,' she says, still picking. She looks up again. 'But don't worry, I'm not backing out. I know you didn't exactly give me much choice, but even so. If I say I'll do something, I'll do it. How are you going to get your hands on this drug though, if you're not at work? It doesn't exactly sound like the kind of thing you can buy online.'

I shake my head.

'Definitely not. But I know where we can get it. Or I should say, where *you* can get it. You're going to have to do that bit for me, Ella.'

Chapter Forty-Three

NISHA

I've been on a high all week. It's happening. It's really happening, after all this time. I couldn't quite believe it when Harriet transferred that money to my account. Up until then, I still had my doubts; although she'd sounded beaten when I spoke to her on the phone, I wondered if she might find some way of backtracking, of wriggling out of our agreement. But clearly, she's realised it's in her own best interests to keep me happy. And now, probably for the first time since I was a kid, I have *no* money worries. So much cash, just sitting there, waiting for me to spend it! I had a couple of bills to settle, so I did that first, and then I paid Polly and Jake for the bus thing and Letisha and Toby for the hospital thing. Debts settled. Toby was over the moon with his new games console in particular; I got him the very latest model in the end, the one above the one he'd asked me for. He deserves it. But other than that, I haven't spent much. Well, there was a pair of shoes I couldn't resist in Selfridges. Louboutins, spiky little black numbers, just under seven hundred quid. A girl needs a treat now and again. But otherwise, I'm biding my time. I'll wait until it's all there, all that lovely cash, and then I'll have a proper splurge. I'll go house-shopping too. I'm already looking, seriously this time, earmarking a few possibilities. It's so exciting I'm struggling to focus on work, but I need to try, so now I sit down at my desk to check my schedule for this afternoon, and as I slide my chair in and tap my mouse to wake up my computer, an email notification pops up on my mobile. Harriet. Again, so soon? My stomach rolls – I'm not sure why – and I pick up the phone and open the message.

Hi Nisha,

Just to let you know I accepted an offer on the Gloucester apartment this morning. We got 5k over the asking price so I'm pretty happy with that. There's no chain so we're estimating eight to 12 weeks for the sale to go through, meaning it should easily be done by our agreed date. I'll keep you posted.

Regards
Harriet

GET IN! I fist-bump myself, then realise that Gav, who's on the phone at his desk on the other side of the office, is eyeing me strangely. I don't even care; I just grin and wink at him, and he rolls his eyes and turns his attention back to his conversation. I read the email again, just to make sure, then pick up the bottle of water next to my keyboard and take a long drink, trying to compose myself. It's going almost too well, and I can't quite believe it. That was *such* a quick sale. I mean, she did tell me she thought it would go fast, and it did look decent online, but it's literally only been one week…

Just to check, I bring up the Gloucester estate agent's website and search for the listing. There it is, and she's not lying. It's marked 'SOLD, STC'. Sold, subject to contract. It's real. The flat is effectively off the market, and as long as the buyers have their mortgage in place, and the conveyancing process all goes smoothly, and there are no problems with surveys and searches, well … eight to twelve weeks, as Harriet said. Bingo.

I haven't seen *her* place on the market yet though. I've been checking all the property websites, and no sign of it. Maybe she's got a private buyer lined up. Maybe she's worked out some other way of raising my money, and doesn't need to sell after all. Maybe she's decided to release some equity from the place or something. Maybe I should ask her.

I sit and think about that. Then I think about the one hundred grand, and the flat she's already sold, and I decide to leave it. She's proved herself enough for now. Maybe I'll actually back off, leave her to get on with it. She's been pretty good at keeping me updated so far. If it all goes quiet, I'll chivvy her along a bit. But I won't ask Letisha to withdraw the complaint to the hospital, not just yet. If that happens too soon, it might stall or even stop this lovely process that Harriet's started so well. But for now, the girl's doing OK. I'm not good at being patient, that's the only thing. But it's already … I check my calendar … the twentieth of March. That's … I count the weeks. Just under fifteen weeks to go. Less than four months to financial freedom. I've waited this long. *Years.* What's fifteen weeks? Roll on July. I smile, then jump as my desk phone rings. OK. Concentrate. Back to work. It's all going to be fine. Better than fine. It's going to be FUCKING FANTASTIC.

I smile again, then grab the phone.

'Hello, Nisha Cartwright speaking, how can I help?'

Chapter Forty-Four

ELLA

Six weeks later

I pass through the main doors of MediWest Hospital, and walk briskly through reception, not glancing right or left. It's busy as always – staff, visitors, the odd patient in pyjamas making their way towards the entrance for an illicit smoke – and nobody's looking at me. I'm wearing hospital scrubs, just another doctor: that's what I'm supposed to be anyway, but as I hit the button for the lift to the second floor, my mouth feels dry and my stomach is fluttering. What if someone recognises me? Can I really get away with this? Harriet seems to think I can.

'You always wore make-up to work in the canteen,' she said this morning, as she helped me get ready. 'It's been a couple of months now anyway, and you do look quite different bare-faced, and with all your hair piled up under the scrub cap, and the glasses … here, put them on.'

I took the black, square-framed glasses from her. She'd

ordered them online, with clear lenses, no prescription. We'd had to hide them from George when they arrived; we've been hiding a lot from George recently and doing a very good job of it. The poor man is still completely clueless. I did think, briefly, about telling him everything. Telling him what his wife is really like. Telling him everything she's done to me recently, and what she's planning to do next. But I quickly changed my mind again. I can't, can I? Because I *did* bring some of this on myself. Because I can't risk Harriet getting me into serious trouble with the police, which she's clearly more than capable of doing. Because if I just keep my head down now, I at least have a chance of walking away into a brighter future. I'm in this up to my neck, and I just need to put my big girl pants on and get on with it. And so this morning I took the specs from Harriet and pushed them onto my nose, and she took a step backwards and surveyed me critically.

'I think that's pretty darn good. Honestly, *I* wouldn't even recognise you if you passed me in the corridor. You're going to be fine.'

She'd convinced me she'd never get away with doing this herself; that she was so familiar to all the medics that one of them would be bound to spot her and wonder why she was at the hospital when she was still on suspension, and that's probably true, to be fair. And so here *I* am, disguised as a doctor and about to attempt an audacious theft. What has my life become?

The past six weeks have been so strange. Harriet had said she'd pay my way while we waited for the fourth of July and D-Day, but quite unexpectedly I heard from that old modelling agency days after I agreed to help her with Nisha, and suddenly I was back in front of the camera again. It's been nothing major, just a few shoots for the website of a gothic and grunge fashion brand who liked the look of my tattoo, but it's been fun, plus it's meant I've been earning some money and not having to spend every day hanging around the apartment with Harriet. That's been uncomfortable, at times, even though we've both clearly been trying to rub along together without too much friction; but quite apart from what's going on with me and her, she and George still don't seem terribly happy, and she's drinking too much, often opening a bottle at three or four in the afternoon when he's at work. I've been trying to stay out of her way as much as possible, going for long walks and retiring to my room early in the evenings to watch TV with a mug of cocoa, counting the days. I did ask her *why* we had to wait until July, if she has no intention of raising the money to pay Nisha: if what we're really going to do is *kill* her, why not just get it over with, and arrange to meet up with her sooner? But she shook her head vehemently.

'I need time, to get all the details right,' she said. 'I need to put some stuff in place for afterwards; I might go away for a bit, just to be on the safe side. And I don't want her to get suspicious. She's not stupid, and she's an estate agent too now; she'll know how long things take with selling property and so on. There's no rush. It'll be worth the wait.'

Harriet's suspension is ongoing indefinitely; to her huge relief, the police finally got in touch to say they wouldn't be proceeding with any criminal charges, as there was no actual evidence she'd touched the teenage boy inappropriately, just his say-so, his word against hers. But there's still the General Medical Council investigation, which as expected is taking a long time. Harriet had hoped that Nisha might have arranged for the complaint to be withdrawn when she received her one hundred thousand pounds, but as yet we're still waiting for her to decide to do that; the Gloucester flat sale, source of *my* payment, is proceeding well though, but it's going to be another four or five weeks before the completion date, so for now, it's all a waiting game. In the meantime, we're polishing our plan, and today is a big one. Today, Harriet has sent me into the hospital to steal the drug we're going to use to kill Nisha.

Now, when I say, 'kill Nisha', I don't really mean that, obviously. That's just me going along with Harriet's narrative. I was so shocked when she first told me that was what she was planning that for a few moments I could barely breathe. She's clearly unhinged; anyone who did what she did to me, no matter what the motive, can't be entirely sane, although I've sort of made my peace with that. But this? To kill another human being, when you're a *doctor*?

Off. The. Scale.

I thought about what to do about it for nearly twenty-four hours after we'd talked. I was awake most of that night, staring into the darkness, the thoughts chasing each other round my head. The murder she was planning, plus the threat she made against me if I refused to help her … what should I do? Go to the police and tell them everything? But I had no proof, no hard evidence she was planning anything at all. She'd just say I was making it all up. So, maybe I should just contact Nisha and warn her? Tell her not to come to the planned meet-up? It was weird, but even though I agreed with Harriet that Nisha was a conniving, nasty person, the story of her life resonated with me. Her lack of a relationship with her mother, her striking out on her own from a young age; so many similarities with my own life. I couldn't let Harriet *kill* her, even if it did mean she'd make even more trouble for me for refusing to help her. But then I thought about the money. One hundred and fifty grand. How could I walk away from that?

And so I came up with my own plan. A way to stop the killing, but still get the money. I *think* it will work. I hope it will. But for now, I have to make it appear as if I'm committed to Harriet's vision of how this is going to pan out, and that's what's brought me here, stepping out of the lift now onto the second floor, turning left and then left again, keeping my head down, not making eye contact with anyone. Following the map that Harriet had drawn and had made me memorise, heading for the corridor she marked with an X, where the operating theatres are, and their adjoining anaesthetics rooms.

'I promise you, people are in and out all the time. Nobody will bat an eyelid,' she said, when I expressed serious doubts about what she was asking me to do. 'I was in a theatre a while back and a member of the public just wandered in. His face when he realised someone was being cut open on the table! So honestly, just act as if you're meant to be there and you'll be fine. There's surprisingly little security. And don't worry about bumping into George, either. I've checked his schedule. He'll be busy on the other side of the building at the time I'm sending you in. Just chill, OK?'

I'm here. I pause, getting my bearings, looking at the doors opening off the corridor, making sure I identify the one Harriet circled on her map correctly, envisaging the layout inside the room in my mind's eye. She drew it in detail; the exact location of the fridge, the precise shelf I can expect to find the drug I need on.

It's a long name beginning with S, that's what I'm looking for. I've memorised the exact spelling, because I really don't want to get this wrong. Harriet explained it's a drug anaesthetists use to paralyse patients for operations, and then – because it paralyses *all* the muscles, including those used to breathe – the patient is intubated and their breathing is done for them. Except, of course, in Nisha's case, that latter part won't happen. She'll just stop breathing, and that will be that. It sounds horrific, and if I thought it would actually happen, I would have no part in this. But, as I said, just playing along for now…

I take a couple of seconds to gather my thoughts, then walk towards the door. I've just reached out a hand to push it open when a voice behind me makes my heart thump.

'Excuse me,' it says.

I whirl around. It's a young man, in similar scrubs to mine, and he's looking at me questioningly.

'Yes? What is it, I'm in a bit of a hurry?' I say brusquely.

It's what Harriet told me to do if I was challenged in any way.

'Be rude,' she said. 'Act as if you're on urgent business. As if someone's life might be in danger if you don't get on with what you're doing…'

The man holds up a hand.

'Gosh, sorry, it's just that it's my first day and I'm a bit lost. Can you tell me how to get to Maternity?'

I point vaguely in the direction I've just come from.

'Down that way to the lifts and go up to the fifth floor. It'll be signposted outside the lifts. Now I really must get on,' I say, and he smiles gratefully, already backing away.

'Thanks *so* much,' he says, and I nod and open the door, closing it quickly behind me. The room is empty, and I emit a soft moan and lean against the wall for a few moments, trying to regain my composure.

In truth, I have no clue where Maternity is; I can't remember if this building even *has* a fifth floor. In fact, now I think about it, I have a horrible feeling it might only be four storeys high. But hey … if I happen to bump into him again on the way out, and he says something, I'll say I misheard him, or he misheard me, or whatever. I don't care. I just need to get this done and get out of here.

Right. The fridge. I see it in the far corner, just as Harriet described, and walk quickly across the room. The fridge shelves are lined with neat rows of boxes, all labelled, and within seconds I spot it. That's it, definitely. Plenty of it, but I only need one dose. It's in small glass ampoules, and I lift one out carefully and slip it into my right trouser pocket, my fingers damp with sweat. I exhale, realising I've been holding my breath. I've done it. I've bloody done it. Now I just have to get out of here again…

I'm almost back at the door when it opens, and I can't help it – I let out a little yelp of shock. The two people who've just walked into the room, a man and a woman, stop abruptly and laugh.

'Whoops, sorry, didn't mean to scare you!' says the woman, and I lower my head and mumble:

'No problem, my fault, half asleep!' then push past them and rush from the room, my heart hammering.

Shit. *Shit*. Please don't come after me, don't look at me, please…

'Hang on a minute…' I hear the man say, but I'm practically running now, and when I get back to the lift lobby I pause for a second then turn and open the door to the stairs instead. I run down them so quickly I nearly trip twice, somehow managing to right myself, and by the time I get back to the ground floor I'm breathless with panic. I erupt through the doors to reception, then risk a look over my shoulder.

Nobody.

Nobody behind me, nobody paying me any attention whatsoever. I run my sleeve across my sweaty brow, then force myself to walk calmly and steadily across the busy space and out through the main doors, still half expecting to hear someone calling my name, to feel a heavy hand on my shoulder. It doesn't happen, but it's not until I'm sitting on the bus and heading back to the penthouse that I can actually breathe normally again.

God. That was close, I think.

I slip my hand into my pocket and feel the smooth glass of the ampoule. Harriet will be pleased. I'm one step closer to getting that money, and to getting my life back.

Chapter Forty-Five

HARRIET

Four weeks later

I t's the second of June, just over a month to D-Day. I can barely remember what it's like to have a job now; my days have taken on a strange, slow rhythm, so different from the manic nature of my life at the hospital. I get up late – nine, sometimes ten – shower and eat breakfast, then go for a walk along the river, occasionally with Ella, more often alone. Chores come next; cleaning a room of the apartment, maybe a trip to the supermarket or, on Fridays, the food market that takes over a nearby street with colourful stalls of cheese, meat, fish, sweet treats. I enjoy those markets, the bustle, the noise, the aromas, the cheerfulness of the stallholders. It lifts my mood, gives me a little spark of joy, and there isn't *much* joy in my life right now.

For the first few weeks of my suspension, I got into the dreadful habit of opening a bottle of wine mid-afternoon, slumping on the sofa with a glass in my hand and an old movie on the TV. I told myself I deserved it, that I'd been through a terrible time and that I might as well make the most of this unexpected break from work, because who knew how long it would be before I had another one? But after a while it stopped being pleasurable, and just started to feel sad. Ella never wanted to join me – she's been getting the odd modelling gig again. Even when she is home, she's spending more and more time alone in her room, which isn't surprising given she now knows what I'm really like – and day drinking on your own just isn't much fun. George was getting pretty fed up with it too. I thought I was hiding it well, but he saw the empty bottles piling up in the recycling bin, of course, and when two days in a row he accused me angrily of slurring my words and looking like, as he charmingly put it, 'a two-bottle-a-day alkie' when he got in from work, I decided it was time to pull myself together. I'm still drinking most days, but only in the evening and only a couple of glasses. Things still aren't great with George though. I think he still loves me – of course he does – but I feel like he no longer entirely *trusts* me, that he still has doubts about my behaviour in the days that preceded my suspension. And when you're so used to being a couple who both have full-time, crazy busy jobs, I also get the sense that me being here all the time and doing so little with my day irritates him. I don't blame him – this is all my fault, after all – but it upsets me.

Once this is over, once I'm working again, it will all be OK, I keep telling myself. *Just a little while longer…*

I'm trying to stay positive. The Gloucester flat sale is moving along well, but to keep Nisha at bay I've told her it's hit an unexpected snag.

It's infuriating! I wrote. *The survey found a small amount of*

Japanese knotweed in the courtyard garden at the rear of the apartment building. Now they say it's more pervasive than first realised, and so the buyers have delayed completion until it's sorted. It should be done in a couple of weeks, I'm so sorry.

She's obviously used to this sort of thing, in her job – she agreed it was annoying, but didn't seem too put out. She's still holding off on retracting the complaint to the hospital though. Although – and this feels like a strange thing to say, even to me – there are days when I don't even care about that any more. I've always said how much I love my job; love being surrounded by children, helping them through tough times in their young lives. But there've been many days, I realise now, when I've spent most of my working hours in pain. Not physical pain; I'm talking *emotional* pain, which is worse, because no number of painkiller drugs can ease it. It's the pain of yearning, that hopeless aching need I try so hard to suppress, but that never really goes away. The pain of mourning the death of my child, the agony of losing someone I never even knew but who meant so much to me. All this pain made worse, so much worse, on my bad days, by being surrounded by other people's children. Now that I'm away from the job, from those daily reminders of what I could have had, I've been astounded to realise I'm wondering if I chose the wrong career after all. I thought, at the time, that it would be the next best thing to motherhood. Now, I think I just might have got that terribly wrong. And so, slowly, my plan for Nisha, and after Nisha, is changing yet again. Nothing's definite yet – who knows, I may change my mind again a dozen times between now and the fourth of July – but I'm just letting it all gently percolate, confident that one of these days I'll wake up in the morning and PING ... I'll suddenly know exactly what to do, know exactly what shape I want my future to take.

Some things are definite though. The date, the location, the details of what will happen when we get there. Or what *Ella* believes will happen, anyway. We haven't spoken about it for a couple of weeks now, both of us quietly getting on with our lives, pretending to George that everything is ticking along nicely. That I'm confident the GMC will find I have no case to answer when their investigation is complete, and that soon I'll be back at work. That Ella is still looking for another full-time job, but that in the meantime she's saving every penny she can from her now semi-regular modelling work and will soon have enough for a deposit on a place of her own. He seems to have accepted all of it – he's even stopped asking me when Ella's moving out. He has no idea whatsoever that when he's not around we've been selling apartments and stealing drugs and planning … well, planning a murder, technically, even though it's a murder that won't actually happen.

I'm sitting out on the terrace now, running over it all in my head, enjoying the gentle breeze caressing my bare arms and legs. It's the second of June, warm enough to wear T-shirts and shorts, and this outside space that runs the length of our indoor living area is bathed in sunshine this afternoon, the sky a cloudless tanzanite. Ella has transformed the terrace in recent weeks; first, she built a little potted herb garden, then started coming home with some bigger plants: a bay tree, a bamboo, a red cordyline. Tending them gave her something to do on days when she wasn't working, she told me, and I was happy to let her get on with it. I like it. It's strangely soothing, listening to the breeze gently rustling the leaves, watching these new arrivals slowly grow and change. Now, a pigeon lands briefly on the edge of one of the planters a few metres away, tilting its head on one side and looking at me expectantly with sharp, orange-red eyes, and I smile and shrug.

'No food on me. Sorry, Pidgy,' I say and, appearing to comprehend perfectly, it turns its head, flaps its wings once as if testing them, then takes off again. I watch it vanish around the corner of the building, and then realise that Ella is standing right behind me, watching it too. She went out earlier, I'm not sure where, and I didn't hear her return but she's obviously been back long enough to get changed; earlier, she was in a striped shirt and wide-leg trousers, but now she's barefoot, hair pulled back into a loose ponytail, sunglasses perched on her nose, and she's wearing an empire line mint green sundress that stops mid-thigh. She looks stunning.

'Hi,' I say. 'Coming to get some sun? It's gorgeous out here. And I wondered if we could maybe have a chat. You know, about ... we haven't talked about it for a bit.'

I make a vague gesture with my hands, and she nods her understanding.

'We could,' she says. 'But we have a few weeks yet. And ... is that wise, out here? What about ... you know, the neighbours?'

She hisses the last few words conspiratorially.

She's right, I think, so I stand up and peer over the guard rail, looking first down then to the left and right. The place is deserted on this Monday afternoon, all the terraces and balconies empty. This building is largely occupied by young to middle-aged working people, mostly nine-to-fivers, and we rarely see a soul on weekdays.

'All clear,' I say, as I sit back down again. 'We can keep our voices down just in case, but I really wouldn't mind doing this now and it's too nice to sit inside.'

She shrugs.

'OK, whatever you want.'

She settles herself in the nearest chair, and I move mine a few inches closer, then lean forwards, closing the gap between us.

'Right,' I say. 'So, the hotel room at The Hill is booked. Thanks for that, by the way.'

'No problem,' she says.

I'd persuaded her to do that bit too. The story I've come up with is this: that Nisha is an old friend of ours, the daughter of my former next-door neighbour (at least that bit's true), and that we gave her a night away in a boutique hotel in Richmond as a treat because we both missed her last birthday. We'll say we popped in to surprise her with a bottle of champagne, and then … well, the exact wording of what happens next is yet to be decided, but I'll work it out. I told Ella it was too risky for me to book the hotel room: that I'm the one who's going to be carrying out the murder, the one who has the knowledge of the drug they're going to find in Nisha's system, the one who is more likely to be suspected of wrongdoing if something in our plan goes wrong.

'I'm paying you a lot of money,' I told her. 'So I want to spread the risk a bit, just in case. But nothing's going to go wrong, I promise you.'

She looked wary, but she did it anyway. Money really does talk, doesn't it?

'So, she won't be able to check in until three, but I'm going to tell her to be there just before so she gets settled as soon as she can and then texts us the room number. We'll arrive at three-thirty, and go straight up to the room, bypassing reception. There'll be CCTV cameras in the lobby, I'm sure, but that's OK. All we'll be doing is bringing a friend a gift, and we need to go in there laughing and smiling and looking, you know, all relaxed and happy, as if we're on a nice day out. If we go skulking in looking nervous and on edge, that's going to look very dodgy if they ever feel the need to check the footage. Sound OK so far? Ella?'

She's staring into space, her expression unreadable. Then she turns her head and nods.

'Sorry. Yes, fine.'

'Great.'

I pause for a moment, as a police siren shrieks down on the road below, then rapidly fades into the distance.

'And then…' I say and look sideways at her.

She looks back at me, saying nothing.

'And then,' I repeat, 'the *real* fun will begin.'

Chapter Forty-Six

ELLA

'... The real fun will begin,' Harriet says, and I feel a shiver run down my back.

I still can't quite believe she's planning this; I can't quite believe I'm helping her, even if I still have no intention of actually letting her go through with it. She's chattering away now, going through the details with me, and I'm having to force myself to concentrate. I have a lot on my mind, especially after something that happened earlier today, something I can't tell Harriet – can't tell *anyone* – about, and it's distracting me, but I try to push it to the back of my mind for now. I can dwell on it later, in the privacy of my room.

'So, obviously, Nisha's going to think she's there to sign the final paperwork,' Harriet's saying. 'I'll make some on the computer to bring with us, make it look like official documents, so she won't suspect anything too soon. We'll say we brought the champagne to toast to the future, to the end of the feud, to us all moving forward. And then—'

'And then I do my little bit,' I say, interrupting her, wanting this to be over. 'We'll have a bag of ice cubes with us too, in that insulated tote, and I'll say I'll make a sort of ice bucket in the bathroom sink and that I'll go and pour the bubbly in there while you two go through the paperwork. I'll have the drug in my pocket. I'll go in there and pour the drinks, crack open the ampoule and add it to her drink. Then I'll emerge again and…'

'…and make sure you don't mix those glasses up and she gets the right one!'

Harriet laughs, and I force myself to smile back at her.

'Of course, don't worry!' I say, feeling slightly sick.

'OK,' she says. 'So, she drinks it, and … anyway, we leave. We come home – you can leave whenever you like after this, obviously, you'll have your money! – and then a few hours later I ring the hotel reception and say I'm a bit concerned about my friend Nisha in room whatever. I'll say we popped in earlier with some champagne but she seemed very low and depressed, and then we had to leave but we left her with the rest of the bubbly, and now she's not answering her phone, and would they mind going to check on her. There's no getting out of making that call, because they'll have seen us at the hotel earlier. So, they'll go to the room and find her and … well, the police will be called, obviously.'

'They'll definitely want to question us,' I say. 'So you're going to say – what?'

She turns her head to the sky for a few moments, closing her eyes, as if savouring the warmth. Then she says, 'I'll tell them you were with me to say goodbye to Nisha, because you're moving abroad. And I'll say that I'm a paediatrician, currently not working – I'll have to be honest about that. And that I had to leave work in a hurry and threw a load of stuff in my bag and that ampoule somehow got picked up by accident – I mean, that's not very likely at all, but they won't know that … and that I'd met up with Nisha a while ago and while I was with her I discovered it at the bottom of my bag and showed it to her, and told her what it was and what it does, and what am I like! And then she must have taken it from my bag when I nipped to the loo, and I totally forgot about it and didn't even notice…'

'It's a bit convoluted,' I say. 'Do you really think they'll buy it? And what about fingerprints?'

'We'll make sure it's completely clean before we go. And then you'll need to wear gloves,' she says. 'Pop a pair of those disposable ones into the bag with the ice. We can add Nisha's fingerprints afterwards. Put it into her hand for a minute when she's … you know.'

I nod, but the nausea is back. She sounds so casual, so … so *cold*.

How can someone who spends her days making sick kids better be so callous, so evil, I think. What's happened to you, Harriet? Is this what losing your baby did to you? Or is there something else?

'And I don't know if they'll buy it, but I think I can persuade them,' she says. 'I'll make sure I wipe all the email correspondence between us and any phone messages that might look suspicious in advance though. And she's not stupid. I'm quite sure she's long ago got rid of her threatening emails to me. She won't have kept any evidence of her extortion. The police won't be able to find any evidence of any bad blood between us. It'll be fine. It'll just look like another sad suicide.'

You can wipe emails and messages from your phone, from your computer, but the police will still be able to find them, you fool, I think. *Don't you watch TV crime shows? Doesn't everyone know that?*

I don't say it though. Nisha isn't going to die, I'll make sure of that. None of this will really matter in the end. I just need to get my money, and get out of here…

'Fine. You're right, I'm sure that will work,' I say. 'And I think I'm going to leave straightaway, actually. That evening. I'll bring my stuff with me and head straight to the airport when we're done. But Harriet…'

I hesitate, wondering how she's going to react when I say this. I decided to ask her on my way back to the penthouse after my little trip out this morning, but I'm not entirely sure she's going to go for it.

'I'm going to need the money in advance. You want me out of your hair, and I want to leave, but I need to see that money in my account before I go. It's a big thing I'm doing here, and I'm definitely doing it, don't worry, I'm not going to pull out. I can't, can I? But I just need to know that money's there. That *you're* not going to change your mind.'

She's been leaning back in her deckchair, looking quite relaxed, but now she sits up straight and looks at me. For several seconds there's silence. Then she says:

'Half. I'll pay you half the day before, and half on the day, after it's done. Seventy-five thousand in advance. Will that do? You'll get your money, Ella. A promise is a promise.'

'OK. OK, thanks,' I reply. It's as good as I'm going to get; I can tell by the tone of her voice.

'Great,' she says. She leans back in her chair again, closing her eyes.

'So we're sorted then. We know what we're doing,' she adds, almost in a whisper. 'Bring. It. On.'

Chapter Forty-Seven

NISHA

The fourth of July

Today's the day. My very own Independence Day. I'm on my way to Richmond, to meet Harriet Hart and her friend Ella at a hotel, and I've even treated myself to a taxi instead of using public transport. A proper London black cab too, not an Uber. It just felt more appropriate, for a big day like this. It's a cultural icon, isn't it, a black cab? People all over the world, if shown a photo of one, would instantly say, 'That's a London cab, innit?' or whatever the local language equivalent might be. Anyway, I feel it's giving me more a sense of occasion, riding in one of these. Plenty of space to stretch my legs out. Privacy from the driver, courtesy of the sliding glass partition in front of me. No need to chat, just to be polite. I usually don't mind a natter with a cab driver, but today I'm not in the mood. I'm jittery, a combination of nerves and excitement. Because today is meant to go a certain way, and I already know it won't.

This is what I do know. A hotel room has been booked for me, and shortly after I've checked in, Harriet and Ella will arrive, Harriet bearing paperwork that will officially sign that huge amount of money over to me, no going back. A document too that Harriet and I will *both* sign, confirming that going forward neither of us will make any further claims, harass each other in any way or take any legal action. A permanent ceasefire. That's fine by me. I still don't really know how she's managed to raise the cash; I've kept a close eye, but her Teddington penthouse was never put up for sale publicly, so maybe she *did* arrange a private sale, or maybe it *has* been an equity release. Or maybe she has even more cash than I knew about, and lied when she said she'd have to sell her home to raise the amount I demanded. Maybe she inherited more, from some other poor sucker, who knows? Maybe *he* did, the husband. The Gloucester flat sale got held up – bloody knotweed – but completion day was Wednesday, so that's all done now, and to be fair, she's been pretty good, Harriet, at staying in touch, keeping me updated, so when she said it would be easier to arrange a single bank transfer for today instead of two separate ones, and asked if I could wait just those two extra days for the proceeds from the flat and have one big lump sum, I was happy enough to agree. I feel like we understand each other now. Yes, I had to threaten her, blackmail her, to get her to finally give in. But I think what really happened is that she ultimately realised I was in the right and she hadn't played fair. And once she handed over that first instalment, that hundred grand, I *knew* I'd won. I did still feel a bit guilty though, about the kids. That's why I decided to get Letisha to withdraw Toby's allegations two weeks ago, just after contracts were finally exchanged on the

Gloucester property. I was pretty sure the sale would go through to completion, and my conscience was nagging me.

Harriet was very grateful. She emailed to say she'd been told Toby had apparently confessed he'd been anxious and confused on the day she'd examined him, because in the days leading up to it he'd been trying to Google his symptoms and had fallen into an internet rabbit hole, reading articles about patients who'd been assaulted during hospital visits. In retrospect, he didn't think Harriet had actually touched him inappropriately at all, and he was now horrified at the upset his allegations had caused. The hospital had been obliged to pass this information on to the police, who considered prosecuting him for wasting their time, then had decided it wouldn't be in the public interest, and had let it go, which was what I had assumed – and very much hoped – would happen when we got to this stage. Harriet's now in the process of negotiating her return to work, but apparently taking some annual leave first, just to get over the trauma of it all. All's well that ends well, eh?

The cab slows, and I look out the window. We've just passed Dukes Meadows, the riverside park. Just a couple of miles to go. I shift in my seat, and feel a ripple of apprehension. As I said, today is meant to go a certain way, and I already know it won't, and I'm trying to play that out in my head now, wondering if it's going to go to plan, thinking about the ways it could go wrong. The faces of the two women I'm about to meet in that hotel room float into my mind: Harriet, with that long silky dark hair. And Ella. Ella Leonard, the friend is called; I looked her up. She used to be a model; still is, on and off. The pictures of her online are stunning: green eyes, blonde mane, edgy tattoo. Together, they make a striking pair. A clever pair too. But not quite as clever as they think. Well, one of them isn't, anyway.

One of them has no idea what she's actually going to face today. She'll walk into that hotel room, and we'll start proceedings as scheduled, and everything will seem fine, and everyone will relax. And then … BAM.

I take a few slow, deep breaths. In, out. In, out.

Independence Day. It's been a long time coming. And if it all goes as I hope it will, it's going to be even better than I dreamed.

Chapter Forty-Eight

ELLA

The fourth of July

'Nisha. How are you?'

Harriet's tone is one of forced jollity, and as we step inside the hotel room and I see Nisha Cartwright's face for the first time, the trepidation which has been building for days now suddenly turns into full-blown terror. It's all I can do not to turn and run, but it's too late now. I'm here, we're all here. I have no idea how this day is going to end, but I have no choice. I have to play my part, and play it well, otherwise ... well, I don't want to think about what might happen. I grip the handle of my new wheeled suitcase with a hand clammy with sweat, pull it into the room and close the door, then turn to the others.

'I'm OK,' says Nisha. 'Big day. Long time coming.'

She's tall, taller than both me and Harriet – five eleven maybe. She has short black hair, one side tucked behind her ear, olive skin, dark brown eyes. She looks tense, unsmiling, but then we all do. This is such a strange, strange encounter. One woman who believes her rightful inheritance has been stolen from her, and who's resorted to seriously dirty tricks and blackmail to retrieve it. One woman who's determined *not* to let her have it, and is prepared to commit murder to get her tormentor off her back. And me, who's being paid a lot of money to help with a truly heinous crime. Me, who did something horrible years ago, and has now been punished for that in the most unexpected and deeply unpleasant way. Me, who, unbeknownst to both of these women, is here to stop one in her tracks and save the life of the other.

I'm heading straight to Heathrow when we're done here. My flight to Paris and my first three nights' accommodation are booked, courtesy of the money from my recent modelling work, and my bank account is looking decidedly healthier today after last night Harriet transferred, as promised, half of my 'fee'. Then, this morning, I told her that instead of waiting until afterwards, I wanted the other half immediately, before we left.

'I'm not going to pull out, Harriet,' I said. 'I promise you, I'm coming with you. I'm doing this. But I'm just thinking we're probably going to be in a bit of a state afterwards, you know, when … well, I don't need to spell it out. And the last thing you're going to want to do at that point is sit down and start sorting out a bank transfer.'

She'd hesitated for a few moments, clearly thinking, then nodded slowly.

'Fine. I'll sort it now,' she said.

I watched her do it, and when the confirmation notice flashed up on her banking app I thanked her and headed back to my room, where I'd been cramming the last few items into my suitcase.

'It'll take a few hours to clear, but it's gone through,' she called after me.

I've already said goodbye to George; he was leaving for work early this morning, and I knew I wouldn't get to see him today, so last night after dinner I told him how grateful I was for everything.

'You've been very tolerant, and I very much appreciate it, but Paris calls,' I said, and he smiled and pulled me in for a slightly awkward hug, as Harriet, still keeping up our 'great buddies' act in front of her husband, said, 'The apartment is going to be very quiet without you. But it's a much greener place than it was when you arrived, so thanks for that.'

'We'll make a gardener of you yet,' I said.

'I'll need an actual garden first, not just a balcony,' she replied. 'But maybe one day, eh?'

She smiled at me, and, for a fleeting moment it felt … *genuine*. I think she really *does* appreciate the plants. I've watched her sometimes, looking at them, gently brushing specks of dust from their leaves. I even heard her talking to them once, like I often do.

How strange life is, that even two people like me and Harriet can have a connection over something, despite everything that's gone on between us, I thought.

Soon, I'll walk away and never see her again. But there *have* been little moments of joy in amongst all the madness, even over the past few months. Moments when I've wondered what might have been if I'd never slept with Felix that night. Nothing's ever truly black and white, is it?

Today though, the craziness continues, and now Harriet reaches into her bag and pulls out a manila folder.

'Everything's here,' she says to Nisha. 'You'd better read through it all first though, just so you know what you're signing. And then I'll do the transfer, and … well, that will be it. We brought some champagne, actually. To celebrate. You're right, it's been a long and rocky road to get to this point, so…'

She turns to me and, as rehearsed, I pull the bottle of champagne out of the insulated bag that's slung over my shoulder.

'I have ice too,' I say. 'Maybe I'll stick it in the bathroom sink? It's chilled, but a few minutes in ice would do it good.'

'Knock yourself out,' says Nisha, gesturing towards the door to her right. She's already focused on the sheaf of documents Harriet's just handed her, not really interested in me. Harriet and I make brief eye contact, an acknowledgment that all is proceeding smoothly, and I head into the bathroom, pushing the door almost closed behind me. Swiftly, I close the sink plughole, tip the ice in and plunge the bottle into it. Then I pull the three plastic champagne flutes – Harriet has a stash of them in her kitchen, for picnics apparently – out of the bag and line them up neatly on the countertop. Not bothering to put on the gloves she insisted I bring, I slip my hand into my jacket pocket, checking that the ampoule's still there, feeling the coolness of the glass between my fingers. OK, good.

I go back out into the bedroom, where Nisha appears to be reading carefully, Harriet giving her space, staring blankly out of the window. I perch on the end of the bed and wait too, my stomach churning. I feel slightly light-headed with anxiety, and it seems like an age before Nisha looks up and nods.

'OK, it all seems in order. I'm happy to sign,' she says.

'Great!' Harriet turns and smiles at Nisha, proffering a pen, then looks at me.

'Bubbly time, I reckon,' she says.

'On it,' I say.

My heart is thudding against the wall of my chest as I walk back into the bathroom, my hands shaking as I peel the foil off the bottle and pop the cork, then carefully fill the glasses. This is where I'm supposed to put the gloves on, crack open the ampoule and pour the contents into Nisha's drink. Harriet's assured me it's tasteless, but fast-acting; all I have to do is add it to the champagne, put the broken ampoule in my pocket for disposal later, and serve the fizz. I stand there for a moment, bracing myself. Then I snap the top off the ampoule and, fearfully checking over my shoulder in the mirror to make sure neither of the others has stepped into the room for any reason, I pour the drug into the sink, where it swirls between the ice cubes for a few seconds then disappears.

I stand there, leaning over the basin, breathing heavily. Then I straighten up, pick up the broken ampoule, slip it back into my pocket, and reach into my other pocket for my phone. This bit is risky. There's an extractor fan in the bathroom, and it's quite loud; I can just about hear Nisha and Harriet talking out in the bedroom, but I can't make out anything they're saying. Will this work in reverse? Will *they* hear *me*, speaking on the phone? I'm going to have to go for it; if I'm in here much longer they're going to wonder what on earth I'm doing. My hands are sweating so much I mistype the number on the first attempt, my finger sliding across the screen of my phone. I try again.

9-9-9.

'Emergency. Which service do you require?'

'Police, please. Quickly,' I say. I'm almost whispering, but it seems the operator can hear me, because seconds later, I'm connected. I speak fast, my words tumbling over each other. The address of the hotel, the room number. A crime in progress. A woman who's plotting to kill another woman, a lethal drug.

'I've managed to tip it down the sink, but I'm scared she'll just come up with something else,' I murmur.

'Help is on its way,' I'm told, and I cut the call, then look at myself in the mirror. My skin looks ashen and sweaty, and I push my hair back off my forehead, forcing a smile onto my face. Then I open the bathroom door, pick up two of the glasses – any two, it doesn't matter, they're all the same – and walk back into the bedroom.

'Here you go,' I say, then hesitate. Nisha and Harriet are standing shoulder to shoulder, looking straight at me with strange expressions on their faces.

Shit. Shit. Harriet heard me on the phone, she knows, oh my God … is my first panicked thought, but no … no, I don't think that *is* what's going on here, because now she's turning to Nisha and smiling, and Nisha is smiling back, and now they're both looking at me again, the smiles fading.

'Right, so – this is where it ends, Ella,' Harriet says.

'What? What ends? I'm sorry, I don't…' I say, but she's holding up a hand.

'Let me explain,' she says, a slightly patronising edge to her voice, as if she's a teacher about to spell out the error of her ways to a misbehaving pupil.

'Today isn't going to end quite as you expected,' she continues. 'Come on – did you really think I was coming here to *kill* Nisha? *Me*? I'm a doctor, you know that. I save lives, I don't take them…'

'But…' I splutter.

What's going on? I think.

'But you…'

She's not listening.

'…so let me tell you exactly what's happening here. We're about to call the police, and tell them that we've just foiled an attempted murder plot, and that the woman who planned it is right here with us. That's you, by the way. And don't try to run. It's two against one – you won't get out of this room.'

'It's … it's … what do you mean, two against one?'

I look frantically from her to Nisha and back again, not understanding, but Harriet keeps talking.

'We've been in touch, you see. Nisha and I. A bit of a collaboration. We decided this would be a much better end to all this.'

'We did,' Nisha chips in. 'Much neater. More financially profitable for me too. Thanks for that, Harriet.'

'Yes, I offered her a … small *extra* incentive to go along with this,' Harriet says to me. 'So … here's the story. *You're* the one who plotted to kill Nisha. *You* booked this hotel room. *You* stole the drug from the hospital. This is all you, Ella. All the evidence points at *you* plotting a murder. No evidence at all that I was involved. And after this, whatever happens, we'll be quits, finally. That OK with you? Oh actually, I don't care. Where's my phone?'

'Here you go,' Nisha says, picking it up off the bed and handing it to her.

'But … but…'

I can barely breathe. How can this have happened? I came

here to stop Harriet from killing Nisha, and now the two of them are somehow in cahoots, and they're going to make it look like it was *me*…? This can't be happening, it *can't*…

But apparently it is, because Harriet's waving her phone at me.

'Time to ring 999,' she says, with a sneer.

'No – stop! *Stop*! You can't because … because I've already called them,' I say.

Chapter Forty-Nine

HARRIET

The fourth of July

'What do you mean you've already called them?'

I stare at Ella, feeling like someone's just punched me in the stomach. She's still clutching the champagne glasses, and I watch as she turns to put them down on a side table, her hands shaking. I'm feeling pretty wobbly myself. When I first got in touch with Nisha to put this new proposition to her, I'd been incredibly nervous. It had been a huge gamble; telling her all about Ella, and what she did to me back then, and my little revenge plot. Offering her an extra two hundred thousand, on top of the one point five million she'd already demanded, to turn the tables on my former housemate, to frame her for planning a murder. I knew Nisha had an extremely devious side; her recent actions have clearly illustrated that. And I knew she wanted as much money from me as she could possibly get. But even so, I wasn't sure she'd go for it. She surprised me in the end, thinking about it for a matter of hours before calling me back and agreeing. But now? Unexpected plot twist.

'I called the cops because, *obviously*, I came here thinking *you* were going to kill her, Harriet!' Ella points at Nisha, her eyes wide. 'And, also obviously, I couldn't let you do that. I threw the drug down the sink, but I thought you might have a back-up plan if it didn't work … shit, I should have known, shouldn't I? You're clearly insane. Everything you've done to me … but I should have known you'd draw the line at actual murder. I am such a … *fuckwit*.'

She groans, covering her face with her hands for a few seconds, then looks at me again.

'And you are such a *bitch*,' she spits.

I'm rapidly recovering my composure as she speaks, my thoughts coalescing.

OK, a slight deviation from the plan. But this can still be fine. The police are already on their way, but it doesn't really matter who called them, does it? I think. *Ella told them I was about to kill Nisha, but all the evidence is still going to point to her…*

'Well, for a start, that drug wouldn't have done much harm even if she had drunk it,' I say. 'Just so you know. It needs to be injected to work. But you wouldn't have known that, would you, when you stole it from the hospital? Whereas I do know that, obviously. Another nail in *your* coffin, Ella. *I'd* never use that drug to try and kill someone in a drink, but *you* might. When the police arrive, we'll just say we rumbled you. We saw you in the bathroom about to pour it into the champagne, so you locked the door and dialled 999 to try to blame me instead…'

'Oh, COME ON!' she shouts, interrupting me.

'Why *would* I? Why would *I* try to kill Nisha? What possible motive would I have? You're the one she's been concocting false allegations against! I'll tell the police that too – you do realise *both* of you are going to be in the shit now, right? She's a blackmailer and you plotted to kill her. You're the only one with a motive for murder, Harriet. I've never even met her until today, for the love of God! Little flaw in your plan there, eh?'

I smile. I've already thought about this, of course.

'I'll tell them you were doing it for me,' I say. 'I'll tell them you caused me to lose my child, and you believed I was having some issues with Nisha over an inheritance, so in some twisted way you thought that if you killed Nisha, that would be helpful for me. It would mean I could keep the money and that might make you and *me* quits. Simple.'

She gapes at me, her mouth actually dropping open, and I turn to Nisha, briefly laying a hand on her arm, then look back at Ella.

'And obviously, I'll tell them that Nisha and I actually have no beef at all, and that I came here today to return some of the money her mum left me because we agreed that was the right thing to do,' I say. 'And Nisha will back me up. Who are they going to believe, Ella?'

'OK, OK.'

There's a note of despair in her voice now, and she turns away, takes a few paces towards the door, then spins back round. I see tears in her eyes, and for a second – just for a second – there it is again, that irritating pang of guilt.

No. Don't weaken now, I tell myself. *It's nearly over, so nearly over…*

Ella takes a deep shuddery breath.

'Look, I didn't want to tell you this. Especially, because,

well … but there's something you need to know, before the police get here. I'm…'

She hesitates, her gaze dropping to the floor for a few seconds. Then her eyes meet mine again.

'I'm pregnant,' she says.

My heart skips a beat.

'You're … you're *what*? Oh piss off, Ella. That's not going to work … it's pathetic. And cruel, actually…'

'I'm not lying, Harriet. Look…'

She crosses to the bed, where she dumped her handbag earlier, picks it up and starts rummaging in it.

'Remember I told you I had a couple of dates at the end of January, just before I left Gloucester, but I decided the guy wasn't a long-term prospect, just a bit of fun? I didn't realise until the end of March … it was so early, and I wasn't showing obviously, and I was lucky, I felt fine, but then I realised I hadn't had a period in ages, which I'd thought was down to stress, but I suddenly thought, *could* I be? So I did a test and … look. Here.'

She pulls something out of her bag, a piece of paper, and waves it at me.

'My scan. I had it the morning of that day we sat on the balcony and went through the plan, do you remember?'

She pushes it into my hands, and I can feel a lump forming in my throat. It's an ultrasound scan image, the grainy outline of a baby, its face squishy, one tiny fist resting on a cheek. My eyes move across the picture. Ella's name and date of birth are clearly visible along the top edge. If this is a fake, it's a good one.

'You would have noticed any day now, though,' she says.

'I've been wearing loose clothes, but I've just popped out in the last week.'

She turns sideways, smoothing the floaty top she's wearing over her usually taut, flat stomach, and there it is. A tiny bump. A perfect, neat bump.

It's real, I think, and suddenly I want to cry. *She really is having a baby...*

How did I not know? The way she quit drinking, the mugs of cocoa instead of the glasses of wine ... and then I think back to that day, the day on the balcony. She *had* been out in the morning; she hadn't said where she'd been, and I didn't ask, but I remember she seemed distracted. And then I remember something else. Something *awful*.

'I ... I drugged you,' I say desperately. 'All that booze was bad enough, but then I ... Ella, I would never have, if I'd known...'

'I know ... I know,' she says, and she gently pulls the ultrasound picture from my fingers, running a hand over it, smoothing it where my grip has creased it.

'It's fine. The scan showed no abnormalities. It's OK. But Harriet, please ... if you tell the police I plotted to kill Nisha, and they believe you, I could go to prison. *Please*. I'm keeping this baby. I never knew I wanted one, but suddenly ... and I can do it on my own, I don't need the father. Please, don't do this to me. Don't do it to *us*.'

She drops the scan onto the bed and puts both hands on her stomach, cradling it protectively, and I stare at her. For a few seconds, I hate her so much I can barely draw breath. After everything, after the agony I went through, and now *she* gets pregnant? Just like that? No effort? Just by accident, with a man she hardly even knew? This isn't fair, none of this is *fair*...

'Harriet … we *can't*.'

Nisha, at my elbow, has been silent for so long, simply observing, that I'd almost forgotten she was there, and I actually jump as she speaks.

'We can't,' she says again. 'Not if … not if there's a *kid*…'

I swallow hard, still trying to stop bursting into tears.

'I know,' I whisper.

I inhale slowly, rub my eyes, exhale. Nisha's right. We can't do this, not now. At this moment, I hate Ella more than I've ever hated her before, but we can't. We're going to have to let her go, aren't we?

'OK,' I say. 'Go, Ella. But you fuck right off, and you don't come back. I never want to see you or hear from you again, that's the deal. That seventy-five grand will be enough to get you started in Paris, or wherever you're going after that. Because that's all you've got, by the way. That other transfer, the second half of the money, that I sent to your account this morning? I cancelled it after you left the room. My bank gives you a ten-minute window to cancel an online transaction, you know, in case you make a mistake? So I did. I cancelled it.'

Ella rolls her eyes, but she's already on the move, grabbing her bag, pushing her precious scan picture into it, crossing the room to where her suitcase sits.

'Of course you did,' she mutters. 'Fine, whatever. I'll cope. I always do.'

She's at the door now, opening it, but she pauses, then turns, looking back at me.

'But also – and I can't believe I'm saying this, but – thank you,' she says quietly. 'And for what it's worth … I'm sorry, Harriet. I really am sorry, about everything. Goodbye.'

Then she walks through the door, letting it close gently behind her.

Chapter Fifty

NISHA

The fourth of July

We both stand there in silence, staring at the closed bedroom door. Then Harriet walks across to it, turning the handle to lock it, and as she does that, something makes me turn to the window. I peer out of it, and down below, I see them. Two police cars, pulling up at the front of the hotel. *Shit.* Ella phoned them, probably gave her name, but they don't know what she looks like. She's clearly not stupid; she'll just walk calmly past them, out of the building. Just a hotel guest departing, pulling her suitcase behind her. There's a line of taxis right across the road; she'll be in one and on her way to the airport within a minute. How long do *we* have now? One minute, two, before they get inside, find someone to escort them upstairs, to give them access to this room? What's Harriet going to say? What will she do now?

'They're here,' I say to Harriet. 'The cops. They're here.'

She lets out a little moan, takes a step towards the window, then turns and goes back to where she was.

'OK, this is what we do,' she says, and she sounds a little hysterical. 'We say it was all a big, sick joke that backfired. I told Ella I was going to kill you, but we were just winding her up, and we never expected it to go this far. We never thought she'd call the police, right? Or … no, how about this? We say she's a fantasist, that she makes things up all the time, but she went too far today, and now she's done a runner because she's realised she'll be in big trouble. And we just apologise that their time's been wasted and hope they believe us?'

I shrug.

'Either will do. I don't really care. This is between you two, Harriet. As long as I get my money, I couldn't give a monkey's.'

She's silent for a few seconds, then, weirdly, the expression on her face changes from panicked to completely calm. She looks almost serene, a tiny smile playing on her lips.

'Oh. Well, obviously *that's* not going to happen,' she says.

'What's not?'

'You getting any more money. You've already had one hundred grand, Nisha. And I had to pay Ella that seventy-five grand or she wouldn't have come with me today, and now *that's* been a complete waste of money, hasn't it? Although I came here to be rid of her once and for all, and I suppose I still am. She's just not in police custody as I hoped she'd be. But you – you're not getting another penny. I loved my job, Nisha, but it was hard sometimes, really, really hard, you know, being around children all the time. And now – well, you've tarnished it for me. Even though those allegations have been withdrawn, mud sticks, doesn't it? Some people will always have doubts, and this time off I've had recently … I don't know, something's shifted. I'm envisaging a different future now, and that's not something I ever expected to say. Do you know how long it's taken, to get to where I got to? All those years of studying and long hours and … well, I guess you don't care about that, do you? But I've made up my mind. I'm not going back. I have a new life plan, so you can do your worst, Nisha. I'm not scared of you any more. This is where it ends.'

What? What the actual…? I think.

'Are you *kidding* me?' I shout, and I thump the nearest wall hard and instantly regret it. The pain in my hand makes my bubbling anger turn into a blazing fury, and suddenly I have to hold myself back from punching her in the face. The police will be at the door any second now and I do *not* want them to find her on the floor bleeding from a broken nose.

'Seriously? You double-crossed Ella with my help, and now you're trying to double-cross me too? Are you mental? All I have to do is back up Ella's story. I can say you *did* come here to kill me. I demanded back the inheritance you stole from me and you decided to kill me to get rid of me and Ella stopped you. I can back her up and say you forced her to steal the drug. I can tell them all the shit you've done to her too. If they want her to verify it all, they'll find her easily enough. I doubt she's travelling on a false passport, is she? They'll track her down, and I'll back up her story. It'll be two against one. If you want a new life, this is *not* going to be a good way to start it, trust me. Pay me, Harriet. Pay me what you owe me, and I'll play along with whatever you decide to tell the cops. If you don't, you only have yourself to blame for what happens next.'

Harriet smirks.

'Aren't you forgetting something? You made false sexual

assault allegations against me and you *blackmailed* me, Nisha. OK, some of your threats were made in phone calls but I have enough in those threatening emails you sent me to get you in big trouble too. I told Ella I was going to delete all our email correspondence, but I kept *everything*. And I bet those friends of yours who played along with your little games won't be too hard to trace; how sure are you they won't crumble and tell the police everything you asked them to do? I had my reasons for not reporting you to the police before, but now all bets are off. I don't care about my career and I don't care about George finding out about all this. In fact, I'm telling him everything, a clean slate. None of it matters any more. So what's it to be?'

'Oh fuck off! Attempted murder is way more serious than blackmail,' I spit. 'Even if I did try to blackmail you, and sent some friends to piss about with you a bit, you coming here to try to kill me is a bit of an overreaction, isn't it? The cops will come down on you way harder...'

My voice tails off. This is farcical.

You did this, yeah but you did this ... we sound like schoolkids. But she's right. There *is* evidence I tried to blackmail her. I'd lose my job...

We stand there, glaring at each other, both breathing heavily now; seemingly she's as unsure about how to proceed as I am.

'Stalemate,' she says eventually, and then we both jump as there's a loud BANG BANG on the door.

'Police! Open up!' shouts a male voice.

My stomach lurches. The door's locked from the inside, so they won't be able to get in with just a key card, but that won't stop them for long.

'What are we going to do?' I say. 'Quick! We need to decide, now, or we're going to open up a whole world of pain for both of us.'

BANG BANG!

'Police! Open up now, or we're coming in!'

'SHIT! OK, OK, fine. Life's too short. And it *was* your family money ... how about this? Half a million. I'll pay you another half a million, and we're quits, forever. We both move on. I won't tell the police about the false allegations or the blackmail, you say nothing about attempted murder or what I did to Ella. We're friends, this is all a misunderstanding, leave me to do the talking ... deal? DEAL, Nisha?'

She's holding out a hand, looking desperately from the door to me and back again, and for a moment I want to tell her to do one, to take my chances. I *want* my big payout, my promised one point five million. *Plus* the extra she was going to add on for helping her turn the tables on Ella. Then, hastily, I change my mind. It's just not going to happen now, is it? Too risky. I have too much to lose, and half a million is better than prison or whatever the alternative might be.

'Oh fuck it. Deal,' I say.

I take her hand and shake it, just as there's an almighty CRASH and the door bursts open.

Chapter Fifty-One

HARRIET

The fourth of July

I got home an hour ago, and slumped onto the sofa in a state of mild shock. I'm still sitting here now, staring out at the darkening sky, trying to process everything. This is *not* how today should have panned out, nothing like it. I expected Ella to be in custody. I expected Nisha and me to be questioned and to back up each other's stories, then when we were done and she demanded her payout, I was planning to threaten to reveal *her* dodgy deeds to the police, gambling on the fact she would decide to walk away with the money she already had instead of risking her own criminal trial. Instead, Ella's pregnant – *pregnant!* – and free to start a new life, and somehow I've agreed to pay Nisha another half a million, which is going to mean selling this place after all. And yet – is this OK? Is it possibly a *better* outcome than the one I'd planned? Maybe. Maybe not. I still have to face George, and I'm so, so nervous about that. He should be walking through the door any minute now, and I don't even know how I'm going to start...

A little moan escapes me, and I stand up and head for the kitchen. I need a drink; I think George is going to need one too. I open a bottle of chardonnay, pour myself a generous glass and down half of it in one. Then I take the rest back to the sofa and sit down again, my mind replaying the events of the past few hours.

It took a while to convince the police that no crime had been committed. I went for the 'terrible joke that badly backfired' story in the end, telling them that Nisha, Ella and I were old friends and that Ella was always winding us up so we decided to play the ultimate prank, Nisha and I cooking up a plan to make it seem that I was going to kill her in a hotel room. Ella had, it seemed, only given the call operator the bare details, saying something about a crime in progress, a drug intended to do harm washed down the bathroom sink and her fears that I might try another method of killing Nisha instead. They certainly didn't mention anything about any money changing hands, or that I'd persuaded Ella to steal said drug from the hospital, which was lucky. We told them that after she emerged from the bathroom and told us she'd called the police, we confessed that it was all a joke and she'd stormed out, heading to the airport for a preplanned trip, leaving us to deal with the fallout. Nisha and I – she did well, actually – made fervent apologies, agreeing with the unamused officers that it was a stupid, irresponsible thing to do, promising to never do such a thing again. I even admitted that, for extra realism, I'd taken a drug home from the hospital, not strictly legally – I felt I had to, just in case they did decide to do some more investigating and carried out a forensic examination of the bathroom pipework or something. Then I dissolved into tears, saying over and over again how remorseful I now was and begging them not to report the incident to my superiors.

We were so incredibly lucky. I'd begun to panic that they'd demand Ella's details to check her story against ours, but Nisha and I clearly put on such a good show of being close friends that they must have concluded there was no truth in the allegation that one of us was plotting to kill the other. Eventually, still looking deeply unimpressed, and telling us we were just a hair's breadth away from being prosecuted for wasting police time, they suddenly seemed to decide there were more important things they should be doing than hanging out in a hotel room with two silly women who clearly thought crime was a game, and left. Nisha and I left too minutes later, with another oddly formal handshake on the street outside the hotel.

'I'll be in touch, as soon as I can,' I said, and this time she made no further demands, set me no deadline. She simply nodded, said, 'Thanks. Bye for now, Harriet,' and walked away.

The feeling of being in shock is passing; whether it's the wine, or just that the end of all this really is in sight now, I'm not sure, but I can feel a calmness descending on me. It was on that night I spent in Brighton that the idea of quitting medicine first crept into my head. I pushed it away, but it kept coming back over the weeks that followed, initially just a whisper, then a relentless nagging irritant. And then I began to think about Mug & Meadow, the fake business that, so unexpectedly, rapidly became a success. Could I possibly make it a *real* business? I'd learned so much in setting up the deception, and the more I thought about it the more I yearned for the simpler existence of doing something like that for a living. No sick and dying children breaking my heart, no matter how hard I tried to separate the job and my emotions. No life-or-death decisions. Just coffee, and good food, and happy smiling customers. And plants. I've grown quite fond of plants, thanks to Ella. And so I made up my mind. Quit the job, change direction. Change my life.

Today threw me a little curve ball. I hadn't wanted to sell the penthouse, thinking I could use the rest of the proceeds of the Gloucester flat sale – the money I didn't, in the end, pay Ella – to start my new venture, planning to lie to George yet again about where the cash had come from, maybe telling him an old investment had suddenly paid dividends, something like that. But now, after agreeing to pay Nisha another half a million, I have no choice. I'd lied to her when I said I was planning to tell George everything, but now I really *am* going to have to tell my husband the truth, or a version of it anyway. Nothing about Ella, obviously. Just about Nisha, a confession that I've been feeling guilty for years about a daughter who really should have shared my inheritance, and that finally my conscience has won and I'm going to pay her a share. He'll probably be shocked that I didn't do that in the first place, might be very angry, in fact, because he loves this apartment as much as I do, but he'll get over it. He'll get over the fact I'm giving up medicine too. Despite everything that's happened recently, he still loves me, right? I'll win him round.

And now I'm thinking that maybe with the money we have left we move out of London to somewhere a little more rural. It would be hard for George to commute with the hours he works, but maybe we could stretch to a tiny studio flat in the city and a modest home outside it, if the value of this place has increased as much as I hope it has in the time we've lived here. So yes – not the outcome I expected today. But a clearer conscience about Nisha and her inheritance. Ella punished, but now free to bring up her baby. And a different, possibly even better, future for me and my husband.

It's going to be OK, I think. *It is. It's all going to be OK.*

I pick up my glass, raise it in the air in a silent 'cheers' to myself, to our future. Then I swallow the rest of the contents and wait for the sound of George's key in the front door.

Chapter Fifty-Two

ELLA, HARRIET AND NISHA

The fourth of July

It's only nine o'clock, but Nisha feels wrung out. She undresses slowly and crawls into bed without even brushing her teeth, then lies there in the dark staring at the ceiling. What a day. She really, really hadn't been expecting that. She feels strangely impressed, which surprises her. Impressed by Ella, whom Harriet had tried to get into so much trouble. A woman she'd never met before, who'd come to that hotel room to try to save her life. But even more impressed by Harriet. That double bluff. Then to give up her job, her *career*, like that ... to decide she's no longer prepared to be blackmailed. And – the kicker – to still agree to hand over a decent chunk of the money she inherited (to be fair, legally, even if Nisha doesn't always like to admit that)? Wow. OK, it's definitely not as much as she hoped she'd be ending today with, but she's suddenly sick of all this, just like Harriet must be. It's done. And it means this chapter of her life can close. All the anger, the bitterness, the trying to get revenge; it doesn't make you happy, she knows that. She sighs, rolls over onto her side and closes her eyes. She hasn't been happy, not really, not for a long time. Maybe, just maybe, now she can be.

In a Paris hotel room, Ella is in bed too. She feels shattered, but in that good way, the exhaustion that follows a day that's kind of changed your life, a day that's somehow turned out way, way better than you ever dreamed it might. In some ways, she's furious with herself; for her stupidity in believing that Harriet would really kill somebody, and for her naivety about the money. Why didn't she check it actually *was* in her account before they left for Richmond? But what she did after she left Harriet and Nisha, the phone call she had never intended to make but suddenly changed her mind about … *that* had been a good decision. That had been the best decision she's made in a very long time.

She'd arrived at the airport with several hours to spare, having booked an early evening flight just in case things at the hotel took longer than expected. She'd sat in a little coffee shop and nursed a decaf, waiting for check-in to open, running over the events of the day in her mind, and then, almost to her own surprise, she'd picked up her phone. She hadn't been planning to do it; she'd always intended to have this baby alone, from the minute the pregnancy had been confirmed. She didn't *need* anyone. But now…

As she waited for the call to connect, wondering if he'd pick up, or if he'd be too busy to answer, she thought about the first time they'd kissed, on the Saturday Harriet had ended up doing a double shift at work, the day they'd had that chat and he'd asked her about her tattoo. He'd seemed fascinated, and later that evening after they'd eaten the Indian takeaway he'd treated her to, and they were sitting together on the sofa, she'd been surprised by a sudden gentle touch on her right arm, a hesitant finger tracing the outline of the petals etched onto her skin. Their eyes had met, and then, slowly, so slowly, their lips. So unexpected, but so delicious, and over the following few days it had happened again and again; on a walk along the river when Harriet decided not to join them, even once – riskily – in the hallway when they passed each other on the way to their respective rooms. She'd felt guilty at first, horribly so, but she couldn't seem to help herself, and only a week later they'd slept together. The night Harriet went away to Brighton, and they were alone in the apartment. More guilt, until Harriet had made her confession about everything she'd done to Ella, whereupon the guilt had magically eased somewhat. It wasn't purely physical, either, this connection she'd suddenly found. They'd talked more too, talked a lot. Long heart-to-heart conversations, on their walks or in the living room while Harriet was at work or, later, hiding away in the bedroom. He'd told her about his childhood, about his encounter with a dentist who was a sexual predator, about his confused feelings around that and what was happening with Harriet. She talked to him about her mother, and he told her that if she wanted to visit her again before she died, he'd come with her, support her through it. They talked more about children too. How he'd now almost given up hope of being a father; how he was trying desperately to come to terms with it, to convince himself he could live a happy, fulfilled life without being a parent. And then Ella had discovered she was pregnant.

She'd told Harriet it had been four or five weeks earlier, the guy in Gloucester. Most women don't start showing a bump until three or four months anyway, so she was pretty sure she'd get away with it. But it had been that night, the night Harriet had gone away, the tenth of March. That unprotected, passionate, *incredible* sex. She'd started to wonder about three weeks later; when the pregnancy test was positive, she'd at first been horrified, and then, slowly, had come to terms with it.

This is a real *chance for a new life*, she'd thought. *A life where someone else is more important than me. I can do this, I can. And I can do it on my own.*

The day of her first scan was, as she'd told Harriet, the day they'd sat on the balcony together, finalising the plans to 'kill' Nisha. She hadn't been honest about everything, though. She'd let Harriet think that she'd drugged her while she was carrying a child, but that hadn't been true. She'd slept with George *after* that, *after* Harriet had stopped spiking her drinks. But it hadn't hurt to let her think that. She'd clearly felt so guilty about it all that she'd let Ella go, and now she's free to start her new life, albeit with not quite as much money in the bank as she'd hoped. But she has something else instead, something she really wasn't expecting. He's lying here next to her right now, his chest moving gently up and down, already asleep.

George.

When he'd answered her call, she'd asked him to go somewhere quiet, somewhere he could listen without interruption to something that was going to shock him. And then, as quickly as she could, she told him everything. Told him that his wife, Harriet, had actually been behind everything that Ella had been through in Gloucester, because of a stupid fling she'd had with one of Harriet's exes. How Harriet blamed Ella for her miscarriage, and had waited years to enact her extraordinary revenge. About Nisha, and how Harriet had essentially stolen her inheritance, and what Nisha had done to try to get it back. And about today, and how Harriet had convinced Ella she was going to kill Nisha and forced her to help her, and how *she'd* gone to Richmond to stop it happening. About how she was at the airport right now, headed for Paris, leaving the country for good. And about the baby. *His* baby.

She hadn't really known what she wanted the outcome of this call to be. She'd just had the urge to tell him everything and see what happened. It was the baby that did it. He'd listened in stunned silence, interjecting now and again, asking her if she was serious, saying he couldn't believe what she was saying, asking her how, *how*. But when she told him she was pregnant...

He'd arrived at the gate just as the plane was about to board, red-faced and breathless, clutching his passport and a small carry-on bag he'd rushed home for, stuffing a few clothes and personal items into it before leaping into a cab.

'I'll stay with you for a few days, then I'll go back and move out properly,' he said. 'It's tricky to get medical jobs in Europe post-Brexit but we can go somewhere else – Australia, Canada, maybe? We can talk about it. It'll be all right, Ella. I'm not letting you do this alone, OK?'

When she asked him if he was sure, if he really did want to leave his marriage behind, he hugged her fiercely.

'I'm sure. I've never been more sure about anything,' he said.

He'd loved Harriet so much in the beginning that he'd

convinced himself she was enough, he told her, as they sat on the plane, clutching each other's hands. But as she had slowly changed over the past year, growing gradually more distant – he understood why now – his feelings for her had slowly changed too, *so* slowly he'd barely noticed at first. He'd never looked elsewhere until Ella came along though, when he had, apparently, felt an instant pull. He'd tried to ignore it for a long time; he'd even asked Harriet repeatedly when Ella was moving out, hoping she'd go before his feelings got the better of him.

'When she said you were staying, I just tried to stay away from you as much as possible, you know? And then … well, you know the rest. I sort of gave up,' he said earlier, as they lay wrapped around each other on the hotel room bed. 'But even after we did what we did, I still thought maybe you and I were just a fling, and that me and Harriet could be OK. Christ. Not now though… I still can't believe how horrifically she's behaved. The things she's *done*. But it's not just that. It's you. You're amazing, and you've made me so happy, Ella. It's going to take a while for me to get my head round all this, but I honestly think we can make this work, you and me. We really can.'

He'd kissed her gently on the forehead, and her heart had swelled.

'I thought we were just a fling too. But I think you might be right,' she said.

And she really does. And yet, she does feel a little bad, despite everything Harriet did to her, because she's done it again, hasn't she? Stolen Harriet's partner. When, as she left the Richmond hotel room today, she told her she was sorry for everything, she meant it. She *is* sorry, truly sorry for what happened with Felix, and for what's now happened with George. Although ... maybe not *quite* as sorry now, tonight. Because when she thinks about what Harriet tried to do to her in the last few minutes in that hotel room, what she *would* have done to her if Ella hadn't told her she was pregnant ... *seriously*? Too far, Harriet. Too much, now. And what's done is done, anyway. She can't change it. And Harriet needs to be told. George said he'd call her tomorrow, that he was too angry with her to speak to her tonight. That he didn't care if she'd be worried when he didn't come home from work.

'Let her sweat,' he spat.

But Ella doesn't think that's fair. She wants to get it over with, and she thinks Harriet should know this evening. Now. Slowly, trying not to wake George, she reaches across him to the bedside table, and picks up her phone.

Harriet jumps at the buzz of a message alert. She's been going out of her mind, waiting for George to come home. He should have finished work hours ago, and for a while she just assumed he'd been delayed in surgery, a tricky operation that had taken longer than expected. But when several hours went by and she still couldn't get hold of him, she called the hospital, only to be told he'd actually left *early* today; that he'd rushed off mid-afternoon, citing a family emergency. She'd really started to freak out then – was it his mother, maybe? She hadn't been in the best of health recently, but if something bad had happened, surely he would have phoned her? She called his number again and again, but every time all she got was his voicemail message; she tried texting and WhatsApping, but the messages remained unread. And now, it's nearly midnight, and at last, a message. She grabs her phone, her heartrate speeding up, and then feels a crushing wave of disappointment.

Ella. For fuck's sake ... why is Ella messaging me? I told her I never want to see or hear from her again, and a few hours later she's sending me a WhatsApp? What the hell is wrong with her?

Hugely irritated, she taps on the message, reads it, then frowns. What does that mean? She scrolls down to the attached photo. And then her mouth drops open, and she almost stops breathing.

No. This can't be happening, No, *please*...

There are fifteen words above the photo, followed by an x.

'Paris, right now. First day of the rest of our lives. Love, Mummy and Daddy x'

And then the picture. It's a selfie of Ella, in bed, a white duvet pulled up over her chest, her head on a plump pillow. And next to her is George. George, his eyes closed, asleep, and resting on his chest is a familiar photograph. It's the ultrasound scan picture, the one Ella showed her earlier, in the hotel room. Her unborn baby.

Love, Mummy and Daddy x

Harriet drops the phone onto the hardwood floor, and hears a crack as the glass screen splinters. Then she lets out a howl, as her heart shatters too.

In Paris, Ella switches off her phone. Time to sleep. She picks up the ultrasound photo and runs a finger gently across it. She hasn't actually shown it to George yet. She leans across him again and props it carefully against the glass of water on the table next to him. It will be a nice surprise for him, when he wakes up in the morning. Ella watches him for a moment, listening to the tiny snores now coming from his handsome face. She lies down, closes her eyes and smiles.

Acknowledgments

People often ask me where I get my book ideas from. Sometimes there's a sensible answer; an idea emerging from something I've read or seen or heard, a news article, a true crime podcast, a TV documentary. But often, in the strange mind of a crime writer, ideas appear out of the blue, and the opening of this book – when Ella turns up to find her workplace empty and closed – simply came to me as I drove to work one day and, as I turned into the road the building is on, thought randomly, 'Wouldn't it be mad if it just wasn't there?' And so my seventh thriller was born.

Right – the 'thank yous'. Harriet is a consultant paediatrician; huge thanks to real-life consultant paediatrician Dr Russell Peek for his advice on day-to-day activities in the role, and his patience in answering my multiple weird questions. Thank you to my tattoo artist, the super-talented Ally Lyon-Thomas (yes, I have a couple of tattoos, both book-related; not a lot of people know that, but *you* do now), for her advice on Ella's tattoo. To my friend Sophie Risebero for inspiring one of the moments in this book (you know which one, Soph!). And to my friend Susan Blair, who lent me her name for the hospital's clinical director character – you didn't end up on the cutting room floor this time, Susan!

And then, of course, massive thanks to all the 'book' people. My wonderful literary agent, Clare Hulton. The brilliant team at HarperCollins and One More Chapter. There is a full cast list at the end of this book, but a special big thank you to my two fabulous editors for this novel – Kathryn Cheshire, who departed halfway through to go on maternity leave, and Jennie Rothwell, who picked up the reins. My copyeditor Tony Russell and proofreader Catherine Jackson. The always-so-creative Lucy Bennett, who dreams up my cover designs. The HarperCollins teams in the US, Canada and Australia. Everyone at ILA, who handle my other foreign rights and put up with all my ineptitude when it comes to overseas tax matters. I'm definitely a words person and not a numbers person, so thank you for keeping me on the straight and narrow and for the never-ending thrill of seeing my books published in so many languages around the world. All the book bloggers and reviewers – you ROCK. I've had the pleasure of meeting so many more of you in the past year at various events and I'm now even more in awe of your passion for books and your support for authors than I was before. It means *so* much – thank you. And my fellow writers, crime writers in particular. The friendship, the fun and the genuine and enthusiastic support everyone gives each other's books are phenomenal. The parties and get-togethers aren't bad either.

And finally, of course, huge thanks as always to my husband, my family and friends, including those at my other job on the telly, who continue to be some of my biggest cheerleaders. I love you all very much.

ONE MORE CHAPTER

YOUR NUMBER ONE STOP FOR PAGETURNING BOOKS

The author and One More Chapter would like to thank everyone who contributed to the publication of this story...

Analytics
James Brackin
Abigail Fryer

Audio
Fionnuala Barrett
Ciara Briggs

Contracts
Laura Amos
Laura Evans

Design
Lucy Bennett
Fiona Greenway
Liane Payne
Dean Russell

Digital Sales
Laura Daley
Lydia Grainge
Hannah Lismore

eCommerce
Laura Carpenter
Madeline ODonovan
Charlotte Stevens
Christina Storey
Jo Surman
Rachel Ward

Editorial
Kara Daniel
Catherine Jackson
Charlotte Ledger
Ajebowale Roberts
Jennie Rothwell
Tony Russell
Helen Williams

Harper360
Jennifer Dee
Emily Gerbner
Ariana Juarez
Jean Marie Kelly
emma sullivan
Sophia Wilhelm

International Sales
Peter Borcsok
Ruth Burrow
Colleen Simpson
Ben Wright

Inventory
Sarah Callaghan
Kirsty Norman

Marketing & Publicity
Chloe Cummings
Grace Edwards
Emma Petfield

Operations
Melissa Okusanya
Hannah Stamp

Production
Denis Manson
Simon Moore
Francesca Tuzzeo

Rights
Helena Font Brillas
Ashton Mucha
Zoe Shine
Aisling Smyth
Lucy Vanderbilt

Trade Marketing
Ben Hurd
Eleanor Slater

**The HarperCollins
Distribution Team**

**The HarperCollins
Finance & Royalties
Team**

**The HarperCollins
Legal Team**

**The HarperCollins
Technology Team**

UK Sales
Isabel Coburn
Jay Cochrane
Sabina Lewis
Holly Martin
Harriet Williams
Leah Woods

**And every other
essential link in the
chain from delivery
drivers to booksellers
to librarians and
beyond!**

The Jackie Kabler Thriller Collection

All titles available now in paperback, ebook and audio

BEHIND CLOSED DOORS,
EVERYONE HAS THEIR SECRETS

AM I GUILTY?

USA TODAY **BESTSELLER**

JACKIE KABLER

The PERFECT COUPLE

...OR THE PERFECT LIE?

JACKIE KABLER

USA TODAY **BESTSELLER**
JACKIE KABLER

THEIR LIFE
SEEMS PERFECT...
BUT IS IT?

The
PERFECT
COUPLE

The HAPPY FAMILY

'Suspense, intrigue and engaging characters. Fabulous!'
Lucy Clarke, bestselling author of *The Castaways*

CONVICTED. JAILED.
All for a crime that never even happened...

The LIFE
SENTENCE

JACKIE KABLER

USA TODAY BESTSELLER

ONE MORE CHAPTER

One More Chapter is an
award-winning global
division of HarperCollins.

Subscribe to our newsletter to get our
latest eBook deals and stay up to date
with all our new releases!

signup.harpercollins.co.uk/
join/signup-omc

Meet the team at
www.onemorechapter.com

Follow us!

 @OneMoreChapter_
 @onemorechapterhc
 @onemorechapterhc
 @onemorechapterhc

Do you write unputdownable fiction?
We love to hear from new voices.
Find out how to submit your novel at
www.onemorechapter.com/submissions